THREE SINS AND A SCOUNDREL

#6 The Duchess Society

BY

TRACY SUMNER

WOLF PUBLISHING

Three Sins and a Scoundrel by Tracy Sumner

Published by WOLF Publishing UG

Copyright © 2024 Tracy Sumner
Text by Tracy Sumner
Edited by Chris Hall
Cover Art by Victoria Cooper
Paperback ISBN: 978-3-98536-304-9
Hard Cover ISBN: 978-3-98536-305-6
Ebook ISBN: 978-3-98536-303-2

WOLF Publishing - This is us:

Two sisters, two personalities.. But only one big love!

Diving into a world of dreams..
    ...Romance, heartfelt emotions, lovable and witty characters, some humor, and some mystery! Because we want it all! Historical Romance at its best!

Visit our website to learn all about us, our authors and books!

Sign up to our mailing list to receive first hand information on new releases, freebies and promotions as well as exclusive giveaways and sneak-peeks!

WWW.WOLF-PUBLISHING.COM

Also by Tracy Sumner

The Duchess Society Series

The DUCHESS SOCIETY is a steamy new Regency-era series. Come along for a scandalous ride with the incorrigible ladies of the Duchess Society as they tame the wicked rogues of London! Second chance, marriage of convenience, enemies to lovers, forbidden love, passion, scandal, ROMANCE.

If you enjoy depraved dukes, erstwhile earls and sexy scoundrels, untamed bluestockings and rebellious society misses, the DUCHESS SOCIETY is the series for you!

#1 The Brazen Bluestocking

#2 The Scandalous Vixen

#3 The Wicked Wallflower

#4 One Wedding and an Earl

#5 Two Scandals and a Scot

#6 Three Sins and a Scoundrel

Prequel to the series: The Ice Duchess

Christmas novellas: The Governess Gamble, The Daring Debutante

THREE
SINS
AND A
SCOUNDREL

The true key of the universe is love.
-William Godwin

The Before

Prologue

A hasty marriage appears to be in the cards for Miss Constance Willoughby, the reclusive eldest daughter of the equally reclusive viscount, Lord Smithton. She's landed a proper gent in the Earl of Edgerly, who is seeking devoted companionship from his third countess. Of course, rumors swirl around the mysterious Willoughby family, as they have for decades. Is the earl taking a greater risk than he would on a hand of faro by asking for Miss Willoughby's hand?

This author wonders what mischief a country girl could have gotten into in the wiles of Northumberland to necessitate such a speedy union.

-The City Tattler

A brutally cold winter day
Bamburgh, Northumberland 1815

Cece Willoughby had consumed a lifetime of Crispin Sinclair's sins. Three, to be exact.

When he didn't have many to squander.

Vicar Smith said a man only possessed a few, and he should spread them over the duration. Women were afforded none, according to the cleric, so his little minx was in even worse shape than Crispin.

A concern that kept him up at night.

Nonetheless, the sin-spendings had been glorious—even if he hadn't known what he was doing.

Not once had he been certain he'd handled Cece as a man blind in love ought. In the hayloft, in the luxurious barouche in his father's stable, or that last magnificent episode in her bed, their bodies tangled in sheets warmed with blissful discovery. They'd bumbled and fiddled, tearing clothing, laughing, exploring—then gasping, moaning, *lost*. He'd tried to keep his wits about him, but the experiences had been bewildering and splendid. Miraculous in ways he'd not imagined tupping could be.

Touching Cece had gone beyond anything his youthful mind had seen fit to conjure.

And he'd spent years conjuring.

The encounters had moved him more than he could express, and in a manner men *never* whispered about over billiards and whisky. They boasted of spilling their seed, shoving aside the chit, and falling promptly to sleep. They bragged of desire checked and lust fulfilled.

Nothing, truly, was ever spoken about the chit's yearnings. Of her desire, *her* lust. Which he'd admit matched his in intensity, or so it seemed.

In the end, no one spoke of love.

Which left a young man wondering how to manage *feeling* it.

Cece entranced Crispin, leaving him unguarded to his bones and wishing for more. Of her oft-dogged views, her countless felonious pursuits, her wit, her cunning, her *everything*. Sitting quietly in a salon and watching her stitch would have satisfied should she have been a girl intent upon such inane pursuits. But she wasn't such a girl. She fought for what she wanted—him—and against his better judgment that they wait, he'd caved in the way only a nineteen-year-old passionate fool could.

Regrettably, they'd been careless. And now, they were parted.

His heart gave a thump at the realization of how distanced they were. He was literally watching her life spin away without him.

Crispin scrubbed his gloved knuckle across the icy pane and searched the interior of her mother's garish parlor, the mullioned windows giving him but a watery half view of the proceedings. Cece's head bowed, her slender body curved around the teacup she grasped like a lifeline with both hands, her slipper tapping a rhythm only he knew the true cadence of. She was surrounded with no way out. Her parents, the vicar, and an earl who wanted to make her his wife circling her while she shrank away from them. She needed him—when he'd been advised by her father, rather compellingly, to never speak to her again. A lowly baron's son from a poorly classified family was not a suitable choice for a viscount's daughter.

Crispin sucked a frigid gulp into his lungs, the taste of brine rolling off the churning North Sea and bringing little comfort this day.

This circumstance wasn't what he'd anticipated four years ago when his father won an aging Northumberland manse on a risky bet at Epsom, the only kind of wager the baron involved himself with. The medieval fortress bordered the Willoughby family's estate, a verdant plot they'd inhabited for centuries. Despite the mad dash to the north, a move necessitated by dwindling finances, Northumberland had been a revelation for Crispin. The sting of salty air striking his face, a pantry filled with fresh local produce, country lanes he could travel without fearing a knife being placed in his back, the stink and squalor of London miles upon miles away.

As for his neighbor...

Thirteen to Crispin's sage fifteen, Cece had already crafted a tenacious reputation in the local village. The first time he'd seen her had knocked him silly. Sporting a pair of ripped trousers, her ginger tresses trailing down her back like strands set aflame, she'd displayed a bearing similar to the wild lads he'd run with in London. Sensing his presence, she'd glanced over her shoulder, given him a knowing smirk, and let the arrow she was holding punch directly through the center of her target.

That, as they say, had been that.

Two nights later, when they'd been formally introduced at a country party—her boisterousness hidden beneath a snug chignon that didn't suit and a stunning ivory gown that did—he'd been set adrift across turbulent waters for good.

As women who knew they'd hooked a man but good tended to do, she'd led him on a merry chase. While dancing circles around her in a mostly prudent manner, Crispin had grown into Northumberland's most celebrated charmer. The ability to spin a story, change a mind, or win a disagreement without a drop of blood being spilled was quite a handsome skill in the temperamental regions close to Scotland. Shockingly, once he overcame his childhood stutter and asthmatic wheeze, he couldn't seem to keep his mouth shut. Last winter, for instance, he'd convinced a public house full of drunken chaps to jump in the Tyne for an invigorating midnight swim.

While he stood, grinning, from the shore.

He tucked away the seasoned part of him crafted on city streets. Northumberland didn't require ruthlessness, although he could *be* ruthless. Crispin preferred solving problems using charisma and his remarkably nimble mind. Proclaiming yourself the smartest individual in the room, even if you were, put people off.

Only dullards didn't realize this.

Crispin Jasper Sinclair, heir to a ragged barony, was no dullard.

Shivering beneath the only greatcoat he owned, a cast-off of his father's that was years out of fashion and tattered at the cuffs, Crispin waited. Patience was a gift he possessed in spades.

By Hades, he'd stay until he had a bloody word with her.

The second her father escorted their guests from the parlor, leveling a vicious look at his eldest daughter on the way out, Cece turned to the window, having known all along he was there. Of course, she had. She gave her knees a hard squeeze, then shoved to her feet, and crossed to him. His heart chimed in dull beats against his ribs because hers was the walk of a soul heading to the gallows. She halted before him and, with a quick glance thrown over her shoulder, went to her knees to level their gazes. Even in a crisis, she never backed down.

Working the rusted metal latch free, she opened the window

enough to allow her scent to tangle with his senses. He'd never known her to be absent from the fragrance of orange blossoms. Behind her ears, between her breasts, at her wrist.

He'd tried them all, *tasted* them all.

Seeing where his mind had gone, the stubborn pleat he adored settled between her brows. Cece's eyes were the color of wilted grass this morn when he preferred them dark and smoky from his touch. "You must leave, Cris. Now, *today*. My father is furious, my mother more so. Go home, or better yet, go to London until the ceremony is over and done with. Stay with that cousin of yours, the shifty one you like so much. My family isn't going to stop until it's done, until I'm married to that horrid Edgerly. My father threatened to revoke my sister's chance at a Season next year if I don't comply. He'll force her to marry someone worse. He gave me names of men he would consider appropriate, and they're unspeakable. It's safer if you're nowhere near me. Earls have power in this country, more than we can fight."

He palmed the rough stone bordering the window ledge, his lungs caught in a familiar and embarrassing twist. He held the breath until he was certain a cough wasn't going to spill out atop his words. His asthma wasn't going to be the last thing she recalled about him. "So, you're going to go through with it."

When, of course, she was going through with it.

Crispin's offer of marriage, rushed and with nothing behind it, *less* than nothing, wasn't a feasible option for the daughter of a viscount. The Willoughby's weren't a respected family, but meager sons of faithless barons didn't waltz into society and seize the eligible women—even if the woman in question was found in a compromising position. Furthermore, Cece had a younger sister to worry about, the main reason for selfless choices. She and her sister, Rose, were close, and ruining her family for her own sake wasn't like Cece at all.

He supposed he'd merely wanted her to tell him to his face.

Cece gave him a defeated study, her upper lip quivering. She reached, then pulled back before she touched his bruised face. "Who did this to you?"

Crispin dusted his hand over his aching cheekbone. He blinked the only eye he could; the right was swollen shut. "My father isn't any happier about the situation. The difference is, yours uses words to persuade while mine uses his fists. Men who've crawled from the gutter don't actually crawl that far from it despite useless titles conferred due to military service. We're only able to milk my grandfather's relationship with King George II for so long before the well runs dry. A return to balance, some in the *ton* would claim. I'm not considered good enough for you, minx, even by my own family."

"I've ruined us both," she whispered, the first hint of true grief showing on her face.

Love for her whispered through Crispin in pulsing strokes. If she cried, a deed he'd only witnessed as they lay curled around each other in her grand tester bed, he was going to climb through her window and damn them all. If the dimple in her left cheek entered the conversation, he would be a goner. She'd best hide it.

"*I* ruined us," he vowed, when in actuality, he'd said no to her impassioned advances for going on a year. The hardest feat of his life— until it wasn't hard in the slightest. Months of heated kisses and ardent caresses could only lead to doom for a young man as desperate for her as he was. Ultimately, a piece of clothing was removed, and his hand made its way beneath her skirts, hers sneaking inside his trousers. Then...

Doom. Glorious, spellbinding doom.

She'd promised they would survive the encounter, and he'd believed her.

"London," he whispered, searching for any indication to stay in Northumberland when it appeared she was refusing to fight for them. "Is that what you're telling me to do? Go back from where I came and leave you to Edgerly?"

"*Yes,*" she whispered, sinking his heart like a stone. "If you stay, I won't be able to do what I must. I'll run to you in the dead of the night, and all will truly be lost. My sister's chances destroyed. You can't save me from this, but I can save *her.*"

Crispin glanced at his muddy boots to get away from her probing gaze. He imagined slamming his fist into the brick and howling out his anguish. Imagined what he'd do if he had a brother or sister to save. A dream because he had almost no family. No siblings, his mother long gone, his father...

He swallowed hard, palming his chest, pushing back the ache. *It's time to grow up, Cris, right now. Show her you can.*

He had opportunities. Skills he hadn't told her about. The desperate sort of talents one acquires after growing up two streets over from the roughest slum in the city. His shifty cousin, Arthur, *was* absurdly connected—strange that this is who Cece thought he should go to for help. The two years he and his father had lived with him before coming to Northumberland had indeed been interesting ones. Arthur had told him many times to look him up when he finally had enough of his father's abuse, that he had prime arrangements with higher ups for a chap who looked like a gentleman but wasn't. Who could pick a lock with his eyes closed and was, perhaps, the keenest shot in England. He'd reasoned Crispin's pale complexion and slight asthmatic wheeze were grand subterfuges. Disguises in a natural sort of sense.

Decided, he caught her gaze. "Fine," he whispered, unable to add another word.

She inhaled a full breath, lifting those gorgeous breasts he'd suckled beneath her modest bodice, this day a dreary shade of cream her mother had no doubt selected for her. Cece preferred jewel tones, crimson and gold and deep blue like the sea. Colors matching her spirit. His fingertips tingled inside moist kidskin as he struggled to contain the impulse to reach for her. Crispin understood, on the cruelest day in the cruelest spot in England, that despite his broken heart, he'd never forget her.

But he would do what she asked of him until he drew his last.

At least, at the time, he believed he would.

"Leave me, leave this. Leave your nightmare of a father in the manse across the way. Leave it *all*." She gestured to them with a tightly drawn fist. Back and forth, back and forth with her fierce breaths. "We're a lifetime too late. The world we inhabit won't allow for dreams. You know this. Women have few choices, and sometimes, unseen men have fewer."

He gripped the frame to keep her from closing the window. "I

7

won't be around to protect you. You've got to stop the mischief-making. Promise me, minx, or I won't be able to leave."

A rosy flush spilled across her cheeks. But there was ire beneath it, sturdy as the stone beneath his hand. "I never asked you to protect me."

He clenched his jaw, his own anger brewing. Rage was rare—but poisonous when it hit. Proof positive that Sinclair blood pulsed through his veins. He'd hidden this from her, the only thing about himself he'd hidden. "Promise me, right this bloody *minute*, or I march to your front door and announce myself while they nibble on crumpets and wreck your future. I'll destroy this entire setup in seconds flat, create the biggest scandal England has ever seen. I have base compulsions racing beneath the surface that are innate to my heritage. Don't make me reveal them. You might not like what you see."

Crispin needn't remind her she had base compulsions racing beneath the surface, too. A unique ability combined with an appetite for adventure that set her apart from any female he'd ever known. Perhaps someone in her family had once been a pirate.

She'd be a proper delinquent in another life, in another locale, and no one but him knew it.

Cece swallowed hard, tossing a last look over her shoulder. Her ginger strands dazzled in the dull lamplight, the fiery color beckoning to him. Her eyes when they met his were closer to what he desired—a murky, emerald green. He trusted this color. Mostly. Only a girl who couldn't entirely be trusted would be able to steal his heart. "No more misconduct. No more schemes. Not as long as I'm married."

He recognized the catch in her pledge. Edgerly wasn't a young man, and she'd outlive her spouse by decades if the gods were with her. Though, once Cece had children—which made Crispin's stomach positively *ache* to imagine—she'd turn into another dull society chit. There was no help for it. Many independent women before her had been broken by the system.

In any case, how many countesses went around forging signatures like they'd been born to the trade?

The end of their relationship in plain view, they stared, gazes misty, so close yet a thousand miles apart.

THREE SINS AND A SCOUNDREL

Before he could utter another word—plead with her to find him someday, to never forget him, to leave with him, *now*, to let him love her as he longed to—she secured the window latch with a decisive pop. Dragged a knuckle beneath each eye to vanquish her emotions and turned away.

Crispin watched her rally. Shoulders back, spine rigid. A smooth stroke over one of those stiff chignons he loathed, a shake of her skirt, then a departure befitting a future countess. Damned if he wasn't in awe of her daring while he stood there shivering like a lovesick lad.

Because love him or not, Constance Willoughby exited his life without a backward glance.

The Now

Chapter One

Let him go. Secrets develop a life of their own once they're told. And these secrets, we don't want told.

-Chief Intelligence Officer Browning on the abrupt retirement of Agent Noble

A cozy distillery where business partners discuss the day
Limehouse, London 1831

H is finger ached like the very devil, meaning foul weather was on the horizon.

Since he'd become friendly with this eccentric group of knaves, overturned carriages, stolen telescopes, and convoluted love affairs had become the norm. With a scowl, Jasper Noble tossed a sullen glance at the man responsible for his painfully crooked digit.

Dash Campbell stood before a barrel jammed in the corner of the distillery's main salon, scribbling on a folio laid atop it. His waistcoat was a blinding plaid explosion that rather suited him. He had a pending deadline for his next book, or so he claimed, and was furiously insistent that everyone let him work. The first two volumes he'd written on techniques to cheat at gambling had made him quite the fashionable character. A bloke every hostess in England wanted gracing her parlor when Jasper had never been able to decide if Dash's scandalous manuscripts or his once-in-a-lifetime face had made him so popular.

London loved nothing more than a stunning cad.

Jasper flexed his hand with a grimace, feeling rather uncharitable at the moment. *He* was a cad with a fairly fine face—but the invites didn't come his way as furiously.

Sensing attention like a fox routed from the bush, Dash's quill stalled on the page. "I begged you not to set it yourself, Noble. The sawbones woulda done a proper job and not left you with such a deformity. Nonetheless, you helped me secure the love of me life, my darling Theo, and for that, I'm forever grateful. Hideous finger or no."

Reluctant to fall for Dash's charm or his baiting, Jasper massaged his finger, the boiler clanging in the back of the building providing a comforting vibration beneath his bum. Picking locks didn't come as easily as it once had due to the injury, he'd love to tell the swaggering Scot. Although he didn't share much about his former profession, even if his friends suspected plenty. "I barely remember your sage advice," he said instead, searching his waistcoat pocket for his flask. "The knock to my head when we landed in the ditch thankfully muffled your words. Seeing stars does that to a man, your efforts to woo your wife a race I sorrowfully got involved in."

While Dash laughed, Jasper imbibed, the whisky rolling down his throat in a smooth burst. A prideful burst because he was an investor in not only this distillery but two others the Leighton Cluster—his friends' official name in the *ton* thanks to the Duke of Leighton—owned. Three hundred thousand gallons of exceptional liquor produced last year with projections to go a solid five hundred thousand this year.

Jasper had been working since dawn, checking casks for leakage, overseeing the examination of corn for rotten kernels, and supervising the loading of wagons bound for public houses throughout England. It was backbreaking work at times, physical and grueling, a step below the duties he performed for his own shipping concerns. But he loved it. And it was leagues removed from his past. At the end of the day, there were no governmental summary reports to file. No intelligence officers to pacify. No bullets to dodge. No fabrications to construct—or not many.

He never worried about waking to a blade at his throat.

Trade was child's play compared to espionage. And, by *God*, did it pay better.

Ridiculously, he was making more blunt on an investment in prams than he was on liquor. Every expectant mother in London wanted one of the damned carriages Dash had inadvertently designed for his wee babe, the bolt of tartan lining the interior proclaiming them to be an authentic Scottish creation.

Hence, the Leighton Cluster's new and unexpected business venture.

Why Jasper had wanted to be a spy when he could make boundless money on baby carts, he couldn't recall.

Jasper frowned and sucked down the last of his drink. Actually, he could recall. A naïve young man with few options fleeing a failed love affair rang a bell. He palmed his chest, forcing back the asthmatic flutter. That only bloody happened when he thought of *her*.

"Ah, Campbell, me lad, you've said something to anger the beast," Xander Macauley murmured as he strolled into the room. He wiped his grease-streaked hands on a rag, then stuffed the length of linen in the waistband of his trousers, where it fluttered like a flag with his every step. He was forever making adjustments to their whisky stills, never completely happy with the product when the product was the finest in England. "Your frown could crack ice, Noble. Miserable bit of melancholy to be giving on this fine day on the docks, innit?"

Jasper's closest partner and friend was a rookery urchin, a man who'd built an empire from less than humble beginnings. Although Jasper's fabricated backstory was that he, too, had been born in the stews, his narrative had actually been created during his nineteenth year by a government contact. Shoreditch had been selected as his home since he'd spent two years in his youth close to the borough, his speech altered for the worse to fit the environs until he almost forgot the *true* place of his heart, the coastal vistas of Northumberland.

Although he couldn't lie to himself about his vaguely aristocratic heritage, Jasper was happy, more than, to lie to everyone else. He was honored to be considered a gutter rat. People accepted what they were told, what they were *presented*. If he tied his cravat a little straighter and roamed Mayfair parlors using that name from long ago, they'd accept him without a care.

A baron was the lowest step, but it was on the bloody staircase.

As it was, a man of wits and intimidation, society stayed out of his way—and he theirs.

Remarkably, Xander Macauley had called his bluff from day one. The innate grace Jasper had hidden beneath a half-arsed rookery accent not enough to fool the man. Despite arguments over the shipping contracts they'd tried to steal from each other and the women they'd once competed for, Xander had reluctantly allowed Jasper into their circle, trusting him with his family and his businesses. Given him friendship, the genuine article. If Xander had Tobias Streeter's wife, Hildy, owner of the Duchess Society, investigate him, Jasper couldn't blame him.

Better, he didn't care.

There was no way to find what His Majesty's secret service had hidden.

If the Leighton Cluster continued to welcome the asthmatic, stuttering son of a dissolute baron who was known to be someone else entirely, Jasper would remain with them for *life*.

Feeling a rare zing of sentimentality, he glanced around the whisky-scented space. This was age, he suspected, catching up with him.

Tobias Streeter's corpulent cat, Nick Bottom, was dozing on a blanket in the corner, while Buttons, a mangy hound who'd wandered into the alley two months ago, lounged on a heap of empty barley sacks. Children of various ages were scattered about on the scarred plank floor and the sagging sofa. Their fathers rarely went anywhere without them, girl or boy. Enough that Jasper knew each by name. Kit, Nigel, Arabella, Tate, Kieran. The infants were at home with their mothers, of course.

The many, many babies.

His friends were productive in more ways than one.

Thoughtful, Jasper grazed the flask's rim across his lips. It was time —but for *what*? Last month, his mistress had departed after tossing a lamp at his head, and he had no inclination to replace her or the bit of flooring she'd cooked. Gray was streaking the hair at his temples, and his left knee ached when it rained. He couldn't remember what he ate for breakfast if asked on command. He needed spectacles to read in dim light.

He was almost thirty-six, for blood's sake. Positively ancient.

He was too old for love. Marriage. Children. Certain things in life had passed him by. Besides, he had too many secrets to start over. Too many instances he wished to forget. There were parts of his past he couldn't share, and he wasn't entering a union built on lies. Frankly, he'd rather be alone than live a charade.

Which was what he was doing inhabiting two grossly different worlds. He felt most at home in Shoreditch, among the rabble... but his bedside table in Bloomsbury was strewn with books written in Latin. He spoke imperfect but passable French. Played billiards like a criminal but rode his mount like a duke. Tied the smartest cravat this side of Christendom when he chose to. He had a valet, a baron's signet ring he'd not worn in nearly twenty years, and a minor notation on page 733 of *Debrett's*.

Jasper Noble was a fabrication—but he contained many pieces of the man left behind.

Nevertheless, and this was the change, both of them wished whole-heartedly to stop pretending.

Dispirited, Jasper propped his jaw on his fist and tracked a bead of rain as it slid down the windowpane, the rumble of conversation in the room swimming past without comprehension. He'd find another mistress. Maybe one with ginger tresses this time. Something novel. Something to keep him interested. He didn't need his own children. There were enough tots in the Cluster for him to feel like a beloved uncle. Xander had even let him host his eldest boy, Kit, one weekend last summer, where they'd talked shipping and commerce late into the night. He hadn't realized until that moment how much company a growing lad could be. The house had been positively deadly after Kit left.

Xander kicked the leg of his chair as he passed, startling Jasper from his musing. "I hate to draw you from your misery, but you wouldn't happen to have any experience with forgeries, would you, mate?"

Jasper blinked, his whisky haze leaving him in a rush. Sitting up, he started to speak, then recognized a stutter sat on the tip of his tongue. Coughing lightly, he tried again. "Why would I?"

Xander's gaze glimmered, a cool, steely gray. He shrugged and adjusted a coat lapel that needed no adjustment. "Just thought I'd ask."

They stared for a lingering moment, silently acknowledging a weighty respect between two men who'd started as enemies. "I might, *mate*, now that you mention it," Jasper finally said.

Xander grinned and rocked back on his heels. "Your expertise in so many areas of criminal activity never ceases to amaze me, Noble. It surpasses even my shady knowledge."

Jasper sighed and jammed his flask in his pocket. He should have lied and said he didn't know a bloody damned thing about forgery. However, this topic, this very *one*, he'd never be able to leave behind. "Out with it, then."

The details were scant but troubling. A document submitted to the Customs House for a recent shipment had been signed by Tobias Streeter when he'd never once seen the paperwork. Everyone in their line of business created a signature that wasn't easily reproduced, making forgeries a rare occurrence.

Unless one was dealing with a skilled professional.

Jasper shoved to his feet, the hair on the back of his neck prickling. "Copies of *The Times* lying about anywhere?"

Xander gestured to a crate wedged behind a row of whisky casks. "That and the *Gazette*. A few others. We keep them to line the cat box. Streeter doesn't like Nick Bottom roaming the alleyways at night, so we created inside facilities."

Jasper laughed into his fist. *Fucking hell.* Tobias Streeter, a man once regarded as a formidable rookery thug, the so-called Rogue King of

Limehouse, treated his felines like princes. Along with his beloved wife and children.

And his friends, Jasper noted with heartwarming clarity.

Going to his knee beside the crate, Jasper flipped through the broadsheets. Each had a society column or five, drivel he never read. He didn't want news of Cece, updates on her life, her children, her bloody husband. Or, frankly, updates on *himself*. The gossip printed about him was usually much too close to the truth.

Yet, there it was, in the fifth edition he scanned. The hawks were indeed circling.

The Countess of Edgerly was widowed and residing in the family's London terrace after years spent in the backwoods of Northumberland. This was regarded as a surprise since she'd not often joined her elderly husband in the city.

Jasper should have had his contacts alert him the moment her name hit the broadsheets. By damn, he had emissaries at every printer in England, Wales, and Scotland. Even a few scattered about France and Italy. This was an amateurish mistake on his part. What kind of spy *was* he if he let his long ago love slip into the city without his knowing it?

A sad excuse for one, that's what.

Only, he hadn't wanted to know. Hadn't been able to *endure* the knowing.

Jasper shot an aggrieved breath through his teeth, the flutter in his chest a complaint soon demanding a coughing fit he'd rather his friends not hear. He had yet to tell a soul about his asthma because he'd be damned if Jasper Noble got saddled with that charming childhood bit.

The biggest issue, however, was that he was trying to stay out of trouble. Walk the straight path. Remake the scoundrel. Like the rest in this room, though they'd done it for love when he was doing it for friendship. A man honorable enough to please the Duchess Society ladies was required for Leighton Cluster membership—because that's just the way it was.

With a curse, Jasper tossed the newspapers in the crate, despite his resistance feeling himself being dragged back into the mire. The reliable ping in his gut said life was about to get interesting. *Damn her.*

Cece had promised to leave mischief behind. In all fairness, the vow was only valid during her titled tenure.

The earl was dead. The countess no more.

All bets were off.

⁓

Swearing softly, Jasper shook out the match before it singed his kidskin glove. The stone façade of the Mayfair terrace tossed off wonderful shadows for him to disappear into, a veritable crevasse of invincibility.

He sniffled, choking back a cough. The smell of sulfur carried good memories and bad. Of his work, his many schemes, of a gorgeous young woman, candlelight spilling free to skim her flushed cheeks and the curve of her bare hip. A sweet settle over those incredible auburn-ginger tresses.

He'd dragged the match's tip over her collarbone, leaving an ashen streak he'd later licked away. Hence, the taste of charred ash, not merely the aroma of sulfur, stung his senses like no other. *Aroused* his senses like no other.

At one time, he'd imagined sexual congress with Cece to be the most provoking of his life, certainly a memory stamped with youthful fondness and sentimentality. It simply wasn't possible to stumble upon the key to your soul at fifteen, the lone person meant for you. He didn't believe in such mawkishness. Although he was presented with fine examples on a daily basis as a member of a group of men who loved their wives. *Adored*, in fact. Each and every one of them.

Jamming the match's metal tin in his coat pocket, he ground the smoking bamboo stub beneath his boot. Regrettably, there wasn't enough moonlight to see the lock on the servants' door, therefore the need for a sulfur stick. Antimony sulfide and potassium chlorate only burned for thirty seconds or so, but the chemicals left a perceptible scent, making them a risk in any secret endeavor. No matter. A robust breeze was funneling down the Grosvenor Square alley he stood in with enough vigor to clear the aroma in seconds, leaving behind a rancid city stink neither he nor God could do a blasted thing about.

He would get inside the manse he'd prowled about for the last hour, of course. There wasn't a lock—outside a royal's—he couldn't pick. Jasper's tools were smooth from use, and the finest in the business. Made by Christian Bainbridge, the supreme watchmaker in England. (Also, a manufacturer of top-quality burgling gear, a profitable and extremely clandestine side business.)

His Majesty only employed the best.

Jasper flexed his hand, his finger jamming as it tended to on humid evenings. That's what he got for participating in Dash Campbell's race for true love. Partaking in bloody matchmaking efforts. Although Dash and Theo were the happiest couple inhabiting his universe. Or maybe it was Tobias Streeter and Hildy. Or Xander and Pippa. Xander's brother, Ollie, appeared equally content with his wife, Necessity, an infamous landscape artist who was one of Jasper's old rookery friends. Last spring, she'd done a truly gorgeous job on the gardens at his Bloomsbury flat that he'd been neglectful about maintaining. Then there were the joyful dukes, Leighton and Markham, and their similarly joyful duchesses.

How had a former spy-cum-rookery-thug come to find himself carousing with dukes? Not one, but *two*?

"Come on, luv, work with me," he whispered, negotiating the lock's tumblers, this little project taking longer than it should. Standing there thinking about all the blissful couples in his life was making him soft, his brain sluggish. "You're getting too old for this shite, Noble."

And he was. He knew it. His weak knee made it hard to run as fast as he'd need to if he still took cases, the zigzagging effort meant to evade bullets discharged at short range, a trick that was surprisingly hard on the joints. Not to mention his vision, which wasn't as crystal clear as in his earlier years. His confidence, too, had taken a beating on his last case. He'd gotten out of the embassy with the documents intact, but the recovery period in hospital had been the longest of his career. Three days without a clue who he was from the hard knock to his head. He could have ended up telling the world about Crispin Sinclair that day and been forced into a baron's role he didn't for one second desire.

Thank you, but no.

His retirement appeal had been delivered to his superior two hours after his discharge. Where he'd begun to become Jasper Noble, rookery rat and astute, slightly crooked entrepreneur, in earnest.

Nonetheless, achy and ancient of mind and body, he was inside the manse in less than three minutes. Possibly two and a half, a calculation he'd have measured if he had his Bainbridge in hand. He'd waited until every light dimmed and the house quieted, then delayed an hour more. Servants rose early and were rarely up late. He'd built his investigative enterprise on calculating routines and schedules, the basic rhythms of households. Although he usually observed for a day or two, a week if there were intricacies, before breaking into a place.

This was a dangerous gambit because he was going with his gut.

Now, didn't *that* make sense considering the person he was tracking?

Jasper paused when a hallway floorboard squealed beneath his boot, another mistake on his part. He should have tested each before placing his full weight on it. To stay safe, nothing about these endeavors should come as a surprise—when everything concerning Cece Willoughby was a surprise—because it involved his bloody feelings.

His brain behind his cock behind his heart.

What the hell kind of spy led with his *heart*?

Chuckling, when the remembrances weren't particularly amusing, he crept down the corridor. The wall sconces flickered as he passed them, tossing random slices of helpful light across his path. Parlor, breakfast room, music room. No, no, no. There was one room in every home that held its master's secrets. The study, the office, whatever a gentleman called it. Or in this case, the lady. He'd find the damning goods, then he'd find *her*.

Naturally, the sensual secrets were located in the bedchamber.

Jasper could write a scandalous tome to rival Dash's about the things he'd found in bedside tables.

The room he sought was located at the end of the passage. Dark-paneled, officious, redolent of leather spines, ink, and linseed oil. Beneath these sedate layers was the citrus splendor he'd bathed in years ago. Oranges were still his favorite. Shoving aside the hard pinch of yearning, he closed the door behind him with a soft *snick* and went into factfinding mode.

Little bits of the countess were scattered haphazardly about. A woman settling into a space she hadn't long inhabited.

An emerald hair clip he pocketed without remorse. A bone china teacup with a splash of tea lingering in the bottom. A half-eaten scone on a chipped saucer. A folio littered with crumbs. Ink splattered on a sheet of wrinkled foolscap. Same girl, years later. As he recalled, Cece hadn't been a well-ordered person, rather a spontaneous one.

Which appealed to the passionate boy but would not to the circumspect man.

Jasper picked every lock on the escritoire in seconds. Riffled through items of scant interest to his current pursuit. Mounds of unpaid invoices and the accompanying notices demanding payment. Paltry bank statements, pleas for assistance from tenants of the Derbyshire estate and the majordomo at the cottage in Bath. London's finest clothier was no longer willing to attire the earl—nor was George Hoby, who crafted the finest boots in England.

Jasper still remembered his first pair, buttery black Wellingtons purchased after completion of a preliminary assignment for the Crown. Though he'd had to store the beauties in his wardrobe rather than wear them, pride in ownership and that sort of thing.

Rookery spies didn't wear Hoby.

Now, of course, he wore whatever he *liked*.

It took less than sixty seconds to ascertain the Earl of Edgerly's dire financial straits, leaving his countess to deal with the mess upon his death.

Other than that, he didn't find what he was looking for because Cece was cleverer than this.

She would never hide her dirty goods in a *desk*.

Jasper paced the room until he found the slight, almost unnoticeable ripple in a ragged Aubusson. The floorboard beneath the rug shifted when he stepped on it, enticement enough for him to drop to the troublesome knee he'd taken a bullet in years ago. Better this location, however, than the gut or chest. Ripping aside the carpet, he located the lip of what he suspected was a hidden chamber. He and Cece had secreted all manner of treasures in one such as this in his Northumberland bedchamber. Every space had a loose board hanging about that, with a little craftmanship, could be fashioned into a handy floor safe.

He selected a tool from his leather-bound set and went to work, edging the polished metal edge into the narrow gap in the planks. With a gentle twist, *very* gentle because he wanted to cover his work when he left, the board popped free. A puff of grimy dust rose with it, filling his nose and lungs. He held back a cough with a choked gasp, once again reminded of that pathetic sack of a gagging boy.

A satchel rested in the darkened cavity. Jasper wouldn't have been surprised to find Cece's initials neatly burned into the leather. The papers inside were varied—letters, contracts, statements—and more troubling than Xander Macauley's meager piece of information. Shoving to his feet, he crossed to the window, and held the correspondences in the watery sliver of moonlight. Patting his waistcoat pocket, Jasper wriggled his spectacles free, and slipped them on his face. Another nod to age, by hell. Nonetheless, the lenses cleared up the situation Cece had gotten herself in quite nicely. Forgeries of multiple documents proving Tobias Streeter to be far from her only target.

His heart kicking, Jasper scrubbed his hand over the nape of his neck.

Her promises were about as good as his, weren't they? Grifters, both of them.

This was when he caught sight of a woman wiggling through the hedges at the back edge of the property, a chit unaccountably outfitted in black from head to toe. He'd know her shape, her height, the way she moved, anywhere—even *with* the innumerable changes time had wrought.

At least she was wearing a gown and not the lad's trousers she'd loved so much. Trousers he'd admittedly been fond of as well.

Unable to tear his gaze away, he recorded her meandering journey in a direction that didn't lead to the front of the house, her spencer fluttering behind her like a phantom. She snuck in side entrances, too, as most scoundrels were wont to do. Exactly as he'd done.

When she got closer, her features materialized, a positively haunting portrait in the mist-laden night. Her hair was curling madly about her face, dense locks he'd wound about his fingers while he thrust inside her. Back in the day, he'd been unable to contain the strands, the woman, or his fucking obsession. Thank God times had changed. Dangerously, the glint of moonlight kissing her cheek, her bottom lip, the generous curves of a mature body, sent his stomach to his knees. She was *smiling*, proud of whatever mischief she'd gotten into. Same girl, all right.

Memories of their glorious, youthful summer rose from the fog to choke him, no grit from hidden storage chambers to blame.

He'd suppressed what he could of the past using the standard methods.

Time, liquor, women.

So many women in a desperate struggle to forget the *one*.

Crushing her papers in his fist, Jasper stalked down the corridor, determined to beat her to the pass. Leaning, he wrenched his pistol from his boot and emptied the chamber, hurling the lone bullet aside.

If Cece wanted to dance with criminals, she must learn how criminals *danced*.

He had her chest pressed to the wall seconds after she traversed the entranceway, the butt of the cocked pistol digging into her spine. A whispery breeze snaked inside the open door, wrapping her skirt about his legs and rushing the scent of orange blossoms into his nostrils for the first time in years, a tangle that sent his senses soaring. In response to his hold, she took a halting breath but didn't move an inch. Tossing her head, she purposely tumbled her glorious hair into his field of vision, blinding him. Though she was tall for a woman, he'd grown since their last meeting and gained two stone of muscle, giving him a distinct advantage. Not to mention the skills of defense he'd learned the hard way.

They held steady, pressed together like two pages in a book. Fighting a battle that was much more than physical. Realizing she was crawling inside his head like always, his blood pulsed, his chest tightening.

The jolt to his cock was unwelcome, but the jolt to his heart was *unacceptable*.

Worse, he had no free hand to capture the sneeze that echoed down the corridor.

Cece tilted her chin high, her lips compressing. If she smiled, he couldn't say what he'd do to her. "Oh, Crispin, is this any way to greet an old friend? And you're still sneezing at every hint of dust about a place. One would hope to outgrow asthma after all this time."

He shook her off like a fever, backing up a step, then another, until his back met the wall. He calmly released the pistol's hammer, letting her hear how close she'd been to disaster.

"You brought a pistol to this engagement? My, those rumors about you must be true."

Tucking his weapon away, he studied her back in increasing uneasiness. Honestly, he wasn't sure he was prepared to face her. "It's empty. This time. With the games you're playing, the next it won't be. No 'old friend' to save you from yourself."

Stepping to the side, she tidied her spencer like nothing unusual had occurred, then turned to face him with the grace of her station and the courage of the hellion he'd once known.

That's my girl, he thought before he could stop it. Grief had been grueling work, far more difficult than spying. Worse than death or so close to it a man couldn't see the difference. Regrettably or not, he'd never get over the burn of walking away from her that day in Northumberland and giving her to another man. Never.

"The earl's locks are pathetic," he murmured and arranged his coat over his pistol. He winced and flexed his throbbing finger. He would need to bind it when he got home. Ripping his glove off with his teeth, he stilled, finding her gaze fixed upon him.

Her eyes were the simmering green of dead seas and forgotten lakes, dark as peat, as he liked them. Perhaps he was crawling into her head as well. The scar splitting her eyebrow was there, attached to the memory of her tumbling from her mount when she was fifteen and slicing her brow on a stone. *Christ*, he'd been scared that day. Until she rolled over and issued a delighted gasp, calming him as nothing had before or since. He'd kissed her for the first time two days later, starting an affair that had nearly destroyed him.

As they stared, the world around them dissolved. The sounds of an aging house in repose, an exquisite woman's faint exhalations slipping past her lips, the tick of a clock all seeping into the nether as a familiar chemical wonder vibrated, thriving even if he'd wished it away with his every breath.

He was mad to think attraction disappeared because a desperate soul willed it to.

Her attention lowered to the bulge from the weapon he'd hastily concealed. "You're intent on fulfilling this thug persona, aren't you? You can drop the rookery accent while you're at it. I remember the real one, you see."

With a guttural curse, Jasper shoved his glove under his armpit and wrenched his gaze from her. Her bloody forgeries were still clutched in his fist, and he tightened his fingers around them to keep himself from doing treacherous things his body desired but his heart did not. "I know about the trickery, Countess. Now, sadly, you're playing with people who won't find your nefarious skill as charming as I did. A lead barrel jammed in your back will be the least of it."

She ripped the documents free as she brushed past him. "I'm not a countess anymore. I never really was."

Jasper snorted, right on her heels. He wished he didn't want to stay close. Because staying close meant hanging on to the scent of oranges, an aroma that had the power to slay him. "You'll be a countess until you drop, minx."

She stumbled but corrected her measured stride almost before he noticed. *Minx.* A nickname he'd never meant to utter again in this lifetime. Damn, damn, *damn* her. "Like you'll be Crispin Sinclair, Baron Never-do-well until *you* drop."

"That nipper's been dead for years, Cece. The title's in abeyance, though I've kept up maintenance on the Northumberland estate through my solicitors. An anonymous arrangement."

Stunned, she glanced back. Her grip loosened and one of the sheets fluttered away like a feather. "You've been to Northumberland?"

He worked his other glove off with a grimace, his tone harsher than he'd like. Anger meant caring, in his book. And caring meant not getting the job done without wounds inflicted upon oneself. He'd had enough wounds imposed on his body and heart for a lifetime. "Not since that day. There wasn't any reason to return, was there? I could have dropped in for tea and inquired after your marriage, I suppose."

She hummed in reply, which was *no* reply, and entered the earl's study.

Fighting that annoying tickle in his throat, Jasper halted in the doorway, mortified to see the state he'd left the room in. The Aubusson in an awkward fold, the plank to the floor safe tossed negligently to the side. Cece went to her haunches, secreted the papers inside the satchel, worked the board into place, and smoothed the carpet over it. "Some emissary you are. The scent of sulfur lingering in the doorway, a fresh scratch on the lock. I knew you were inside before I fit the key to the tumblers."

He pushed off the jamb, forcing back a stutter. His glove tumbled to the floor. "How do you know about that?"

Cece tilted her head, her gaze sweeping him before drifting away. "I kept up with the London newspapers. A week or two delayed in the hinterlands but delivered eventually. Something about this person mentioned repeatedly in the scandal rags struck a chord. Jasper was your middle name and Noble was your mother's maiden name, wasn't it? I put two and two together. The rest are speculations, though I thank you for substantiating them."

"Noble was my grandmother's surname," he whispered, desperately uncomfortable with how well she knew him. How *much* she knew.

"I read a letter from your cousin, the devious one you said was a ragtag investigator of some sort. Snuck it right out of your desk drawer that weekend you were off on a hunting adventure with the vicar and his son. Your cousin said you had skills a government agency might want, and that he knew people. In the event your father's 'black moods' finally drove you away." She shrugged a slim shoulder and rose. A stray flutter of moonlight whispered over her, dust motes glinting as the beam settled around her. Jasper decided he couldn't have looked away if the barrel of a pistol had been jammed in *his* back.

She fluttered her hand, as if the discussion wasn't that important when every word pierced him like a needle. "It wasn't hard to figure out where you'd disappeared to, Crispin. Another life. Engaged to the famous gardener, Necessity Byrne. Lost her to the Earl of Stanford, didn't you? A baron might be able to steal a girl from an earl, but not this Shoreditch hooligan you've become. That is an impressive feat. I wonder which of your talents you used to convince her."

Jasper tunneled his hands in his trouser pockets and rocked back on his heels, ignoring the prickle of heat to his cheeks. This interrogation was almost worse than the one in the medieval dungeon in Derbyshire, when he'd been interrupted while searching for falsified letters from a senior association of the King. It had been six weeks before he was healthy enough to accept another assignment. Broken bones never healed as fast as you wanted them to. "I was never engaged to anyone. I stole a telescope to help Necessity secure her earl, in fact. I still get questions about the bloody thing. Who knew it was the rarest specimen in Christendom?"

Cece unfurled her spencer and pitched it over the nearest chair like an actress walking onstage. She could be melodramatic when the situation called for it. "I have no idea what that means."

"Probably for the best," Jasper murmured, trying industriously to ignore the changes time had welcomed. The countess was fuller of hip and plumper of bosom. Her hair a bit longer and escaping its tight confines, the moonlight only serving to turn the ginger tresses aflame. He needed to remind himself these emotions were a lad's obsession, youthful passion, and idiocy tied in a knot around a tangle of loose memories. He'd done the infatuation dance with this woman before, and he wasn't doing it again.

A heart, after all, could only be broken once.

"Does this Leighton crew—two dukes, a viscount, and an earl among them—know you were brought up as a gentleman? So-called." Turning, Cece leaned her hip on the desk, her skirts settling around her. She was dressed for intrigue in varying shades of midnight, and she'd yet to whisper a word of her activities this eve to him. Maybe she considered slinking through hedges and slipping in side doors a normal occurrence. "Funny. You ran from that world only to land right back in it."

"My position required I *be* someone else, Countess. And truthfully, I liked him better."

She raised her arms, removing one hair clip, then another. They pinged on the desktop as she dropped them like coins down a well.

Released, her hair collapsed in a molten cascade down her back, the final unfurling streaking temptingly along his spine as her fingertips might. "Gone is the sticky grip of family. And the past."

"They're quite my family now," he said, knowing when he was being seduced. Successfully. Beneath the thankfully concealing swing of his greatcoat, his cock was as hard as a brick. Come to think of it, which he tried to avoid on good days, he'd not had the opportunity to take her in the many ways he'd dreamed. Pleasuring her over that ancient desk of hers, for example, would check one item off an insanely long list.

She tapped her slipper, also dark as night, without comment.

"I wasn't the one who got married," he murmured flatly, changing tactics, disgusted he was unable to let the matter drop when he'd had years to get over it. "I had to find a family somewhere as the one in Northumberland was no longer an option."

She curled her fingers around a hair clip she'd yet to release. "I had no choice. Do you recall how we were found, tangled like two cats around each other?"

He did recall. A thousand times since, at least. Glancing to the mantel clock, Jasper told himself he'd allow this disaster of a conversation two more minutes.

Two minutes to warn her.

Two minutes to forgive her.

He wished to tell her he'd done better than forgive, he'd *forgotten*. However, lies were off his docket as he was trying like hell to become a changed man.

She didn't back away when he crossed to her. The hard swallow she took was the only indication of her unease. Jasper tipped her chin high, bringing her eyes to his. They sparked with fury and a bottomless emotion he didn't have the wherewithal to manage. He simply couldn't after what she'd once meant to him.

Despite this avowal, he wasn't departing Mayfair without touching her.

Proving to himself that he *could* walk away.

"I have contacts in every ballroom, parlor, and bawdy house in this city, Cece. The newspapers, the House of Lords, and the Commons aren't out of range. I'll be alerted if you think to do more of whatever it is you've been doing with these forgeries. I've already put out the word. If it's money you need to keep the earl's ship afloat, there are other ways to locate it. Find a wealthy husband, for one." He smoothed his thumb over her jaw, his hidden heart racing, realizing he was nearing the end of his stamina. Her skin was as soft as gossamer beneath his calloused fingertips, five points of astounding contact. "If you wanted my attention, you've got it. But awareness comes at a price."

She drew her tongue along her bottom lip, her breath a rasp that streaked across his cheek. "You could help me, Crispin, like you used to. We made exceptional partners."

He shook his head, fighting his attraction to not only her but that life. They'd been children, their antics hurting no one. Forged letters, correspondences, and the like. Pranks for the most part with no true intent. He was the first to admit it had been astounding what she could do, replicating any inscription placed before her. Now, it was dangerous business she was involved in. He could ask questions and try to ease the burning ember in the pit of his belly, a part of him reignited, but he didn't want the particulars of how she'd found herself embroiled in goings-on beyond her reach.

Not from her. She'd twist the truth into a pretzel and choke him with it.

Nonetheless, his men were already on the case. He was going to crush this mischief into dust whether she liked it or not. She had no idea the favors owed him from gutter to Crown.

Temper pinkened her cheeks as he delayed, warming his palm and sending desperate little flutters through him. "You were always ready for a bit of mischief. Don't tell me you've changed that much. I know you want to."

"You knew the boy, not the man." He released his hold on her and stepped back. He did *want*, frantically enough to have him considering taking her up on her offer to spend another second with her. "And the man is considering tying you to a chair to stop you. If you recall, we talked about that once. I never got the chance," he whispered, leaning in until her teasing scent stung his senses, "but I might like to."

31

Her gasp was low, raw, *there*. A solid burst of awakening settled between them.

His breath leaked away as realization dawned. She wasn't immune to him, which made him deadly happy.

If he could ever be happy about her marrying another man and only now, too many years later, thinking to track him down.

The sound of feet pounding on the staircase and along the corridor had them swinging toward the door. Cece grabbed his wrist, her first display of true agitation. Tremors slipped past her fingers and raced up his arm. "Hide, Cris, *please*. I'll take him back to bed. His governess must be sleeping."

Jasper blinked in confusion as he stepped behind the open door and out of sight, following her command without hesitation. "*Who?*"

"My son."

Chapter Two

The neighbor girl beat me soundly at chess. Somehow, I must better my game. Everyone knows girls mustn't be allowed to win.
  -Crispin Sinclair's journal entry, 1811

Streeter, Macauley & Company
Limehouse Basin Lock, London

Her plan had almost worked.

Cece frowned, her fingers curling around the cup's delicate bone handle. Until the reprobate everyone in England called Jasper Noble was nowhere to be found when she returned from escorting Josiah to bed, thereby destroying weeks of effort to gain his attention.

Attention that came with a price. A price she was willing to pay.

It stung to have her offer rejected—and from a man who'd once given her anything she asked for, including her request to let her go years ago. Despite her pleas, she'd searched for him in the shadowy corners of the church the morning of her wedding, only realizing as Edgerly pressed an arid kiss to her cheek that Crispin Sinclair wasn't stepping in to save her.

Though he'd liked saving her once upon a time, the core strategy of her current plan.

Cece took a sip of tepid tea and considered her dilemma. She'd not imagined government moles or whatever it was Crispin had been to have such high moral standards. She fondly recalled the times he'd agreed to any gambit she suggested, traveling to the ends of the earth when she asked him to.

Her powers of persuasion over that young man had been formidable.

As his had been over her.

The contrast between past and present verified his statement from the previous evening. She'd known the boy, not the man.

The man...

Ah, the pinch to Cece's heart was brutal. Jasper Noble's romantic forays were legendary, spilled-ink-across-a-thousand-broadsheets renowned. Actresses, opera singers, bored wives, dispassionate widows, with a stunning mistress thrown in here and there for excitement. She was nothing to him, the unsophisticated chit from Northumberland who'd rejected him in the worst way possible. Fragile male egos often never recovered from such a slight even if the reasons were numerable and unconquerable. She'd had no choice when faced with the threat of her family's ruin.

The truth was, Crispin didn't trust her and never would again.

Twisting the conundrum into a knot, around him, she didn't trust herself.

Nevertheless, she'd waited, communicating her plans to return to the city with a few loose-tongued members of society, thereby ensuring her name was mentioned in the London newspapers. If Crispin had been waiting for her to be free, she was. Edgerly had been dead for almost two years, yet he'd never come to her.

So, she would come to *him*.

Determined, Cece settled the cup in the saucer with a *click*. The vision of Crispin ripping off his glove with his teeth flashed through her mind, sending a jolt to every forgotten, lonesome part of her body. What a feral specimen he'd grown into, this rookery business perhaps not simply for show. There was a predatory glimmer about him, elegance with an edge. A menacing persona softened by innate refinement he carried about like his portmanteau. His eyes so blue they'd looked black in the hellish, golden lamplight, his gaze focused solely on her.

Oh, she'd once loved that absorption.

Although he'd changed in a multitude of ways. She'd never had to tilt her head to gaze into his lovely face. Never feared her hands couldn't span the width of his shoulders if she clasped them during a heated kiss. His adorable sneeze and the hiss when he'd exhaled were the only familiar pieces, perhaps pieces only familiar to *her*.

When she was much the same: a hoyden who cleaned up well.

Cece snaked her hand in her reticule and fingered the bullet she'd retrieved from the hallway the previous evening. She clamped her thighs together to halt the tremors. She still desired him. One look across Edgerly's darkened corridor had revealed that not so surprising fact. His gentle shove, pressing her into the wall, had done marvelous things to her. Their friendship was dead, certainly, but the inexplicable yearning she'd always experienced around him was alive. His body had spoken to hers in a silent, sensual whisper, much to his chagrin, she imagined.

The brackish scent of the Thames sat solidly in the steadying breath she took, as the office she inhabited was less than two hundred yards off Dunbar Wharf and the Limehouse mudflats, an area no lady in her right mind ventured to. The space was teeming with aromas both expected and not: rotting fish, tea, freshly sawn wood, and linseed oil. The sound of a working dock outside was an unusual but comforting pulse. This unconventional warehouse, decorated in splashes of crimson and black that looked more gentlemen's club than rookery business, was part of Crispin's new life as a member of the Leighton Cluster.

Rugged yet sophisticated, like he was.

With a sigh, Cece tucked the bullet in a secreted nook in her reticule. What if this new existence of his was more enticing than any she could offer? His sea-blue eyes full of secrets, his hair streaked with gray, Crispin had changed more than she had. He was a man, when she'd never escaped being that raggedy, dirt-streaked girl. At least it felt this way to her.

Hell's teeth, Constance, buck up.

She'd come this far to snag his attention, and she wasn't stopping now.

"I propose a house party, a solid strategy for introducing you to eligible men, my lady."

Snatched from her daydreams, Cece glanced into the face of the most beautiful woman she'd ever seen. Hildegard Streeter sat behind a massive mahogany desk, her composed smile intimidating *and* welcoming, a neat trick. She ran a matchmaking enterprise with her partner, the Duchess of Markham, though the pair refused to describe the Duchess Society as such. The daughter of an earl who'd married brilliantly beneath her, Cece had engaged Mrs. Streeter's services as part two of her plan to step into Jasper Noble's line of sight and stay there. She and her husband, Tobias, were quite the stunning pair. And gloriously happy, go figure. Cece figured a woman who'd made a wise and courageous choice in her selection of a spouse would agree with Cece's plan to do the same if given the chance.

Clutching her reticule as Hildy's words penetrated her consciousness, she edged forward in her chair. "House party?"

Regrettably, this suggestion wasn't a valid one.

Cece wasn't a competent hostess. Edgerly hadn't liked socializing, and they'd spent so little time together after grasping how unsuitable they were that repeat performances as the entertaining countess hadn't been an issue. Cece rode a horse as well as any man, played exceptional chess and passable billiards, and she could pin an archery target dead-center with her eyes closed. If world affairs or the latest literary goings-on were brought into a conversation, she was ready.

Skills no one in society appreciated in a woman.

Forget even *thinking* about the forgery business.

She was hopeless with place settings, flower arrangements, and menu planning. Watercolors, needlepoint, and delicate conversations were not a strength. Her mother hadn't cared to teach her, and frankly, she hadn't cared to learn. Due to her transgressions with Crispin, she'd never had a Season on the marriage mart, nor had she wanted one. Ballroom conversation wasn't a talent. "I'm afraid my seclusion in Northumberland means I don't have experience organizing parties. Or attending them."

Mrs. Streeter raised her hand with a pained grimace. "Hildy, please."

"Constance, then." She smiled, never one to lean on formality herself. "If we're negotiating." The only person who called her Cece was the scoundrel she'd run to London to track down. The previous night had been the first time she'd heard the name whispered in *years*.

Giving her client an inspective glance, Hildy made a notation in her folio. Cece wasn't sure why she'd been asked to meet in Limehouse instead of the Duchess Society's Mayfair offices. It was highly suspect, which Cece adored. She loved nothing more than when her curiosity was engaged. "We can get you up to speed easily, Constance. You're lovely in every way if a bit... novel. You're a mystery, and society appreciates solving them. Or trying to, because they are, in essence, bored silly. The event will be a superb reintroduction to the *ton*, and we can truthfully pose it as such since you've been away for some time. I'll handle coordination of the details, including the guest list. We have files on almost every eligible bachelor in London for the past fifteen years. It pays to retain the notes because the knaves often outlive their spouses, then we're on to round two when they're back on the market."

Cece gave her teacup a gentle turn, striving to appear calm about a topic that scared her more than forging documents did. "I'm not acquainted with many families in the city."

"Leave that to me. I promise, no scoundrels seeking a wealthy widow are receiving this invitation. *They* will be on display, not you. Parading before us for our consideration." She smiled in a dazzling show of authority and confidence. "Although they may not realize it, which is the most enjoyable part of my job. I married a self-made man and have come to appreciate hanging the born-into-wealth ones out to dry."

Cece trailed a gloved finger along the scrolled lip of the desk in mild agitation. Hildy had a flowing style of penmanship that would be easy to replicate. Nothing like her husband's signature and the crafty curl he added to the S. His had taken a full week and many sheets of foolscap to learn how to reproduce. The loupe in her pocket warmed to the thought of a new adventure. "There may be a misunderstanding. I'm not wealthy."

Hildy paused, her brow lifting. "How *not* wealthy? It will help to identify what you require from this union. All you require if you please. Unfortunately, many of the men on the hunt are seeking financial salvation, though not all."

Cece shrugged, fighting the urge to lift her thumb to her lips and chew on her nail. "I'm living on borrowed time at the London terrace. The earl's cousin, Archibald, appropriated the entailed properties in short order. I'm surprised it's taken him this long to reach the city. He signed over the Northumberland estate because, like most, he cares little for visiting that far north, much less living. An agreement reached if I waived plans to reside in the various dowager cottages dotted across England. I live frugally, and I have funds to maintain my home from a modest stipend left me by my grandmother. You see, I come to you not for money but *companionship*."

Hildy stilled, her startled gaze meeting Cece's. Her eyes were a soothing indigo, far from Crispin's turbulent blue, but second in beauty to her mind. "I admit to not hearing that often."

Cece flicked her fingers, not wanting to delve too deeply into this topic. "My marriage was a lonely one. Let's keep it at that."

Hildy pressed her lips together, perhaps to contain a show of sympathy. "In my experience, most are."

Cece gazed lazily about the gorgeous space as if this next bit wasn't the most critical. "One trivial matter." She glanced at Hildy, nerves dancing beneath her skin. "I would like your brethren to attend."

Sitting back, Hildy let her grin fly free. A laugh soon followed, delightful to the extreme. In her courting days, she must have beaten suitors off with a parasol. If Cece had friends in the city, if she knew *how* to make friends, she hoped this woman would become one of them. "Brethren?"

"The, um"—Cece gave her cup another spin in its saucer—"Leighton Cluster."

"Oh, my," Hildy murmured and brought her hand to her mouth to hold back her mirth. "Don't let my husband hear you call them that. He loathes the moniker."

Cece straightened the seam of her glove, unsure how to respond. She found the name silly too, of course, but it's what the *ton* called the motley group surrounding the Duke of Leighton and had for years. She should know. She'd been searching the scandal rags since the hour she forced Crispin from her life, waiting for news of him. Somewhere along the way, once she connected him to the infamous Jasper Noble, his association with this group began to crop up with regularity. All told, they'd blazed a raucous trail through London.

Her gut told her if *they* attended this ridiculous event, *he* would attend.

Seeing the doubtful expression on Hildy's face, Cece tried another ploy. "It will add legitimacy, won't it? A duke, a viscount, that celebrated Scottish author tossed in for amusement."

Hildy's smile grew, her eyes glowing. "I can secure the Duke and Duchess of Markham because this is Duchess Society business, and if Her Grace asks His Grace to attend a function for one of her clients, he will without question. Lord Remington is at his country estate as his wife is expecting and close to labor." She sighed, knocking her quill against the folio with hard taps. "That's too bad because Chance is a marvelous conversation starter. Dashiell Campbell, the author you mentioned, is a dead certainty. He'll charm the clothing off everyone. All I have to do is tell him he can prepare a short reading from his latest book, and he's there. The Duke and Duchess of Leighton are in Ireland, so they're out. This may be for the best because Leighton can be temperamental," she said, her voice lowering with confidence, "and often starts brawls with his friends when he's wearied. He and Dash got in a huge row last month over something horribly trivial and ruined a marvelous dinner party in the making. I'll never get the plum stains out of that carpet. In any case, they made up the following day, the childish fools."

Beginning to perspire, Cece shifted her legs beneath her skirt. The room was warm, her nerves were racing, and the air snaking through the open window was damp and uncompromising. London in the summer was insufferable when the sea breezes of Northumberland would have soothed. "The others, perhaps they can attend. The Earl of Stanford?"

Who would bring his countess, the woman rumored to have been engaged to Crispin.

Hildy leaned forward on her elbows, her smirk five shades past cheeky. "You realize the remaining Leighton Cluster aren't going to give this party any shine, my husband, Tobias, among them. In fact, the risk for disruption rises with their attendance. Xander Macauley likes nothing more than bruising highborn cheeks. Although Stanford attending decreases the probability that Xander will get in a muddle." Sitting back, she clicked her tongue against her teeth. "A calming presence on his brother, that one."

Cece clenched her fingers in silk and released a hushed breath. This was it. Time to roll the dice. "What about Jasper Noble?"

"Noble?" Hildy glowered. Exhaled softly. Rolled her shoulders. Flattened her hands to the desktop. "I suppose, yes. Apparently, he's here to stay. Xander heartily approves of him, as does Tobias. Dash worships him, follows him around like a pup, in fact. Showed him those pram designs before anyone, I believe. And there *was* the telescope affair, a favor for the Countess of Stanford when she was trying to make the biggest apology of her life to the man she loved." With a huff, she snapped her folio shut. "Although Noble's horrid on paper, my dear, with a shadowy set of credentials my investigators have been unable to verify. A first in my business. He's the only unattached member of the brethren, as you called them, but he's not one to concern yourself with. I can add his name for spice to the stew only."

He'd be fine on paper if he told the truth about who he is.

Instead of sharing this wisdom, Cece merely nodded. "I understand. A blackguard, when we're crossing those off your, um, my list. Though he could be a beneficial guest for people who like a little scandal at their house parties. Better entertainment than the author, perchance?"

Hildy's spine straightened, awareness capturing her porcelain features. She paused a lingering moment before replying, "Blackguard may be too harsh a word, though scoundrel is not. And scandalous describes his brand of charm perfectly. An *available* female enticement or two to capture his fancy might be a way to keep him out of trouble, otherwise he'll be a fox in a henhouse with the jaded wives in attendance. It's vexing, truly. If he gave me half a chance, I'd locate the ideal wife for him, but that's another struggle. He claims marriage is not for him." She tapped her quill to the desk like a judge handing down a verdict. "Not that we're matchmakers, mind you. We introduce, we arrange, but we never solicit."

Fox in a henhouse. Cece lost her breath but recovered nicely.

Never mind the scandal rags, his friends thought this of him!

She tightened her hands into fists, crumpling her skirt. She could do this. She could play the grieving widow in need of a husband if it allowed her a private conversation with Crispin. Despite the attraction she worried would stay with her until she kicked, perhaps she'd find she didn't like him anymore.

If their previous encounter was any indication, he didn't seem to like her.

These were dangerous waters she'd decided to dive into. Aside from her illicit hobby, she wasn't accustomed to duplicity. Northumberland didn't offer opportunities for anything more sensational than a gallop across her estate, mounted astride whilst wearing boy's trousers. Too, she didn't win every contest she entered, unlike her childhood friend.

She was rather used to *losing*. Her heart, her hopes, her dreams.

Maybe it wasn't a bad idea to follow Crispin's example. If he'd successfully pretended to be someone else for years, Cece could certainly manage such a pretense for a few measly days.

Heart thumping, Hildy strode across her bedchamber, her eyes fatigued from reading for hours by dull lamplight. Dawn was announcing itself in the crimson glow edging around the curtains, and the echoes of a waking house were sneaking into the room. Her research project had allowed little time to prepare for the coming morning. Too soon, children, cats, and dogs would be demanding sustenance, attention, *love*.

Thankfully, she had loads of each to share.

"Darling, wake up," she whispered, dropping her book on the bedside table and giving her husband's shoulder a gentle shake. The man who'd once ruled the Limehouse docks and claimed to have enemies on every corner was sleeping deeply, another beautiful thing he'd said their marriage, their life, had given him. Now a self-taught architect, Tobias Streeter obliged clients at every level of society, the most dangerous thing to occur in his day might be a boisterous disagreement over a floor plan.

"Kittens," Tobias mumbled drowsily. "Crate. Kitchen." He'd been up half the night himself with a newly adopted cat, Darcy, who'd wandered onto their property months ago and promptly gotten in the family way. Adorably, Toby tended to name them after fictional male characters because he invariably guessed incorrectly about their sex. They'd switched to Austen because everyone had gotten sick of Shakespeare. "Three orange, two black as sin. The mum is fine. Nick Bottom is guarding the door. If he wasn't so old, I'd guess he was the proud papa."

"I found him," Hildy whispered and slipped into bed, curling her body around her husband's and hugging him tightly. He typically slept in the buff, and her body heated as tenderness thrummed through her. He was still the most gorgeous man she'd ever seen and would *ever* see. This was fact, as she'd assessed every rascal on the market for years. "It took me months upon months, and heaven knows, someone highly connected hid his identity as well as any soul I've come across, but I prevailed. You don't call me your stubborn missus without reason."

Tobias took her hand and dragged it beneath the counterpane, pressing her fingers over his rigid shaft. "Ah, luv, you found him, dead certain. You know I fancy the devil out of waking up this way."

Hildy laughed, tossing a quick glance at the fragile light seeping into the room. If they were swift, perhaps they had time for a quick romp. *After* she told him. Nudging him to his back, she settled her legs astride his lean hips, her favored position. He was hard and ready beneath her. "News first, lovemaking second."

With a sigh, his lashes lifted, a dreamy smile spreading across his face. Stunned, Hildy stared in wonder, amazed he had the power to make her melt after all these years. He was graying at the temple and crown, tiny grooves streaking from his apple-green eyes, his olive skin gently sun-kissed—the color speaking of his Romani heritage—and he was *hers*. She'd made the best decision of her life forcing his hand and making him accept he was falling for her. She appreciated being a ruffian's wife much more than she had being an earl's daughter.

"Luv," he whispered, shifting his hips to nudge his cock against her folds, "if you keep looking at me like that, this conversation is going to be very, very short. Only, I can see you have a bit between your teeth this morn. Let's get talk out of the way, so I can soundly tup my delectable wife."

Provoked, Hildy leaned to dust her lips across his but pulled away when his fingers snaked into her hair and tugged, a potent threat to deepen the kiss. He growled and anchored her hips against his. "Three minutes, Hildy girl, that's what I'm giving."

Hildy braced her palm on his chest, knowing he could take control in seconds should he choose to. In fact, she hoped he would. "I've found him."

Tobias released a fatigued breath. "You've lost me, luv. Which happens with regularity."

"Jasper Noble. I've found out who he is."

Tobias rolled his eyes in characteristic masculine disdain. He considered some of the Duchess Society's investigative work to be a shade on the gossipy side. "So, he comes from Five Points instead of Shoreditch? Has a mistress you didn't note on the first fact check? Each of us has things we'd not wish snatched from a locked trunk. I bloody well did. Leave it be."

Hildy felt a nip, rarely suffered, mind you, of annoyance. Her work was as important as his. She had clients by the plenty, a waiting list even! A marquess had come calling last week, she could tell him.

"Oh, no, *Gadji*, don't go getting that way," he said and lunged for her when she leaned away from him. "I didn't mean it, however it came out and whatever I said."

Her husband knew when he called her this Romani term endearment, she'd crumble. Giving in, she grasped the book she'd left on the table, laid it on his chest, and began to flip pages.

Tobias glanced down. "You brought *Debrett's* to bed?"

His father, Viscount Craven, had an entry—a circumstance they rarely talked about. Tobias, a by-blow who'd only been acknowledged on his sire's deathbed, had buried those ghosts long ago. "Look," she said and tapped her finger to the page.

Tobias groaned and held out his hand. Smothering a smile, she reached for his spectacles, watching as he fit a metal arm over each ear.

Yes, she thought, *I'll ask him to leave them on.*

Unaware of her lusty planning, he shot a quick glance at the book, then flopped back, thoroughly unimpressed. "Who the hell is Baron Neeley?" He scowled, and she traced her fingertip along his bottom lip until his eyes darkened another degree. "You woke me for *this* after I've been tending a birthing feline for hours?"

"You missed the best part, Toby." With a huff, she closed the book and dumped it on the bed beside him. "I swear, you'd make a horrible investigator. I'm glad I have a ready stable of them for Duchess Society business."

He shifted his hips to remind her that her time was up. "You tell me what I missed while I lie here imagining how you're soon going to make me the happiest man in London. Do you recall what I whispered to you this morning over tea? I'd love to take you that way, luv, fast and furiously."

Hildy swatted his chest, her cheeks catching fire. She'd been thinking about his naughty suggestion for the better part of the day, exactly his plan. "The baron's name is Crispin *Jasper* Sinclair. A man we've found hasn't been heard from since 1815. The title's in abeyance, in actuality, though the lone property attached to it is being managed through an anonymous benefactor. No one seems to care because the family has about as much clout as, well, a cobbler's. The maternal grandmother's surname was Noble, darling. It took quite a lot of digging to come up with *that* tasty morsel because she was as far from nobility as one can get. The daughter of a butcher, I believe."

Tobias stilled, a spark of interest finally entering his gaze. Aside from being the most stunning man in England, he was the cleverest.

He didn't welcome being outwitted. "Maybe you got a rubbish report from those fiends you employ. You want me to believe that rookery filcher is a *baron?*"

Hildy clicked her tongue against her teeth, a habit she'd been unable to break no matter how hard she tried. "His gutter accent slips when he's foxed, leaving him sounding like a prince. His bearing speaks of ballrooms, not docksides. We've all witnessed the transformation when he lets his guard down. He speaks French, darling. When we had that associate of yours over for dinner, I decided he understood every-thing the comte said after he laughed at a joke before the translator explained it. Don't you grasp what I'm saying? He isn't who anyone thinks he is. No one knows." Leaning down, she kissed his cheek in delight. "Except *her*. And me. And now you, you lucky devil."

Tobias turned her head and whispered against her lips, "Her?"

"The Countess of Edgerly, my new client. Crispin Sinclair's neighbor in Northumberland." Hildy giggled, unable to hold it back. She didn't think of herself as a giggler. "I think she's the one Jasper told Necessity about when he was busy stealing that telescope. A sad speech about lost loves and such."

"Here we go again," Tobias muttered gloomily.

"This isn't some silly matchmaking foray we're talking about," she bit out, struggling to rise. She would sleep in one of the guest cham-bers tonight and show him but good. Although she'd have to pleasure herself at this rate because, as usual, he'd gotten her worked up by doing almost nothing. "If I'm correct, this is the discovery of the century."

Laughing, Tobias snaked his arm around her waist and rolled her beneath him, knocking the copy of *Debrett's* to the floor. He seized her mouth in a kiss that left her breathless before lifting his head just enough for her to witness his appalling smirk. "Take it easy, *Gadji*. No one believes in your silly matchmaking more than I do."

"You should have seen her when I said Jasper would be a fox in a henhouse among so many women." She nibbled on his jaw until he settled firmly between her thighs and issued one of those rusty groans that drove her mad with want. "I almost felt bad for making the comment when I was merely testing the waters. Her interest in him was masked but apparent. She suggested he be invited to the country party, after all. I had to see if my suspicion was right, didn't I? I can only do my best for her if I know what the true situation is. And she left out a lot when I demanded everything."

He sighed, realizing he had to ask. "Such as?"

"There's a little boy, not her son, but a lad rumored to be a cast-off of her husband's. This information my runner got from the cousin of a sister of a maid in the late earl's employ. It says so much about her, wonderful things to my mind, that she took him in. Most women in her position wouldn't."

"Certainly, that was my experience. My father's wife loathed me from the first moment she learned of my existence. It's likely part of the reason he chooses never to acknowledge me."

Hildy's heart squeezed for the scared boy he'd once been. She laid her brow to his, hoping he could feel her heart beating in love against his chest because he would not want her sympathy. "I had to find out, Toby."

"Your persistence scares me, luv." He palmed her cheek and shifted her gaze to his. "He won't like your meddling. If you've hit the mark, a fine deduction, I'll admit, but Noble created another life for a reason. Mac estimates he worked for the Crown at a dangerously high level, and I tend to believe him. I've seen the man do things no regular bloke should know how to do. He can shoot the wings off a fly. Dead center, every bullet. There's skill and then there's training, a monumental difference. I saw him break a man's wrist in seconds when he tried to rob him in the street."

He believed her! "Then—"

Tobias pressed his thumb to her lips. "This information stays with us, do you understand? Until we know what's going on. Why this countess chit has shown up in London, requesting your services and the attention of a supposed spy. I don't like walking into traps, and I for damned sure don't like *you* walking into them. Truth be bloody told, I won't allow it."

She started to argue, but the hard edge in his emerald eyes swayed her. He was a rookery thug beneath his gorgeous polish, she must remember. A fighter first, a lover second. "Fine, but I won't budge on holding the outing at Leighton's estate. Invitations are sent, the planning complete. The countess came to me, and I mean to help her. With what, I'm not yet sure. You can stay by my side every second if that's what it takes. I'm going to tell her to bring the boy to the house party to let the suitable men see the full package they'd be getting."

"Let Jasper see, you're meaning. Your schemes don't fly far past me, luv."

Hildy didn't respond, only smiled beneath his caressing fingertip.

Tobias's chest rose and fell, his keen mind churning in that wonderful way. In the end, he didn't speak, but merely laid his body across her and gave her pleasure of the wildest kind.

And... he left his spectacles on.

Chapter Three

Meet me by the fountain at midnight, Ce.
    -Note to a neighbor, 1814

J asper gave his portmanteau a punitive kick, then sent the
invitation waiting patiently on the escritoire an acid glance. The
emerald hair clip atop it added a dollop of vexation, much like a
cherry slapped atop a stale slice of cake.

He didn't want to go to this goddamn affair. His gut had determined it was dangerous—and he trusted his gut above all. *A countess's
reintroduction to society*, the flowery script claimed.

The Duchess Society's name for this disaster in the making.

Cece was a crafty one; he'd almost forgotten how devious.
Demanding without actually demanding—and in a way he wouldn't be
able to refuse. There wasn't a more tenacious woman in England, he
knew for a fact.

She'd gone through those blasted marriage brokers, making herself a proper client.

When he'd never been able to tell Hildegard Streeter no. Rolling his shoulders with a sigh, Jasper glanced at the window and the mist-laden lane beyond his Bloomsbury terrace. The sky was a fierce shade of gray that matched his mood. Hildy was as frightening as her husband, and this judgment coming from an emissary who'd been in more terrifying situations than everyone in the Leighton Cluster *combined*.

With her winning smile, Streeter's wife had requested he join the country party she was hosting. She'd even added "darling friend" at the end of the attack. Support for her business and some such blather. As many suitable men in attendance as possible, she'd claimed, when he wasn't suitable, and they both knew it.

He didn't miss the verbal blade held sweetly to his neck.

Jasper dragged his knuckle across a streak on the windowpane, detesting his preference for strong women, friend or lover, when weak-willed ones were so much easier to manage. Regrettably, he held Hildy in great affection for her savvy *and* her excellent choice in spouses. Tobias was the brightest bulb in the city for securing her as far as Jasper was concerned. When his own dreams had slipped away without him fighting hard enough to snatch them up.

He guessed he liked them both more than any couple he'd ever known.

Shite. He flipped the portmanteau's brass lock, spilling it wide. A miserable afternoon spent packing formal blacks for a dreary party teaming with toffs, dandies, and dupes. Dejection his boon companion as he watched Cece parade around while chaps of a certain station vied for a spot on her dance card. Scoundrels like him wouldn't be allowed within two feet of a countess, invitation or no. Jasper understood Hildy had invited him to entertain, not to actually *partake*. At one time, with the baron bit, he might've been permitted more leeway, but even then, his humble title hadn't been enough to lay claim to a viscount's daughter. When he'd gotten quite skillful at not fixating on the chit, here she was, in his life again.

He could make an excuse, he reasoned, buffing the toe of his neatly polished boot across a gold thread in the rug. A business emergency of some sort. A sick friend. Although all his friends would be at the damned party.

"Quit your complaining, will ye?" His valet hobbled into the chamber, a superfine coat hanging from his crooked index finger. His rheumy brown eyes took in the half-packed scene with a grimace. "Tasty food and drink for days at a duke's. Ladies in posh gowns gushing over your sad self. Billiards and hunting and such. Games for men with time on their wee hands." Nelson tossed the garment atop the open luggage with a huff. "The pampered life you lead, laddie, is beyond me."

Jasper turned from the animated display on the lane outside— vendors hawking roasted nuts, meat pies, and flowers in the misty rain —a scene he wished he could disappear into. A dead baron beckoned lately, and he wasn't up to answering the call. "You don't know how challenging society gatherings are to bear. The simpering wives, the curious ingénues, the offers I'll have to brush off. You recognize they enjoy a slice of the stews as a diversion. Rough handling isn't appropriate for musicales but works well in the bedchamber." He gave the cuff of the coat lying atop his portmanteau a twist, smoothing out a wrinkle. "It isn't as if I won't be slipped a note or two. Or ten. Even without a bloody title, I'm sought-after. The shadowy rumors about my past have only increased my popularity. Society likes a puzzle, don't they?"

Nelson limped across the chamber, his stride a relic from an injury sustained during his time as a lieutenant in the Napoleonic Wars. Grabbing two cravats and a pair of buff riding trousers from the wardrobe, his lips tilted in the sardonic twist Jasper well recognized. "Why brush 'em off? Ain't wedded, are ye? Trip through the offerings like you was dancing through a field of daisies, I say."

Jasper hummed without reply, reluctant to take romantic advice from a man who'd been married to the same woman for going on forty years. Nelson's tripping through the offering days were so far in the past, they were petrified.

"*Eh*, I begin to get the picture," the valet replied in a rusty murmur, giving the trousers an awkward fold and shoving them in Jasper's luggage. "That rowdy Willoughby gel is back in yer life. I seen the papers, you know. I don't read fast, but I can read, thanks to you."

"Don't start," Jasper growled, although he'd tolerate the intrusion from his closest confidant. The only person, aside from Cece, who knew about his former life.

An aging groom of his father's, Nelson wasn't anyone's idea of a valet, making him the ideal choice for Jasper. He was hard-nosed yet kindhearted, loyal to those he loved, and the closest thing to a father that Jasper had ever had. The moment Jasper was settled in London and paid his first wage, he'd sent for Nelson and his wife. His father had begun to harass his groom about his son's whereabouts, and the retribution to follow would have been brutal. The baron wasn't known for a light touch in his negotiations.

Even at the tender age of nineteen, Jasper had decided he'd given up the last person he loved in letting Cece go. The remaining few in his life, he'd hold close to the end.

Following form, Nelson had hired a ragtag band of misfits for his staff. His housekeeper a light-skirt who had aged out of the position, his majordomo a dockworker with a bum leg, his lone footman a miner with troublesome lungs, his groom an orphan who was blind in one eye.

A toff's staff they were not. Though it warmed Jasper's heart to have a family, of sorts.

"I always liked that gel. Tough as buckskin, a might saucy, but with a fond heart," Nelson said and rummaged through the books Jasper kept on his bedside table. With a decisive sniff, he jammed *The Pickwick Papers* next to the trousers, wrinkling them horribly. "Sure as the night is long, there'll be a sovereign's library in that palace you're headed to, but better secure than regretful, I say. Reading helps a man sleep. I'm glad you made me see the pleasure of escaping into other worlds when the one we live in is a blimey dismal lot some days."

"It's not a palace. And she's not my problem." His tone was harsh, his temper washing over a man he claimed as a true friend, his only until the Leighton Cluster came along.

Undaunted, Nelson shrugged a bony shoulder, going after a stack of cravats this time. He folded the sleek silks with improper care, leaving

Jasper to wonder how long it was going to take him to repack his portmanteau. "She was once. I remember, laddie, when you didn't let anyone forget it. Crickey, when she hit her head on that wee stone, I thought you'd expire from *her* wound. A spot of blood sent you into the faints."

Jasper flipped through the correspondence littering his escritoire to avoid citing the gaping chasm that lay between the idealistic young man's heart and the calcified one he now owned. Dreams were dashed upon the rocks of life, and a grown man realized true love wasn't attainable. Besides, there were attentive women and sexual adventures around every corner. If he left the random bedchamber with a heavy heart, so be it.

This wasn't to say he was discontented. His life had entered a bountiful stage, his professional successes at an all-time high. He had engagements, professional and personal, scheduled until November and beyond. Engagements absent of a blade against his neck or a pistol discharged in his direction. Brewing whisky, shipping goods, and selling baby prams was a bloody wondrous deal. If he'd had the wherewithal as a young man, he'd have told the Crown's commissioners to jump off Waterloo Bridge. Jasper traced the gilded edge of a missive from the Duke of Markham while debating the purpose of convincing himself of his happiness.

It seemed a great waste of time.

Done with his dreadful packing, Nelson crossed to the window and flipped the copper latch to open the pane. A gust of coal-laden air snaked into the room to tangle about Jasper's throat. He swallowed past the tickle and a frustrating urge to cough.

"I miss the briny breezes, laddie, and them sunsets that ripped across the sky like a raging beast. Quality air might work wonders on yer lingering touch of asthma."

Jasper missed Northumberland as well, but he wasn't starting a conversation that invariably ended with an argument about a lost life he'd batted away like a flaming ember. His Bloomsbury home wasn't an inherited castle, granted, but the residence sat on a lovely square that housed two members of Parliament and a rather dubious viscount, which was good enough for Jasper. "I'll pension you and Myra to the estate, if that's your choice, as I've offered five times at last count. There's a charming dowager cottage sitting unattended but ready."

Nelson pitched a wizened russet gaze his way. "My family has been with yours in some capacity, low as buckets most, since the reign of George two, so here me and my beloved Myra stay. Until your direction changes course." He frowned and gave his sun-spotted balding head a scratch. "Or was it George three? I get those royal grandees confused, I do."

Jasper didn't care to mention the relief he felt at hearing those words, as Nelson and Myra were the only family he had. "Then we'll table this discussion until you're ready to withdraw. Which at some point, you'll have to."

Nelson retied the curtain sash, busywork as he sought to elbow his advice into the conversation. "Mayhap when you make amends with the past and find a proper wife, I'll feel safe to. Dropping that base-born accent and telling them rowdy friends of yours the truth would be a start."

"I became what the situation required," he whispered, confident this was an accurate assessment. Cowardice wasn't a realism he was comfortable accepting.

"I admire a good performance, always have," Nelson said with another scratch, this time beneath his armpit. "One that goes on this long gets a tinge maddening, though, don't it?"

Indeed, it does, Jasper thought with a beaten sigh.

With this notion resting heavily on his shoulders, he set off for a deuced house party and a lost but not forgotten love.

Chapter Four

Mrs. Crispin Sinclair. Baroness Neeley. Cece Sinclair.
~Scribblings in a young woman's diary, 1814

The gathering started swimmingly.

The Duke of Markham's expansive estate was located in Richmond, close enough to London's city center to allow for no more than a three-hour carriage ride in even the worst of conditions. Upon review of the guest list, it appeared a diverse but congenial group had been invited. No rabble-rousers aside from the Leighton Cluster. Suitable bachelors, society matrons, affable couples, and an exquisite widow or two for the scoundrels in attendance to entertain. The planned activities each day were expected or would have been if Cece knew what to expect. Lavish buffet breakfasts followed by lawn picnics followed by formal dinners. Afternoon teas for the ladies, fox hunts and shooting competitions for the men. Croquet, lawn bowls, archery, shuttlecock. A musicale the first night, a dance Hildy had promised wouldn't be as decorous as a proper ball the second, and a final closing evening of card games with prizes open to both men *and* women, owing to the Duchess Society's belief that women were as important in the scheme of things.

Without incident, Cece arrived a day before the attendees, allowing time to discuss details with Hildy and her partner, Georgie, the Duchess of Markham. They'd thought of everything, from the songs the orchestra would play, to lists of activities detailed for guests, to accommodating Cece in a private section of the house containing the nursery. She really had no skills available to help them, her knowledge of party planning paltry at best.

Hildy had admitted to finding out about Josiah during her investigations, which was fine with Cece because the boy wasn't a secret. She refused to let him be. Moreover, she appreciated Hildy's honesty and her lack of censure about the topic.

Cece knew what people suspected, and what they suspected was true, so to hell with them.

An aged servant had arrived on her Northumberland portico mere days after Edgerly's death, clutching a boy's trembling hand and a dew-stained letter. A note from the lad's mother written hours before she passed, begging Cece to take pity and open her home to her son now that the earl was dead. One look into a pair of brown eyes matching her husband's, and Cece's heart sprang into action. A nursery had been prepared, books and toys purchased, an additional cook to make sweets and foods a child would appreciate hired. She'd always wanted children, although the few times she'd tried with Edgerly had been mortifying and wholly unproductive, leaving her motherless at the positively ancient age of thirty-three.

Josiah filled her empty heart with his adorable smiles and affectionate happiness, although deep, unfulfilled spaces only a man's love would satisfy remained.

This she could live with—because she must. Unless... unless the one man her heart longed for could be reclaimed.

Hence this ridiculous society circus she'd thrown herself into.

With a dawning sense of dread the morning of the country party's commencement, Cece recorded the entrance of one lavish carriage after another from her bedchamber window, none bearing the person she actually *wanted* to see. The buttered toast she'd eaten for breakfast was a looming weight in her belly, the few sips of tea she'd drunk not enough to ease her parched throat. Maybe Crispin had decided to stay in London with his latest tasty sweet, an actress rumored to collect more men than a cobbler collected shoes.

Why in heaven's name would he want to get mixed up with this aristocratic charade when he'd desired to escape it so badly he'd created another identity?

Cece rested her brow on the windowpane as the sounds from the courtyard below filtered past. Rushed conversation, boisterous laughter, the crunch of boots and hooves on the pebbled drive announced a household preparing for adventure. A realm she'd never inhabited but, regrettably, had been born into. Her parents had loathed city life, and perhaps they'd transferred this aversion to her. During her mother's bad spells, the countess often hadn't left her chamber for weeks, much less thought to travel to London or take care of her daughters.

Although Cece hadn't minded staying in Northumberland as there'd been no desire on her part to search for a life beyond.

She'd had everything she wanted.

Until he arrived. Until he *left*.

"I might like another cocoa, Mum. The first went down faster than a storm."

Startled, Cece turned, the hem of dressing gown whipping her ankles. Josiah stood by the end of the bed, his slender arm circling the scrolled cherrywood post. His cheeks were flushed, his ashen hair disheveled, a streak of chocolate delightfully cutting his jaw in two. He'd been racing the length of the hallway for the past half an hour, pushing a wooden train they'd found at a delightful shop on Bond Street. The boy held her heart in his fist, and if she weren't the greediest of creatures, he would have been enough.

If not for the love she'd tossed aside to save her family, she wouldn't have longed for more. If nothing else, her brief time with Crispin had given her insight into a true relationship. Without him, she'd have believed her passionless marriage the most she could hope for.

Her heart giving an achy twist in her chest, she went to her knees before her son, cradled his face, and placed a kiss on his sweaty brow. She needed him. "My darling boy, I thought Mara was giving you a bath."

Josiah yawned and scrubbed his fist across his chin. His nursemaid had taken him on a long walk across the estate grounds to prepare him for bed. *Hopefully* prepare, as the boy had a boisterous spirit. "I'm hardly filthy enough for that. Not one trace of dirt beneath my nails this time. And my trousers are only a tad stained from the puddle I stomped through."

"If I promise to play a game of croquet with you tomorrow, will you agree to the bath and an early dinner? You can take the train to bed with you. The musicale tonight promises to be more boring than a maths lesson."

Josiah wagged his head in consideration, gauging what else he could ask for, the little devil. Tracing his toe across a scrolled design in the carpet, he murmured, "There's a billiards table in a lower parlor. Just like the one in my castle book."

Billiards were not appropriate pursuits for women or children. However, those spaces were generally deserted before guests awakened, especially after a late evening. "Tomorrow morning, bright and early. A short game if I remember how to play."

Her cheeks burned. She remembered how to play and who'd taught her.

Josiah grinned, his missing tooth giving him a charmingly crooked smile. "I suppose that'll do, though girls are known to be rubbish at games." He shrugged and gave his chest a scratch. "But who else can teach me?"

A memory whispered through Cece, of Crispin's arms coming around her, his hands covering hers as he explained how to hold a cue stick. The lesson had led to their first kiss. And that kiss had eventually led to disaster. "There was a young man, a friend, who showed me," she whispered, pulling herself from the remembrance before it swept her under.

Josiah squinted dubiously. "Were you rats at it? Was he?"

She laughed and gave him a squeeze he immediately wriggled away from. "I was fairly *rats*, as you call it, but he was patient... and wonderful at everything he tried. I've never known a person to be good at so many things." *So. Many. Things.*

The memory of a passion-laced afternoon in a baron's billiards room in the lazy summer of 1814 circled her mind for the rest of the day. As did the lovely boy who'd become an unreachable man.

Consequently, hours later, in a brief respite from the madness of the party, Cece found herself hiding in a shadowy alcove outside a duke's billiards room. She'd been unable to suppress the inclination to find the parlor, one of those gut feelings she rarely ignored. Instead of the boy's trousers she'd worn that day with Crispin, this evening a dazzling ivory frock fashioned by Hildy Streeter's personal modiste shimmered down her body. Her slippers pinched, and her head ached. Cece gave the pearls swimming through her braided strands a nervous pat, wishing they weren't wound so tightly. She didn't look or feel herself. Truly, the only recognizable piece was the faint aroma of orange blossoms drifting from her skin, her grandmother's favorite scent that she'd taken as her own. A dreadful tune floated down the corridor, courtesy of Lady Chambers-Taft, who placed a higher value on her pianoforte expertise than was warranted. Cece made it out before the third atrocious attempt at fashioning Beethoven's *Moonlight Sonata* with the excuse of a ripped hem in need of repair.

Dinner had been a whirlwind of conversation about politics, fashion, and the pathetic state of England's roadways, discussions she'd been expected to take part in with interest—when the only person of interest, the knave she'd enacted this farce for, had failed to attend. Names and faces had skipped around her brain like rocks tossed in a pond, a point of panic when she was forced to address a comment from a "prospective" suitor. Lord This, Viscount That. Handsome, witty, dry as toast. Tall, short, pudgy—men somehow strangely attentive to the woman the *ton* had begun to call the Veiled Countess.

When she'd never worn a veil in her life.

She understood, however, a moniker attached to her meant her popularity was rising.

Cece decided before the apricot ice cream and baked apples were served that she didn't enjoy country parties. Or society life. Or gowns that itched. Or slippers that squeezed. Or pearls that pinched. She didn't like being the center of attention or pretending to be the proper countess they thought she was. She missed her horse, Champion, and her lumpy feather bed that slumped on one side. She missed the gusty sea breezes and the scent of brine in the air. She missed Mrs. Amberton's freshly baked bread and the host of lilacs she was tending on the back lawn. She missed her tattered gowns and scuffed boots.

If these people really knew her, they would be appalled.

If they heard the curses she uttered when she stumped her toe, observed her drinking her weekly glass of brandy, or found out about the love affair she'd had and did not regret—they would detest her.

The sound of breaking glass and raised voices had her peeking into the gaming parlor and witnessing a sight that dropped her stomach to her knees. Crispin stood clothed in formal black attire in the middle of the room, his hand clenched around the shirt of a man swaying on his feet from drink. *The scoundrel must have sneaked in the back to avoid dinner and the horrid receiving line,* she thought.

Shocked, Cece swallowed one of those swear words she loved so much.

At least he'd showed up.

Dash Campbell—whose literary reading had been the only highlight of the evening—stood with arms outstretched between the livid men, in a half-hearted attempt to halt what appeared to soon be a brawl.

"Don't ruin another gathering," Dash whispered to Crispin, his lips curled in a smirk that stated the situation wasn't bothering him one bit. "Or this poor chap's already kinked nose. Save your ferociousness for the hunt of that sad beast tomorrow. You know what'll happen if Hildy finds out we've gone about this strife again. We'll be relegated to the stables for the night, and my wee wife won't follow me, not this time. The scrap at Leighton's at Christmastide was the last I'm allowed. A solid week passed before I could take a sip of whisky without grimacing, and you were limping for a month. Though the ladies did love your injury, I have to admit."

Crispin took a calming breath that lifted his broad chest, his fingers unfurling one by one. "Right," he murmured before stepping back. "The tea set was of incalculable value, or so the duchess claimed, and we smashed it to bits. I'm still trying to locate a replacement. I have a lead with a family in Wales."

"See here," the drunken chap slurred and leaned in, a daring stance for a man a head shorter than his rival, "this isn't the way to treat your betters, Noble. I'm the son of an earl if you've forgotten. A viscount myself. One of the oldest titles in England, by Jove. We don't fashion mixing with vagabonds from the stews, although it seems the Duke of Markham enjoys diving low. Leighton, too, now I put it forth. I'd not have accepted this invite had I known the assemblage I'd be forced to mix with. A widow with a splendid face might not be worth this. She's said to be quite curious herself, a bit outside the pale, typical for those ginger-haired types, which no one justly wants in a wife."

In seconds, the space erupted in chaos as Crispin grasped the viscount's arm and jerked it high, slamming his body against the nearest wall. "I'll take this moment to ask not for a sincere apology, first offspring of a nob, but your vow to keep your bloody opinions about what is curious to yourself. In fact, it may be wise to keep your mouth shut in London as well. Should you deny my request, I'll find out. Don't imagine a venerable title or a secure lock or even a pistol jammed under your fat-headed feather pillow will save you should we need to have another discussion. You'll wake to find me there."

A middling forger who was evidently dreadful at surveillance, Cece gasped at the sight of Jasper Noble, rumored spy, in full glory, bringing the attention of the six men in the room her way.

Crispin's sizzling sapphire gaze hit her last and held. His curse was vicious, his behavior following the whispered oath reckless. Letting the viscount slide to his knees, he shouldered through the crowd before brushing past her, and turning down the hallway.

She caught him at the end of the murky corridor and yanked him to a stop. His forearm muscles quivered beneath her gloved fingertips, then hardened as he held himself steady. "Crispin, wait."

He turned so suddenly she gulped, the expression on his face lethal. "*Jasper*," he bit out. "Never the other, Countess, do you hear me? It's dangerous for both of us to mix those two in the space of one sentence or one room. He's gone. Please, God above, forget him."

That said, he shoved through the door exiting into the side

60

gardens, sending it popping against the outer wall with a *bang*. Of course, she followed.

She knew where this path led because she'd taken Josiah along it this morning.

She knew where this tantrum led because she'd once loved the man owning it.

Strangely, however, her heart felt lighter.

Because she wasn't sure if she liked this Jasper Noble fellow. Even if he'd defended her in that parlor as well as any knight, he wasn't being very chivalrous *now*.

Stalking along a trail which snaked through a copse of azaleas and hydrangea, Crispin led her to the worst place for unspoken memories. When she stepped inside the stone dwelling, the scents of leather, hay, and brass polish rolled over her. The whinny of a horse in a distant stall echoed through the space. Pausing in the medieval archway of the stable's harness room, she wondered why she and Crispin always seemed to end up in such places. Likely because they were often deserted with nooks perfectly designed for rushed encounters. She'd bet more than one set of lovers had coupled in this very spot.

Powerless, yet intrigued to her bones, Cece leaned on the doorjamb while Crispin prowled the moonlit space, a panther set loose among felines. He paused by a set of straps, drawing the tooled leather through his fist with the gentleness of a brigand. She didn't love that the act shook her as she imagined his hands on *her*.

Being close to this man had always done remarkable things to her mind and body.

His temper was high, so she decided to prick it further, like she had in the olden days. "Venerable is quite a hefty word for a man raised in the rookery, isn't it? You might want to tone down your language whilst you're playing the thug."

Tossing aside the straps, he turned on her. "Advice from the countess or the forger?"

Hiding her smile, she brushed a piece of straw off her bodice and, much to her delight, watched his gaze track the move. *Oh*, how she'd missed tangling with him, this dance she'd never had with anyone else. If memories of his body covering hers intruded, Cece could only guess the two types of sparring—verbal and physical—mated as well as they once had.

Knocking his coattails aside, Crispin growled and shoved his hands in his trouser pockets. A smile that never got close to reaching his gorgeous eyes settled in. It was a staged tactical stance she didn't trust. "Go back to your musicale, Countess. You've got titillating conversations in your future, perhaps a stolen kiss in a dark corner if you're willing. The aroma of horses slides beneath my skin and encourages me to do dangerous things, as you know. It might be prudent to not test me this eve. Getting caught here with me, even for a widow with certain freedoms, isn't wise."

Against her will or because of it, Cece refused, instead taking a moment to drink in the sight of him. Time had added bulk to his frame, silver threads to his hair, and grooves chalked into the skin around his mouth and eyes. If she couldn't tear her gaze away from the sight of Crispin bathed in dull moonlight and tangled in temper, she wouldn't be the first woman to be so entranced. This time, however, she indeed held certain freedoms. Freedoms she'd earned by struggling through an unpleasant marriage and years of loneliness.

She'd paid heartily for every advantage of widowhood. Why not benefit from it?

As she stared across the distance, his gaze darkened to a staggering shade of blue-black, a hue matching the threatening persona he'd assumed. Rough, keen, fierce. Jaw shadowed by stubble his valet hadn't bothered to remove, jet hair overlong and dusting his crisp collar, he no longer looked like that tender young man. Six feet plus of broad shoulder and lean muscle, he appeared leery of his surroundings and ready to attack. She supposed it was a holdover from his rumored profession that no space housing him seemed up to the task.

Nonetheless, if he thought to push her away when she'd fashioned this foolishness for exactly such a chance, he was as mad as her Aunt Matilda, who'd believed she was the Queen of England for the last twenty years of her life.

Aptly reading her rebellious silence, Crispin knocked his bootheel against a flagstone, his frustration coming out in a rushed breath. She loved how he seemed flustered, as if he'd forgotten the rules of his own game. "Look your fill while you can, minx. I don't mind being on display, though I'm only here because Hildy asked it of me. Don't think I don't understand where she got the idea. I'm rarely invited to the Duchess Society's absurd matchmaking affairs as I add little value. Rogues need not apply, you see."

Knowing it would further vex him, Cece drew her loupe from the hidden pocket she had sewn into her gowns and buffed it on her sleeve. She carried it everywhere because a forger without a loupe was like a blacksmith without an anvil. A girl never knew when a private document in need of alteration was going to appear. "What was the argument in the billiards room about?"

His gaze fixed on the tool of her trade as he released another exhalation, the faintest hint of a wheeze attached to the end of it. Holding up his hand, he snapped, "If you mention weak lungs, I can't say what I'll do."

Humming, she gave the loupe another diligent rub. "Is the earl's son chasing after one of the ladies you're hoping to capture for the weekend? Men like to fight over such trivialities, don't they?"

Mirroring her ploy, Crispin's smile tilted at the edges as he slipped a knife from his inner pocket, released the blade, and began to shine it against his superfine cuff. A convenient way to prick her temper right back. "I'd never fight over a woman, minx. I've never found one worth the trouble, but your boy, a child, who I might risk a bruise or two over."

The loupe slipped from her hand to the cobbles with a pop. "Josiah? What did that wretch say?"

He stilled, the blade catching a stray beam and shooting a metallic glow across his fingers. "The speculation is he's Edgerly's by-blow. If it's true—"

"It's true," she said and bent to retrieve the loupe.

Crispin blinked, shocked she'd admit it outright. Wordlessly, he flipped the knife between his hands in a manner that told her he was extremely skilled using it. "It doesn't need repeating in a duke's parlor, though, does it? Among men who might be vying for your hand. I'm no gentleman, but it seemed impudent as hell to me for the viscount to mention it."

The knowledge that he'd protect her in even the humblest of ways swept over her like a caress, stealing her breath. She'd never been safeguarded by anyone, not once in her life. "Thank you," she whispered, depositing the loupe in her pocket where it belonged, done with her effort to torment him. "Frankly, I can't stop the rumors, but I appreciate your attempt. I simply want Josiah to be happy, and I'm doing all in my power to make sure he is. Which includes my not hiding him from plain sight. Let them look. Let them *talk*. They'll find another scandal next week or the week after, and we'll be forgotten."

Clearly unimpressed with her strategy, he grunted as his gaze fixed on her pocket.

"I'm not playing games anymore, Cris—*Jasper*. I only floated the document with Tobias Streeter's signature as a means to reach you. A plan I concocted during my first visit with the Duchess Society after Hildy left a letter on her desk. I would have shown up on your doorway if I'd been certain you'd admit me. Although, why my pride matters at this point is beyond contemplation considering our history. I suppose I've always wondered about you, about *us*. You never came to me, so I'm forced to come to you."

"I beg of you, Cece, go back to that ear-piercing chorale disaster," Crispin said and hurled the knife, impaling it in the wall. He'd positioned it dead center in a knothole in the wood. She watched the blade quiver with a sense of wonder and no little spark of arousal. He might not *want* to feel anything, but this impulsive show meant he felt something. It was almost as if he was trying to show off for her, a tactic of his she'd gotten used to when they were young.

She nodded to the shuddering blade. "You're making too much of my meager side business."

"Says the countess criminal."

"Actually, I've only forged marital documents in Northumberland to keep my skills fresh," she said as he moved past her, wrenched the knife from the wall, and closed it with a snap. "Harmless efforts for couples who want to wed but face familial objections. Some are even being forced into unhappy arrangements, like I was with Edgerly. I'm passionate about keeping this from happening to anyone else, lives ruined with a hasty signature."

"Brilliant," he murmured and shot her an aggrieved sidelong glance.

"It's merely a *hobby*. Like watercolors or knitting. Why must you be so vexed about it? I help people secure matches of their choice, which your Duchess Society friends arrange every day."

His head dipped as he placed his hands in a prayerful pose before his mouth. His fingers were long and slim, no gloves in sight, the silver studs in his cuffs winking in the ghostly light. The scar on his neck was stark against his sun-kissed skin, a mark she longed to bite, then go lower, where she'd pleasure him before making him tell her the story of how he'd gotten the wound. Two lovers tangled up in conversation and silken sheets for days, a luxury they'd never had. A luxury they'd only dreamed about. "If you'd haven't figured it out, Countess, you're fearless in a way that frightens me. Same as always."

"I'm fearless, Jasper Noble, because I've had nothing to chance *losing*." If she repeated this new name of his often enough, she might come to believe it belonged to him.

Sighing, he braced his shoulder on the wall, his gaze glowing a hot blue and focused solely on her. The eyes of a man on a quest he meant to win. "You believe you can dip your toe in a hazardous pond and come out clean while I watch my back every bloody day, never, *ever* daring the gods. Not anymore. And it's not my problem to watch yours. You signed away my concern when you married Edgerly, but I tell you as a friend that Tobias Streeter isn't a man to dally with, even in jest." He dragged his calloused fingertip down the hollow of her throat, halting when he reached the rounded edge of her bodice. In response, her nipples beaded beneath her bodice, and she could only pray he didn't notice. "Nor am I, Cece darling, a change you've yet to accept."

Taking the risk, she flattened her hand on his chest, the uneven beat of his heart beneath her palm giving her courage. The remembrance of what he'd meant to her swirled like mist, clouding her mind but strengthening her reserve. "What if I want to dally? Make use of those freedoms you mentioned?"

Crispin's lids lowered, shielding her from peering into his soul—because they both knew she'd once been able to. "I have options,

Countess. More than I can count. Why delve into a complicated past when a straightforward present is readily available?"

She drew her hand back as an unsavory fact crystalized in her mind.

He wasn't going to forgive her.

And pride was a formidable foe.

"Perhaps I'm indifferent as well. You're merely the easiest arrangement for a curious woman," she murmured, hoping she could pretend for long enough to get to her bedchamber, where the tears stinging her lids could run freely. She had options, too. Her son. Northumberland. Rides through the morning mist astride her horse. A fledgling enterprise devoted to helping young women secure a wedded union they wanted. Independence and enough funds to live the modest life she desired.

She would not wilt before Jasper bloody Noble.

"I'm not indifferent," he whispered when she started to turn from him, *run* from him. "That's a lie I can't let you leave with, God help me."

Then he stepped in, using his broad body to trap her. Rough stone met her back as he guided her into it, his warm breath striking her lips as he lowered his head. "I'll admit I've wondered," he whispered on a lurid suggestion next to her ear. "If wondering means a thousand nights spent recalling the astonishing feel of your body wrapped around mine, your cries of ecstasy ringing in my ears, your nails scoring my back. Indelicate but real truths, minx. We were explosive together, and I've never been able to forget it. I've tried to recreate it and been grossly unsuccessful."

Angry and aroused, she breathed in the tantalizing scent of him. Leather, soap, and the faintest trace of whisky. All the while, his cock was a hardening presence through layers of cotton and silk, proving his assertion that he wasn't indifferent.

The shift to get closer to him was unconscious, instinctive, and the wrong move.

Cupping her cheek, he tilted her face to his, his gaze having gone a stormy near-black. His thumb swept the scar slicing her eyebrow, a wound she'd gotten while riding with him years ago. He'd cried tears for her that day, the first time she realized he loved her as she loved him. "My obsession no longer owns me, *you* no longer own me. So take your false hopes and your curiosity and trot back to Northumberland. Because I'm simply a man in the end, one who will acquiesce if tempted beyond what he's able to endure." A mocking smile tipped his lips, the grooves lining his mouth giving him a sinister appearance. "Is that what you want, Cece? Stolen moments with someone who is long over you?"

"You arrogant beast." She shoved him as hard as she could, barely moving him an inch. "Make me pay, then, Crispin Sinclair. Crush me into bits before us both and be done with it."

He mouthed a soundless plea, his expression bewildered before he took her lips beneath his—although the gentleness of the kiss belied every nasty word he'd uttered. *Too soft*, she silently raged and gripped his face, drawing him into something deeper. Hooking her fingers in the supple strands at his nape, she gave them a yank, entreating. In response, he groaned and gripped her tighter as their tongues touched.

And the dance began.

Her hunger eclipsed any uncertainty, his raw reply any debate.

It was a peculiar sensation, a merging of old and new. Parts of the kiss she recognized, while others were enthrallingly fresh. Jasper Noble didn't hesitate where Crispin would have as he grasped her hips and yanked her against him. His shaft was hard, his lips controlling, his tongue insistent. His hands glided over curves and valleys, tender one moment, forceful the next, persuading when the woman needed no persuasion.

For the first time in memory, a man left no place untouched from hip to brow. His thumb caressed the hard bud of her nipple as his teeth teased the sleek line of her jaw. Her body sang, vibrating with the tremors running through it. The pearls in her hair rained down upon the flagstones beneath his onslaught, their harsh breaths filling the dank space with warnings neither heeded.

With a tangled moan, unsure where she was headed but needing control of some aspect of this liberation, she spun him around until his back was against stone, going on her toes, and bringing his pelvis to hers in mock copulation. Seconds spilled into minutes spilling into an eternity. Growling, he clutched her to him, through layers of cloth still able to do sensual damage. His cock was a hard ridge she rode, awkwardly but with effect. Unbelievably, the pinpricks of light behind her eyelids spelled a rising climax should this continue. *Please, let it continue.*

It wasn't enough, certainly, nothing but him filling her would be enough, but it was glorious, nonetheless.

And she'd waited ages for it.

Years of lonely defeat at the hands of a husband who'd never cared to pleasure her, never cared *period*, roared through her like a train off the tracks. Crispin was the only man who'd ever satisfied her in this way. She'd desired no one else, had dreamed of no one else.

Evidently, it was a request he could not ignore.

He reclaimed her lips and hissed against them, "How close are you? We might not have much time before someone stumbles upon us."

His understanding stunned her. He knew her better than he wished to—or perhaps it was the leagues of women he'd attended, a base thought she shoved from her mind.

She trailed her lips down his cheek, her jagged sigh an admission and a demand. "*Yes,*" she finally added, an answer that didn't match the question.

His chest rose and fell on his own harsh exhalation, a charitable decision made, possibly against his will. Sounds from the musicale had started to intrude, the faint din of laughter and conversation as the doors to the veranda were opened. After glancing to the stable door, Crispin returned his gaze to her, his deadly expression representing a man on a mission. "Think of the time in your bedchamber when I feasted on your lovely quim until you screamed so loudly we had to capture your moans in your pillow. Do that while I touch you."

Everything about him begged her to obey, and for once, she was willing.

Submission with a reward at the end seemed fitting.

The image of his dark head bobbing between her spread thighs arrived as if it were yesterday because she'd never forgotten her fevered cries mixing with his groans of delight, the rough abrasion of stubble on her thighs, her slick wetness coating his lips after. They'd learned a new way to pleasure each other that day, the only time she'd experienced such wondrous bliss. Closing her eyes, she traveled back as the man in the present murmured wicked things in her ear. As he nibbled on her neck and sucked her bottom lip between his teeth. As he slid his hand down her body, finally settling the bony edge of his palm between her legs.

"Grind against me," he rasped, working his hand against her in deliciously languorous circles. "Just like that, as hard as you need to. I would bring you around faster, slide my fingers through the slit in your drawers and truly *feel* you, but there's no time. Only know that it's my desire to taste you until you come. Tup you until we can't stand, breathe, *think*."

His coarse words lit a fire inside her. An elemental fire she'd not felt since he left her.

The world spun away from them as the space filled with the primal elements of their lovemaking. Raw groans of arousal. Bumping bodies. Flushed skin. Sweat trickled between her breasts, her knees trembled. The past faded until there was only the now. The incredible *now*. She found herself wildly kissing him one second, then slumping to his chest the next, as wilted as a daisy. Her blood thumped in her ears and behind her eyes, a pulse of pleasure.

"Come for me, minx," he urged, guiding her down the path. Stroking, pressing, demanding, his long body curled around hers. "They'll find us soon if you don't."

Provoked beyond measure, her release was contained by his hasty kiss as no pillow was in sight. The shudders tore through her, stealing her breath. Toes to knees to thighs to heart, rolling waves of delight with the power to devastate. Words left her lips in a rush, and later, she'd wonder in dread what they were. She'd recall sealing her mouth to his neck and biting, gently, but a bite, nonetheless. Animalistic behavior unlike any she'd previously displayed.

Greedy for every beat of pleasure, she rode Crispin's hand until her legs could no longer support her. There was simply no polite way to describe it. The climax left a spent soul clinging to a man who claimed to no longer care.

Although his actions said he did.

Tenderly, Crispin looped his arm around her waist and held her to him, his mouth at her temple whispering calming words. His breath was gusty, his own body shaking. For a brief time, despite any angst about what they'd done, they were whole again.

United and yielding. A force.

Cece realized it wouldn't be long before this fact incensed him.

It took exactly two minutes.

With an oath, Crispin released her as if she was venomous. Stumbling back, he staggered on a loose pearl beneath his boot. "Damned if that wasn't familiar," he snarled and yanked at his cuffs in seeming need of something to do with his hands. Avoiding her gaze, he worked his fingers through his disordered strands in an effort to repair her enthusiastic damage.

Which only left him looking as ravished as she *felt*.

"We always liked stables, did we not? One of our three sins happened there and so many of the encounters leading up to it. I get aroused by the sound of horses whinnying." He snorted into his closed fist in disgust. "Mad, isn't it?"

Cece refrained from uttering anything she might regret when her brain was the consistency of porridge. "Thank you" sat on the tip of her tongue, but she'd *die* before saying it. Jasper Noble could take his scowls and his crossness and shove them up his handsome, duplicitous arse. She remembered every *sin* she'd committed with him, the lewd memories part of the reason he'd brought her pleasure standing up and fully clothed. Thoroughly vexed, she lowered her gaze, noting that his shaft was holding an arousing show beneath his trouser buttons.

He caught her stare, and his expression dove into a sinister pit. "I'll save my enjoyment for later because my cock will be in my hand before my bedchamber door shuts behind me. Truthfully, I'm amazed I didn't stain my drawers like a lad during his first tumble."

Flustered by the admission, Cece began her own repair, reaching to tidy her sagging chignon. The remaining pearls tumbled to the floor, the sharp pops a blatant reminder of her foolishness. The thick strands had darkened over the years and were no longer a flaming ginger, but they weren't easily overlooked, either. Her hair was her glory and her torment.

Sighing, he made a lazy loop with his hand. "You can't go back like that. It'll upset the husband hunt to have you waltz into the music room looking tumbled but good if I may be so bold."

Cece gave her bodice a helpless press, realizing what he said was true. She was flushed and trembling, wrinkled, ruffled, unnerved. A disaster. Nothing new, actually, where Crispin Sinclair was concerned. They'd ruined each other with a similar performance.

Despite it all, she felt *wonderful*.

His frown was fierce. "Quit fucking smiling, Ce."

She shrugged, her body having dissolved to the consistency of hot wax. When he left her, she was going to puddle to the cobbles and stay there until morning. "I'm not going to apologize for seeking pleasure, Noble. I've had little enough in this life. Hypocritical, isn't it, when the rags devote a paragraph a week to your antics?"

"It's different for a man. We're allowed all sorts of mischief," he said and swiped his hand across his lips. Pausing, his eyes closed as he took the gentlest of breaths.

It was then she realized her scent was clinging to his skin.

He lifted his head, spearing her with a fiery glower that meant her time was up.

She drew her arms around herself to hold back the shiver. "I suppose you're going to turn to one of those tarts Hildy provided to prove how untouched you are by this."

His mouth tensed, his jaw muscles flexing. His hand moved to the spot on his neck she'd bitten in her excitement. "Good idea, minx, thanks for suggesting it."

When she would have kept him talking, kept him *close*, a strident knock intruded. An unnecessary strike on an open stable door.

The protective signal of a friend, a warning that she and Crispin weren't alone.

"Back," Crispin mouthed and motioned her into the shadows.

"Noble? Are you in there?"

Dear heaven, Cece thought and crouched in the shadows until darkness covered her. The voice belonged to a person she desperately wanted to please and was surprisingly intimidated by.

"Hildy, how nice to see you," Crispin murmured with buttery charm.

"Where is she?" The question was as hard-edged as the knock had been. "Oh, you knave. You impossible, unrepentant *knave*. When I warned you, in clear language because I know very well how to deal with reprobates seeing as I married one, about your conduct at this party. You gave me your word you'd stay away from her, far away, signifying no assignations in pitch-black stables. I invited suitable ladies, meaning they are *not* suitable, to keep you occupied. But oh, *no*, you had to grasp the diamond and shove it in your pocket."

Another set of footfalls, heavier these, sounded on the flagstones. "Hildy girl, slow down. It might not be what you think. He learned his lesson after that last debacle, I would guess."

Cece dropped her head to her hands when she realized Tobias Streeter had joined his wife on the hunt—the man whose signature she'd forged to get this insane boulder rolling down a hill.

And what debacle had Crispin been involved in that his friend would think to mention it?

"Don't 'slow down, Hildy girl' me, Tobias Streeter. I have men waiting to talk with the guest of honor when the guest of honor and England's leading scandal are nowhere to be found. My excuse of a torn hem and a slight megrim is losing steam. I must produce a countess, and I must produce her *now*."

"I'm hardly the leading scandal," Crispin returned in a doubtful tone. "Truly, the leading? What about the men who came before me? Xander Macauley, for instance?"

"You fool," Tobias murmured beneath his breath. "Don't you know to calm the beast?"

Cece gave a loose strand a tuck behind her ear and shook out her skirt. There was no help for it, she was doomed. However... these were Crispin's closest friends—his allies—and they wouldn't toss her to the wolves. In addition, she'd *hired* the Duchess Society. Hildegard Streeter might seem a bit like the frightening French governess of her youth when she was, in fact, a consultant. An employee and Cece a client.

Confident in this judgment, Cece took a shaky breath and stepped from the shadows.

The first to react to the sight of her, Tobias cut short his smile and headed for the door. He was as scared of his wife as the rest of them.

After a defeated, head-to-toe review of her charge, Hildy gave Crispin a hostile shove. "Follow my husband to the closest whisky bottle, Noble, and promptly drown yourself in it."

Pausing before he fulfilled her command, Crispin looked back. His face was obscured by shadows, but his protective stance was evident in the tense hold of his shoulders. Cece's heart sang—and sank. He wasn't going to leave without confirming she was fine, proof the young man she'd known existed inside the thug.

It gave her hope she might one day reach him.

"*Out*," Hildy said in a harsh tenor that brooked no argument. Even from England's leading scandal.

Freeing him in this way if she could in no other, Cece gestured for Crispin to go.

Nodding, he followed Tobias Streeter out the door and into the night, leaving *her* to calm the beast.

"I had to fight tooth and nail to get Toby to admit what I meant to him," Hildy shocked her by saying once the men were out of hearing. "It was quite a battle, I admit. And worth every tear I shed during those long weeks."

Cece's cheeks lit, a flush she felt to her toes. She'd shed buckets over Crispin Sinclair. Now, it appeared she'd shed them over Jasper Noble.

Hildy squinted, then bent to retrieve a stray pearl. "I long to throw my endorsement behind one of the men invited to this catastrophe of a party, each approved by the Duchess Society's rigorous investigative review, I might add. But it's hard to do when Noble looks at you like you're something precious he's afraid he'll break. A rare vase that's somehow landed in his possession. It's honestly the first time I've seen him unsure of himself, the bounder. He'd not make it past page two of our inquiry before being tossed out on his swaggering bum." She let the pearl roll off her palm and into a crack in the flagstones. "Yet, here he is, inviting you into dark corners."

Cece decided to omit she'd followed him into that dark corner without a hint of coaxing—and would do so again if asked. The kiss may have even been her idea. What she truly wished to do was ask about the debacle Hildy had mentioned, but she wouldn't dare. She

73

didn't have the stamina to hear about Jasper Noble's escapades when the scent of him lingered in the air as her body thrummed from his touch.

Hildy tilted her head, her smile cunning. "If only he weren't a man with a most unimpressive background, we might consider adding him to your list."

"If only," Cece murmured and directed her attention to retrieving the pearls scattered across the stable floor.

Because Crispin's secret was hers to keep.

Chapter Five

The Earl of Edgerly spends most of his time in London while his wife remains in Northumberland. The reclusive countess is known as somewhat of an oddity.
-Private report to Agent Noble from an intelligence officer assigned to the northeast region

J asper woke the next morning fully clothed and lying on the floor of his bedchamber.

When he recalled starting his slumber on the *settee.*

He rolled to his back, his tattered groan echoing off the walls and through his aching skull. By bloody God, he was getting too old for this. When Hildy had recommended he drown himself in a bottle, he'd held her to her word. At least he could guarantee that Dash Campbell and Xander Macauley—who'd taken pity and joined in his misery—felt like shite this morning, too. They'd run through every ounce of drink in the indigo parlor Hildy had relegated them to, then sent a footman to bring them whatever else he could find.

Jasper flicked the pearl stuck to his cheek off with a factual sense of dismay.

That damned kiss was a problem.

He'd always believed his fascination with Cece derived partly from her being his first. Which he realized was fundamentally a sentimental feminine perspective, but he'd been so taken by her—and not many women had been interested, at the time, in tupping a stuttering asthmatic.

It hadn't hurt that she'd been his every dream realized.

What lad wouldn't fall for such beauty, wit, and courage, with an unflinching sense of bravado tossed into the mix? He'd been captivated from the moment he met his charmingly peculiar neighbor with the lone dimple dinging her cheek. That his father detested her incomparable uniqueness had been a bonus.

Shoving aside the memory of her, Jasper pushed himself to a sit, sending dots swirling across his vision.

Mind over matter would be required to get through this day. And forget that kiss.

He struggled to his feet and began to go through his morning routine without the aid of Nelson, who'd stayed in London because long carriage rides tended to aggravate his hip, a relic of his time in the military. Jasper was cross, queasy, and likely reeked of whisky. He rushed the razor over his skin and cursed as a bubble of blood formed on his cheek.

He was unsteady when he needed to be resolute. The severe discussion he had with himself before running into Cece again required a bloke who was up to listening.

He dabbed blood from his skin and gave the man questioning his life choices an honest talk.

They had no future, he and Cece. She was a countess on the husband hunt, and he was a pensioned spy looking for peace. If he ever married, he'd not stoop to marrying *her*. The troublesome chit who'd had such influence over him that he'd been grievously unhappy for, *oh,* going on two years after leaving Northumberland. Pits of hell unhappy. Blind nights and unseeing mornings unhappy.

Though training to be an operative for the Crown while not caring if one lived or died made for a contented union.

I'm bored, Jasper decided while staring at his grim reflection in the vanity's mirror.

He was exasperated his life had stalled while everyone else's was chugging right along. His friends were finding wives, having children, and adopting kittens faster than he could button his waistcoat. He squinted and trailed the razor's dull edge over a mark on his neck. Turning, he crossed the room and grabbed his spectacles from the bureau top. When they were settled on his face, he returned to the mirror.

A shot of arousal hit him at high speed, his sudden breathlessness doing nothing to relieve his nausea.

The discoloration to his skin was miniscule, one that would be confused with a shaving mishap. He stroked his thumb across the spot in wonder. It had been years, *eons*, since someone had bitten him. An act he'd never enjoyed before. Why did this crude evidence of the previous night's encounter light him up *now*?

Damn that girl, he thought and tossed his razor into the basin with a clatter.

Constance Willoughby stepping back into his life was a test. His famed discipline had vaporized like mist in sturdy sunlight the second she waltzed into the gaming room in a dazzling gown revealing every amazing change time had wrought.

He'd best remember the countess was also a con artist.

Jasper hadn't missed the cunning gleam in her eyes. It was the same spark she'd had twenty years ago during the chase and look how *that* had turned out. Love didn't safeguard a man. In fact, it left one's heart in a snowstorm without an overcoat. There was no place for her in the life he'd created after the other went up in flames.

Letting this verdict settle, Jasper gripped the vanity's cool porcelain and released a ragged breath. The ache in his cock and his temples was too much to fight with a leaden head and an empty stomach.

Take me, Crispin.

That's what she'd whispered before she came.

Or *as* she came. Hell, he'd been half there himself, a piece he'd like to forget as well as hearing that name on her lips. *Crispin*. The only woman ever to call him such in the throes, of course, and it had almost pushed him over the edge.

Imagine that fucking horror of a thought?

He gave the basin a savage swipe with a rag. Did the scheming little counterfeiter think he didn't *want* to take her? Turn her over his knee, bend her over his desk, climb atop her and sink inside, never to leave? Taste her until she screamed, this time knowing what he was about. Once a man had delved deeply into the only woman made specifically for him, the rest were bland versions of reality.

Sadly, he and Cece had been *very* good together.

With time spent reviewing the three introductory lovemaking sessions of his youth, he'd come to realize lust alone wasn't the answer. A simple, deadly truth. There were chemical mysteries at play, and desire was an unspeakably enigmatic thing. *Christ*, brilliant men had lost kingdoms over less than he and Cece had experienced.

Jasper returned his watery gaze to the mirror and recalled the brutality of those first months without her. Waking and wishing he'd not. Walking the streets without notice of the icy chill or the foul stink. He'd gone into another life with barely a recollection of breathing. The numbness had fairly consumed him, but it had helped him survive, like a coma would a grievous injury.

Dredging up techniques from his training, Jasper separated himself from his feelings as another trickle of blood coursed down his jaw like a prophecy. Emotion ruined plans and threw stratagems into the muck. Being able to leave them behind had made him the most successful emissary in the business. A career he'd escaped to then remake himself as a morally questionable entrepreneur. He refused to let Cece come in like a raging squall and distract him from this path, even if that lost boy he'd once been begged him to. He wasn't going back to being a baron's son, back to a world he hadn't been suited to.

Not even for her would he make this sacrifice.

If she was—*hopelessly*—still the chit he longed to stumble upon in a roomful of people, he would feign disinterest until he got the hell back to Bloomsbury. If she was the chit he dreamed of, he would ignore his dreams until he could find someone else to infiltrate them. The process of hardening his heart could be better accomplished in the privacy of his abode. Seeing Cece, *touching* her, was a challenge he wasn't sure he was up to conquering. Every one of his thirty-six years was weighing him down imagining the fight.

Heaped atop this angst were the *memories*, the bloody, fucking memories. And the raging scent of orange blossoms that was forever wedged in his nose.

The passionate girl was indeed the one who haunted his dreams, and she'd never been good at letting him go, nor he her.

Jasper let his head fall back with a groan. He could survive this wretched party for three more days, couldn't he?

Unusual for her, Cece was late to rise.

Sunshine was a violent burst around the closed drapes, a beckon to crawl from beneath the coverlet and find the man who had invaded her dreams and impeded her slumber. She'd heard Mara preparing Josiah for breakfast and pretended to be asleep, making her the worst mother in the history of mothers.

Amazingly, there was a valid reason for her fatigue.

Cece laughed softly and rolled to her back, her hands rising to cover her flushed cheeks. If she tried, she could feel a tremor of sensation between her legs and in the heaviness of her breasts. Crude and positively *decadent*, Crispin's touch. Magic remained despite their years apart. Maybe she didn't like him, maybe he didn't like her. Maybe they'd grown in different directions, paths never to be joined.

Nevertheless, they still desired each other. The quakes racing through his broad body hadn't lied, even if his words had. She giggled breathlessly into her hands, her body overheating. His hard cock hadn't lied. She guessed he'd have tupped her right there if he'd been able, and she wouldn't have put up a fight. The contradictions of the man appealed to her worst qualities—curiosity and rebelliousness—making the situation dangerous and compelling. She was, without question, a defiant woman.

Where Crispin had been entirely reachable, this Jasper Noble fellow was a bit like frost in the spring. A cool exterior, but manifestations that melted upon contact.

She planned to dissolve his resistance in the three remaining days she'd been given.

Scattered plan in place, her step was light as she dressed, her loupe tucked neatly in her skirt pocket for security. Cece lived an independent life with no lady's maid to trouble her. She'd had enough of devious domestics in her youth who'd told awful tales to her parents. In any case, she couldn't afford a governess for Josiah *and* a full staff, so she dressed simply for multiple reasons aside from a practical sense of style.

The gallery corridor was deserted when she arrived, Hildy's guests likely sleeping off their activities of the previous night. She'd forgotten what late hours society kept. She was a morning person, up at dawn to ride across the fields surrounding her home, then back for a hearty breakfast with her son, the loveliest part of her day.

Her slippered footfalls were a dull echo mixing with the sound of pots being emptied in the kitchen, her trip to the breakfast parlor taking her past the infamous gaming room where she'd first encountered Crispin. The voices were low, not much above a whisper, but she recognized both with a sense of awe and dread.

Josiah stood before the billiards table, a cue longer than his body angled in his small hands. Thanks to Mara, his dirty blond hair was neat, his trousers and cotton shirt pressed, unstained, and next to perfect. He wouldn't stay that way for long, she'd bet. His governess sat in an armchair by the fire, knitting what she claimed was a scarf for her sister.

Although Cece's attention was fixed on the scoundrel guiding the boy's shot.

Quite simply, the sight stopped her heart.

"Remember, a balanced stance helps control your movement. One foot slightly in front, like so." Crispin nudged Josiah's boot into more proper alignment and gently curled his hand around the boy's shoulder. His long fingers, she was unsurprised to note, were as gorgeous as the rest of him. And what glories that hand had shared with her last night. "Look across the baize and try to see the shot in your mind. There, that's it."

"Like this?" Josiah popped up on his toes to reach over the table.

Crispin leaned over her son and positioned the boy's arms. "Like this. Slow, steady."

He twisted slightly when Josiah made the attempt, as if he took it himself, presenting his lean hip. She stood riveted, counting the seconds, understanding Crispin would change into someone else when he saw her. His hair looked damp from his morning toilette, the streaks of gray at his temple stark against the jet strands. He wore a simple but smart set of dark clothing, the informal knot at his neck crafted by his hand, not a valet's.

Something, though, was different. Cece stilled, her breath leaking away. He was wearing *spectacles.*

When he turned to her in an elegant pivot, lamplight across his lenses obscured his eyes, the tightening of his lips obscured his thoughts, and she realized *this* was Jasper Noble.

Diplomat, brute, capitalist, charmer.

No sign of the innocent young man anywhere in the parlor.

"Mum, I'm learning to play. And how colored balls aren't the way Mr. Noble played as a boy because there were only two whites and a reddish ball, mostly made of ivory. But now we have ones like a rainbow! I knocked the orange ball in the side pocket all by myself," Josiah said, beaming, waving the cue around like a sword. "Now I have a new nickname, too. Jos! Like my real name, only shorter."

Crispin danced to the side to avoid being struck by the weapon. "Hold up there, lad. According to Miss Mara, you're due for breakfast. Growing boys need food and lots of it."

"Oh, bother," Josiah murmured, his shoulders dropping, the tip of his cue dusting the carpet. "Now I'll be left with my mum to teach me. She promised, and she's kind to offer, but she's still a dumb girl."

With a gusty snort, Crispin crouched before her son, balancing his hand on the floor. Cece couldn't tear her gaze away from the two of them, heads bowed, grins so arrogantly male it made her ache. Men must be born with the inclination. "If your mum agrees, Jos, we'll have another lesson tomorrow morning. We can't leave the teachings of such manly things to dumb girls."

Josiah brightened. "Right-o!"

Laughing, they shook on it. A picture she'd hold dear for *life*.

After delaying as long as he could, Crispin glanced up, his eyes behind his lenses the pale blue of summer skies and shallow seas. His face was clean-shaven this morn but imperfectly, evidenced by the rosy mark on his jaw. As she stared, his mouth tilted down at the corners, highlighting an inner battle between the covert aristocrat and the out-and-out cad.

How many women had he seduced using his unique blend of those remarkably conflicting sides?

Her envy was unwelcome and brought a chill into the room despite the hearth warming her back. It was difficult to deny her possessiveness when she'd once considered the man hers.

Tearing his gaze away, Crispin refocused his attention on Josiah. "Replace your cue in the rack and place the balls in the leather pocket at the end, lad. That's the final step in any game of billiards."

While her son busied himself with his duties, Crispin ambled over as if he'd not a care in the world. His casual stance didn't fool her. Though it had been years, she recognized the tells signaling he was steeling himself against her. Hands shoved in his trouser pockets, shoulders back until he stood that much taller. The muscle ticking in his jaw so *very* Crispin Sinclair. She recalled them well. They'd not gotten along *all* the time back in the day.

He must have felt himself frowning because his lips tipped in a sudden, dishonest smile. Back to the charmer, much to her chagrin. "What's that calculating look, Countess? Or should I be afraid to ask?"

She couldn't help herself—and her inclination was faster than his reflexes. His skin was smooth beneath her fingertip, his jaw rock-solid. "You have a nick."

He closed his hand around her wrist and squeezed none too gently.

"What I have is a love bite that stung like the very devil when I tried shaving over it this morning."

A memory of sucking his skin between her teeth as her release swept her crawled into her mind. *My*, she'd been lost in the man.

Cece recovered quickly, slipping from his hold to massage her wrist as if he'd been too rough. Which he hadn't. She simply needed something to do with her hands to keep them off *him*. "Apologies, Mr. Noble. I let the situation get the better of me. I admit, I've never had a kiss go that far, that fast. It's been years, *oh*... let me think how many." She tilted her head, tapping her fingers and thumb together as if she were counting. "Why, I was a young woman of seventeen the last time I experienced anything like it. An obliging neighbor in Northumberland. A baron's son. He was my dream."

She leaned in as her words hit him like blows to whisper next to his ear, "Not counting the kind of pleasure I give myself, which occurs *often*."

Finally releasing his held breath, he gave his spectacles a vicious nudge. "Playing the game like you were born in the stews, minx. Damned if I'm not impressed."

She lowered her regard to the protrusion denting his trouser close. "An effective strategy, it seems."

Glancing back to ensure they'd retained a modicum of privacy, Crispin knuckled her chin until she was forced to meet his gaze, her eyes traveling along a delicious path up the sleek cords of his neck and over his lovely lips. When the journey ended, she saw herself reflected, dazed and hungry, in his spectacle's lenses.

"You want the truth, Ce?" he murmured in a wicked tone so low she could barely hear it. "I'm tempted by the way your eyes strike me like a slap when I walk into a room. More than tempted, hell, I'm midway to enthralled. It's obvious to me what you're thinking, which has me in return imagining all sorts of obscene things. The scent you wear, your grandmother's fragrance, wasn't it, seems to have embedded itself in my brain, and it's firing off memories of what it was like to touch you. To have you beneath me, pulsing, crying out. Last night, *God*, the wonder of you. I could have taken you there, and we both know it." He laughed, a tendril of mint-tinged air skimming over her cheek. "You see, I want to fuck you as badly as the baron's son did the dazzling girl next door. You said I was your dream. Well, you were a lustful young man's dream as well."

His words lit a fire in her, and Cece tried to respond. Only, reason tangled with yearning until what she'd have uttered would have come out a muddle.

Refusing her time to gather her wits, he flattened his thumb over her mouth as another wave of heat rushed through her. "What's pinking your cheeks and making you wet between your thighs is lust, Countess. As basic a need as hunger. Simple dealings. I've deprived myself of much in this life to get where I'm standing, starting with *you*. Do you know what it was like the day you married Edgerly and the months following? The battle I fought to create a new existence while tossing aside the one I desired with my entire being? To have nothing and no one, not even the home I used to call my own? Sexual thirst one can ignore or *take*. Horrid to admit, but it becomes a bit tedious, actually. I humbly acknowledge what I feel for you in that way because it isn't something I can control. If I could, I'd smash it to bits. *L'acte est fait*."

"But—"

He shushed her with a gentle stroke across her bottom lip.

Flushed with temper and arousal, Cece wondered if his friends in the Leighton Cluster knew Jasper Noble spoke French—and not in some lowbrow accent, either.

He was fooling everyone.

But he wasn't going to fool *her*.

Crispin shook his head, the vehement slash of his mouth overriding any argument. This was a man who'd been trained to reach a deal by forcing a knife to someone's jugular. "I want you *in that way*, I said. Do you understand? I loved the girl. I knew her. It made sense, *we* made sense... until we didn't. I recognize, even if it tore me apart, that I handled it badly, that you were given no choice in marrying Edgerly. I was a boy without power, a good name, or money. Now, here we are. I'll never be a baron's son again, and you can't escape being a countess. I can't go forward, and you can't go back. In my former profession, I'd call our situation an irrevocable impasse."

Witnessing her dogged expression, Crispin repeated the rebuke, his calloused fingertip caressing her lips twice more. Leaving her breathless. Speechless. Needy.

"Jasper Noble—" she started before he cut her off.

"Is a bloke I came to like so much I decided to keep him. And he's decided to avoid trouble in his retirement, which you and your delightful hobby are in spades. I have the life I want, minx, one I worked bloody hard to attain. I'm sorry to say there's no place for yearnings and dreams a man realizes are rubbish the moment they step into the real world."

Cece moved to rip his hand from her mouth, and this time, he let her. Combined with her fury, however, was a breaking heart. Crispin didn't want her, not in a way that mattered, and his decision sounded final. "You're bringing up a difference in *station*? Truly, how frightened are you?"

He blinked twice, his lips parting. He knuckled his spectacles high, a tell she was beginning to see meant he was bewildered. "Of you? Fucking terrified."

"You arrogant knobstick," Cece hissed, glancing around him to find Josiah rolling balls across the billiard table, unaware she was about to take down his new hero. "I only wished to get to know you again. I hate to inform you, the Duchess Society, and every soul in attendance at this social tragedy, but I don't *want* another husband. The first one was abysmal and a lesson learned, thank you. I have funds to live a modest life, one I paid for, and I don't mean in blunt. The place for you was in my bed. Since you're telling me you're beneath consideration, rookery rat that you are, I'll look elsewhere. I'm sure there are any number of suitable men who'd be willing to satisfy my needs whilst keeping their ridiculous titles as I don't require one. I shall live as many widows have before me, a benefit of those freedoms we've discussed."

Crispin stepped in front of her when she tried to circle past. Six feet plus of towering strength and steely reserve. "No," he said in a rough voice absent of a persuasive purr.

A command. A decree. As if he had the right.

85

As if *any* man had the right.

Infuriated, Cece crossed to Josiah and, grasping his hand, exited the parlor with Mara trailing silently in their wake. She saw the fiery glare the governess gave Crispin, nearly singing him where he stood.

Perhaps he'd finally realized his youthful obsession was finished taking orders.

Chapter Six

The Leighton Cluster has ostensibly gained a new member. Jasper Noble was seen at the Duke of Leighton's annual winter ball and, later that week, carousing with celebrated author Dash Campbell at the Hare and Thistle. It's also rumored he's an investor in Tobias Streeter's expanding distillery venture.

This group of low- and high-ranking members of society is known for closing ranks around its own. Will another rogue be inducted and, as has happened before, soon lose his heart to love?

-Newspaper clipping crammed in a hat box under a countess' bed

He didn't particularly like brooding, Jasper decided as he brooded on a duke's veranda later that evening. Flipping his knife open and shut with one hand, a trick he'd taught himself because the action spoke louder than words on the necessary occasion, he guessed this whisky should be his last. The earth beneath his feet was shifting just enough to provide comfort.

Cece was ignoring any effort he'd made to apologize when he wasn't sure what the bloody hell he'd done to make her so angry. He'd been honest about their situation, nothing more.

Not a first, by the by. He recalled many a night he'd sought forgiveness for his transgressions.

Jasper stared into his glass without the liquor answering him back. At this rate, he was going to require a visit to one of those hidden estates up north where one stayed a month or so to dry out.

He rubbed his eyes with a sigh, the tiresome sounds of a ball tainting the air. He'd left his spectacles behind and felt a headache coming on because of it. He wasn't a particularly good dancer, so he'd sat like a wallflower on the sidelines, chalk on the ballroom floor an element that typically brought on a coughing fit. Which made him think of the boy with the sunken chest and dark circles, a lad who'd looked weak and *felt* weak. He stiffened his shoulders and glanced at the moon struggling to be seen through the wispy clouds, light only serving to land in a dull wash over his boot. It didn't help to know he could beat any of the men here in a handsome variety of lethal ways.

Jasper muttered an oath and gave the veranda wall a kick. His pride was smarting; that was the problem.

The countess was currently circling the ballroom with a chap ten years his junior. A reed-thin bloke with hair the color of wheat and a pallor to match. Jasper flipped his blade, a sliver glint in the night, guessing the viscount or marquess, or whatever title the dull sod held, didn't suffer from a shoulder that ached when it rained or a knee that locked up on occasion. He wasn't covered in scars, some of which Jasper couldn't recall how he'd gotten. The man was young enough to start a family and live to see his grandchildren thrive. Not as tall, nor as attractive, Jasper would vainly admit, but he'd do in soothing Cece's curiosity should it come to that.

Which it would at some point. She was too passionate to remain celibate for long.

Jasper polished off his drink with a growl. The youngster seemed smitten, and why not, glancing down Cece's daring neckline every chance he got.

While Jasper contemplated his dilemma, his friends circled him without a hint of subtlety, closing ranks as a gossip rag once claimed they tended to. He fell into the familiar sounds rippling through the night: Xander Macauley's loud curse, Tobias Streeter's low laugh, Dash Campbell's Scottish burr. They'd even dragged the calmest member of the Leighton Cluster away from his own fete. The Duke of Markham was the least likely to engage in the antics they were known for, so his appearance on the veranda was a surprise.

Jasper worried he was becoming too used to their steady friendship.

Dash settled in next to him, levering his polished Hoby boot on the wall. He sipped from his tumbler before speaking, apparently the person nominated to start the conversation. "Scaring me a bit, laddie, with the weapon ye're tossing about. I reckon there's a bloke or two inside you might be considering jabbing a blade into."

"He's in a mood, mate," Macauley murmured and came up on his other side. They were in protective stance, and Jasper couldn't deny the ache this realization sent through him. It had been so long—forever, actually—since he'd been afforded friendship, a thing some claimed a man didn't need in this life. When he'd found he *did*. "Over a woman, no doubt. Hell's teeth, but do I remember those sulks. My beloved Pip cycled me through the races, she did. I about cried in my ale that one night."

"It's the willowy blonde he's eyeing, the actress in"—the Duke of Markham snapped his fingers, trying to recall—"what's the name? Spring something or another, the new production on Drury."

"The chit's been giving more care to the wastrel issue of the Earl of Thandie-Roark, true enough. Might vex an interested man *if* a man were truly interested." Dash hummed, dusting his glass over his lips. "You should check with your bonnie missus, Streeter. The earl shouldn't have passed the Duchess Society's keen examination. I know I didn't."

"Who here except me would have passed?" Markham asked in an utterly nonjudgmental tone, the ruby in his signet ring a fiery spark in the darkness. "And Leighton, of course. The duke factor has pull, I have to admit. Glosses over scandal, lack of finances, or poor dispositions."

"Duke factor." Macauley snorted, casting Markham a wolfish sideglance. "You married in, your wife co-owner of the bleeding matchmaking enterprise. Like you would have been rejected, even without the title."

Tobias Streeter turned to rest his hip on the wall, moonlight an easy wash over his broad form. Thoughtfully, he chewed on the toothpick jutting from his lips, a habit left from his successful battle to quit smoking cheroots long ago. "It's the redhead he's fretting over. The countess we're staging these theatrics for. My wife has a notion, and I've come to greatly respect those."

Conversation ceased, still as death.

The lone member of the Cluster who didn't gossip had spoken.

Jasper stared into his tumbler without comment, which was comment enough. He'd shown blatant fascination, unable to tear his gaze away from a woman he had no business lusting after. Cece's false laughter was a trifle only *he* would notice—and be gutted by. He'd stood too close to her all evening, even tried to make conversation at dinner and been soundly rebuffed. As for her form-fitting-but-positively-stylish gown, well, he'd nearly swallowed his tongue when he'd seen it.

He knew what she looked like beneath it—or he had a long damned time ago.

Taking a sip from an empty glass, he reviewed his options.

What the hell, Jasper decided and tossed the tumbler in the shrubs. They were his friends—and like his persona—he'd decided to keep them.

Besides, he was tired of lying.

"The earl's interest in Lady Edgerly will cease the moment she wipes the floor with him in archery. Or croquet. Shuttlecock. Aren't those on tomorrow's joyful agenda? He'll flirt, then she'll sting him right to his bones with a candid response no other woman in England would dare make. She can shoot as well as any man, should he mistake this as an endeavor meant to impress her. God help him if he takes her riding." Shrugging, he scratched his chin with the dull side of his blade.

"She can't help herself. Letting a man win to gain his consideration has never been Cece's way. She's nothing if not determined, which will make her a societal pariah once they realize who they're dealing with. A lady, truthfully, she's not. Northumberland women are tough stock. Not built for ballrooms, heaven love them."

Though he'd never admit it to this group, it had been much the same when she'd decided about him. Ambitious, driven Constance Willoughby was a sight to behold when she wanted something. She'd broken the mold, ruining him for anyone else.

He'd been doomed to lose his heart from the first second. She'd made sure of it.

"Who the hell is Cece?" Dash asked as he snaked a deck of cards from his waistcoat pocket and began a calming shuffle.

Jasper fidgeted, giving his knife a spin that sent moonlight glinting off the blade. "A girl I grew up with."

"By bloody lord, Hildy was right," Tobias whispered, his toothpick dropping to the flagstones. "That woman is a terror with her estimations."

Macauley turned to him, and Jasper realized it was time. He could be honest, or he could be alone. His friends had given him space enough to come clean. He needed to prove he trusted them. "Who are you, mate?"

Delaying, he glanced over his shoulder. Smoothed his hand down his waistcoat, feeling every bone button knock his palm.

"He's jumpy," Dash said, shocked. "I never figured to see the day. I watched him set his own broken finger without blinking, queasy as hell myself from the sight."

In a quick move, Jasper snapped his knife shut and slipped it into his pocket. "This story is one I'll share with you, then you forget you ever heard it. The knowledge is dangerous to those who retain it if you catch my meaning." He'd made men weep, and for that, there were those who hadn't forgotten. He employed thugs to guard his home and businesses for a reason. He'd never be out of the dark, another rationale to keep Cece away, now that he'd decided he needed another to strengthen his position.

"I told you he was no swindler from the stews. What rookery tough folds his cravat like that? Ever seen the posh way he drinks tea? Like the duke over there, pinkie extended."

Dash held out his hand. Macauley grimaced and slapped a wad of bills into it.

Jasper turned on them, temper flaring. "You've been wagering about me?"

Dash turned his gaze back to his cards. "We wager about everything. I don't own the premiere gaming hell in London for nothing, laddie."

The Duke of Markham clapped his hands, his impatience showing. "I, for one, would like to hear this story if we can cease the damned betting for three seconds."

Jasper respected the hell out of Markham, although he'd yet to call His Grace a close friend. The man supported his duchy through his beloved love of rocks, his knowledge making him the most proficient mining surveyor in England. It was a lesson in respecting your passions and knowing the life you desired above all would follow. Neither his family nor his peers had appreciated his enthusiasm for geology, but he'd remained steady despite that opposition.

Clearing his throat, Jasper reached to adjust spectacles that weren't there, then sighed with a shoulder-rolling stretch. "My father was a baron of absolutely no mention, his only child the same. An unforeseen title bestowed on my grandfather for services given the Queen, a bit of luck most would say. A rotten bit for society. My late childhood was spent in Northumberland after the baron won an estate on a race at Epsom. This is where I met the countess. A brief respite after being asked to leave three boarding schools where, trust me, it was proven I didn't belong in the aristocracy. They knew I was base at my core, and frankly, I agreed."

"A bloody baron," Macauley said, his lips curling, "as I'm guessing your sire has passed on."

"You're the son of an earl, and you married the sister of a duke," Jasper returned, unwilling to buckle. "Let's not cast stones, shall we?"

"*Bastard* son, Noble. Cast out and never acknowledged. There's a key difference."

"The speculation about you has truth, does it?" This from Tobias, his penetrating gaze locked and holding. Tobias's serene nature often left Jasper edgy. He imagined this is how many a man on the other side of the bargaining table had felt.

Jasper hedged, "I assisted the Crown from time to time." Because of a signed agreement upon his retirement, saying more wouldn't be prudent. Or legal. Or *safe*.

Macauley sneaked a tinderbox from his pocket and stuck flint to steel. The aroma of cheroot smoke followed, a rare indulgence and proof that his wife, Pippa, wasn't nearby. "The shipping enterprises? Partnership in our distilleries?"

"Don't misunderstand. Jasper Noble was a front that became very real to me, more so than the baron's spawn who came before him. Except for the brief snatch of time in Northumberland, his life suits me better than the other ever did. I'm entered into no partnership under false pretenses with regard to my faithfulness to the project or business. I can promise you, I'm not going back." *Even for her*, he vowed but didn't utter.

Choosing Cece was choosing the other life, and he wasn't going to do it. She was dangerous for him—and he for her—even if she didn't realize it yet. "I didn't suffer the childhood I would have if I'd been born in the rookery, as Jasper Noble is contended to be, but I suffered, nonetheless. Bruises, black eyes, and the like. My father was an unholy brute, nothing kindhearted about him. I was *glad* to get away when he cast me out, willing to leave his name behind and the memories with it."

Macauley squinted through a plume of smoke as gray as his eyes. "The same, mate, for me. I rejected any connection to my sire after being tossed aside like rubbish. Except for being forced to leave my brother behind, the unburdening was euphoric."

Jasper glanced at his hands, calloused from work dotting his palms. Being judged a hoodlum in this new life gave him pleasure. Unburdening, indeed. "I like what I do. I'm good at bargaining. I'm good at selling. Trade, of all things."

"Trust is mandatory." Tobias wedged another toothpick between his teeth and closed his lips around the bamboo stalk. "Between partners. I won't agree to anything else."

Jasper's gaze touched every man's circling him. "There's nothing false about my friendship or my commitment to our shared endeavors. You have my word, and that's one thing I'll never default on."

Dash grinned and held up the ace of hearts, incapable of focus for long before his mind drifted to other topics. "What about the redhead causing you to hide out in the dark, pining away?"

"I'm not hiding," Jasper lied. "Or pining."

Macauley jabbed the cheroot at him, his smile growing. "Ah, finally the interesting bit. When a bloke starts twitching, it's getting good. It's been years since we had a failed love affair to pick apart. A spot of entertainment's welcome. No babes born in the past six months, no felines adopted in the Streeter home. Damn, this group is dying out."

"New kittens last week," Tobias murmured, his words layered with a shade of mortification. "A batch of three, orange and black."

"The countess is no ordinary woman," Jasper argued weakly, unable to tell them about her hidden talent. Or that incredible summer of his youth. Moreover, perhaps Cece *was* deserving of his fascination—the only woman who'd ever held it—but he thought himself deserving of *peace*. Chasing her down while fearing for her safety seemed a fool's gambit. Suppressing a shudder, he recalled those awful years after she'd married.

Thankfully, things had changed.

Jasper Noble wasn't a fool when Crispin Sinclair had been.

"I get the story, Noble. Making the woman pay for past transgressions." Macauley dropped the cheroot and ground the smoking nub beneath his boot. "You're friendly with my sister-in-law, Necessity, Shoreditch connections and such. She claims there's a lost love who shattered your heart, mate. Though I always took that as female fancy."

Jasper stepped back, resting his bum on the veranda wall. The moon was hanging high in the sky when he checked on it, his imperfect vision adding a misty halo to the scene. Was he making Cece pay? And what about that lightning bolt of a kiss? He'd stumbled to his room last night and, within seconds of entering the chamber, had his cock in his hand, images of Cece in the throes of passion bringing him to a ripping orgasm in fewer than ten strokes.

94

He'd not even made it to the bloody *bed*.

"Take her away instead of trying to solve this dilemma during a country party, of all horrors. She's a widow and can do as she likes, one stellar advantage. As I know from my darling duchess being in the same situation during our courtship. Not that you need to advertise the leave-taking... but nonetheless, it's an admissible option." In a show of expert persuasion, the Duke of Markham glanced away during this advice, removing an exquisitely colored stone from his fob pocket and rolling it between his palms as if he sought to warm it.

His Grace was nothing if not cunning. The first rule of persuasion was stating your case without pinning a man to the wall with a commanding gaze while doing it.

A tremor raced along Jasper's spine and landed right in the hard heart of his belly. One of those fateful sensations a man learned to respect. The duke's stone wasn't far from the color of Cece's eyes when she came, dark green and threaded with golden longing.

Damned if it didn't show how doomed Jasper was when this is what he envisioned upon seeing some silly rock.

"A few days of closed quarters if she's willing to go," Tobias murmured around that dangling toothpick, second most sly in the group. "Proximity often helps a man make a decision. You wouldn't be the first to try it. Once you get her out of here, the rest is up to you. We only aid in the leaving."

"It ain't kidnapping. Her boy might benefit from a man around, even for a short time. You like children. Good with 'em, I've seen it with my own brood." This from Macauley who, despite his keen intellect and ruthless reputation, was the poorest liar among them.

They wanted him to walk the matrimonial plank, every last one of them. Their second name in the *ton* was the Leighton Lovesicks, a salient fact Jasper wasn't soon forgetting.

"You've got that tucked-away cottage in Bloomsbury perfect for the test," Macauley added in a voice threaded with amusement, damn him.

"Test," Jasper repeated, realizing he was being had but allowing it.

Dash slapped him on the back, rocking him forward and off the wall. "I'll assist, seeing as you broke a digit helping me keep my fledgling marriage on a steady path. That bedeviled carriage had a bum axle, though, I'll always contend. It's luck my badly nicked face brought out the tiger in the wee wife, for which I'm thankful."

Jasper flexed his hand, the mention of his injury making it throb. Dash's ungodly visage had never once been injured beyond repair. It was the most flawless face in bloody England, bar none, much to the Leighton Cluster's dismay. "The barouche overturned due to faulty equipment, is that it? Nothing to do with your driver racing hell for leather so you could kiss Theo's slipper the moment we arrived."

Calculating, Tobias shifted his toothpick to the other side of his mouth. "This calls for a diversion. Something to bury this farce of a gathering in an early grave and send these nobs loping back to the city. Enough chaos and no one will know where a misplaced countess ends up. Or with whom."

Markham tossed the rock between his hands. "A diversion could be amusing, though our wives won't think so. This *is* Duchess Society business, Streeter. A misplaced countess as you call it will make my duchess most vexed with her duke. Not to mention what Hildy will think of it."

Tobias frowned, ostensibly considering his wife's displeasure for the first time.

A plan came to Jasper, a ploy he'd used to break into the Italian embassy in 1826. "A fire," he whispered, struggling to remember the particulars of the assignment. Had he used a chemical agent or an incendiary device? He only recalled the nasty burn on his forearm that had blistered for a solid week and the billowing smoke driving everyone into Lower Grosvenor Street without actually harming the building. The ruse had tracked as well as a Bainbridge timepiece, right on the money.

"Now, hold on a minute," Markham said, the stone stilling in his hand.

Jasper smiled, recording their stunned reactions with a pulse of excitement he thought he'd left behind with the emissary business. "A minor disturbance, more smolder than flame. We'll be on the ready to limit the damage, and the wives need never know how it started."

When Jasper could see he hadn't fully convinced the duke, he pushed harder. "I'd be willing to trade your inconvenience for that lavender stone you inquired about, Your Grace."

Markham's breath rushed out in a sigh he likely wished to call back. "The chalcedony? The one with the intergrowths of quartz and morganite?"

Jasper gave a half nod, having no idea what the stone was called or what it was comprised of. He only knew with absolute certainty that he could *get* it. Easier a gambit than stealing the damned telescope for Macauley's brother. He'd had to contact half his list to find the thing and was still fielding questions about what he'd done with it.

Markham loosened his cravat to allow a fast swallow. "The British Museum has that piece in their mineral collection. Don't you recall I was outbid at auction?"

Jasper ran through the particulars in his mind. Diversion. Cece. A possible solution to his angst. Her ginger hair spread across silk sheets as his body trapped hers to the mattress. "The director of the museum owes me a favor, a big one," he finally said.

Tobias snorted, toothpick bobbing. "Of course he does. But this is risky, Noble. You're already on a short leash with my wife."

Jasper waved him away while praying Streeter didn't mention the stable incident.

"A smokescreen, you gits," Macauley murmured, staring sleepily into his glass. "Street, you remember the one in the warehouse in Five Points when we were lads? Got half a shipment of silks out the back door while they were scrambling to get the blaze at the front under control."

Dash gave his cards a quick shuffle. "Why's the spy on a short leash, I wonder? That's the interesting nugget in this conversation."

Markham pocketed his rock with a dogged look no one would mistake for anything *but* ducal determination. "We're planning a renovation of the west wing. My mother had a great attachment to damask wallpaper with large floral patterns. Roses the size of one's head have gotten a bit much. A touch of smoke sent billowing down that hallway would be enough to put an end to the festivities. I can claim it's a worse situation than it is, requiring my staff's undivided attention.

Party over. After all, I might not have another chance with the chalcedony."

Jasper rocked back on his heels, wishing for a folio to get the details out of his head and onto paper. "I have a plan. Enough anarchy to have these blue bloods ready to return to the comforts of London. We'll add someone, I propose it be Dash, to race down the corridors, intensifying the panic. We don't actually need to burn down your estate, Your Grace."

Markham bowed his head in mock agreement.

With a groan, Streeter tossed his toothpick to the flagstones. "Hildy will kill me if she finds out."

Macauley clapped him on the back. "Find your bloody courage, mate."

Laughing, the Leighton Cluster trailed back into the ballroom, able men on a mission.

Jasper would have considered the evening a true victory if Macauley hadn't pulled him aside at the last second and asked to make use of the able talent of his forger.

Chapter Seven

The Leighton Cluster scoundrels are, once again, up to no good.
-Newspaper clipping stuffed in a hat box under a countess' bed

Cece crested the rise leading from the stable and halted in her tracks.

During the hour she'd been riding, chaos had apparently erupted on the Duke of Markham's estate.

The party's attendees were scattered across the lawn in varying states of dress and alarm. Baroness Bradley was slumped against the wall circling the fountain, her maid wiping her flushed brow with a sodden handkerchief. The Earl of Thandie-Roark was attempting to close his trunk by sitting on it, his thinning hair rising like shoots of wheat from his head. Carriages lined the drive in drunken disorder, groomsmen in a flurry as they assisted people inside the conveyances. The odor of burnt furnishings was a lingering but steady presence, as was the gray plume seeping from a lower parlor window. The sound of breaking glass could be heard in the distance.

Cece's thoughts blanked in a moment of panic.

Josiah.

She was running before she knew it, elbowing through the crowd on the lawn, her riding skirt clenched in her fist. When she neared the house, an arm closed about her waist and yanked her into a shadowed recess near the kitchen entrance.

Into a hard body she recognized immediately.

Wrenching from his hold, she stared into Crispin's soot-streaked face. His eyes were a sapphire glow, his mouth a grim slash. He was without coat or waistcoat, his shirt open at the neck, his sun-kissed skin dark against the creamy linen. He looked infuriatingly virile and on the edge of angry, the scar winding beneath his collar giving him the appearance of a brigand.

"I have him," he said in a rough whisper, his gaze fixing on her mouth and holding before moving on.

"Josiah," she breathed, nearly wilting in relief. "You have him."

"He and his governess are in my carriage. Twenty minutes away, at least, that's how long I've been looking for you. You have a loyal companion, I will say. I practically had to sell my soul to get the old bitty to agree to leave without you." He dragged his fist over his cheek, leaving a black smear behind. "I'd protect the boy with my life, you have my word. You know this, even if *she* doesn't."

Despite the chaos, Cece was transfixed, a sturdy pulse of emotion rooting her where she stood. Crispin had safeguarded the most important person in her life when she'd not been there to do it. Long absent and faintly unfamiliar, happiness was a breathtaking sensation. It was as if a layer of ice cracked, allowing sunlight to caress her skin.

Speechless, *breathless*, she gestured inanely to the stable as the chaos continued to swirl about them. "A morning ride."

He coughed into his fist and threw a hasty glance over her shoulder. "I'd forgotten about your penchant for riding, Countess. But now, we must leave."

Without another word, he took her hand and guided her down a foot path leading away from the main drive.

Stumbling along, she yanked from his grasp. "What's this? What is happening?"

Pausing only long enough to seize her elbow this time, he steered her to a waiting barouche parked in a private drive alongside the side garden. An elegant crest on the door of the vehicle confirmed it belonged to the duke. Waving off the coachman when he attempted to scramble down from his seat, Crispin hustled her inside the transport. Crouching to latch the step board, he then leaped in behind her as gracefully as a lion.

It must be something to move like the wind, she thought, dazzled despite her frustration.

Crispin settled himself in the seat across from her, a spent exhalation leaving him. He coughed again, a remnant of the asthma he'd sternly advised she never mention. Flicking the curtain aside, he gazed out, the mayhem on the estate a lessening drone as they entered the roadway. "Bloody poor planning," he whispered, letting the drape fall into place.

Cece studied the interior of the vehicle as her suspicion grew. Her spencer lay in a neat fold in the corner, the battered portmanteau her grandmother had given her on her tenth birthday rested on the floorboard. Anyone who knew her, and this cad *did*, would understand it was a special piece of luggage not to be left behind.

She counted the many things wrong with the picture, most of which centered on the mischief taking up too much space in the tight confines of a duke's barouche. "Did you start a fire to ruin my party?"

He tapped his knuckle to the windowpane three times before speaking. "Hildy's bash, not yours, if we're being precise about it."

"Does she know about this?" Cece slumped back with a sigh, her belly sinking. "I thought I could trust her."

Crispin groaned and massaged the bridge of his nose, refusing to answer.

She noted the silver threads running through his hair and the faint groves shooting from his eyes, changes time had wrought. The brawler was more handsome than the charming young man had been, a shocking truth.

A truth that vexed her to the bone.

She sat forward, daring him to defy her. "I repeat, does Hildegard Streeter know?"

His gaze sliced up, a deep, twilight indigo, intelligence banked hard behind it. "She does now, and she's dying to tell you everything. To claim one spot of joy on this leaden day, I'll strive to beat her to it. I'll start with admitting Dash Campbell is a better writer than he is a criminal even if he's based his silly books on such mischief. Asked to create an adequate but insubstantial blaze, he instead created a *substantial* one. Consequently, Streeter's in a bad way with the wife at the moment, and the duke's missus isn't any happier. His parlor floor will definitely need to be replaced." He frowned and picked at a rip in the carriage cushion. "At my expense. Not to mention the trouble of calling in a prime marker over that damned rock. Retired emissaries only have so many of those as we aren't adding favors to the vault. Invaluable assets I don't trade for gambits that legitimately go up in smoke."

"Rock?" Cece collapsed against the squabs, pressing her fingertips into the velvet's smooth nap to hold herself steady as the carriage took a fast turn. "I'm confused."

"Better that than the truth of the thing," Crispin said and closed his eyes. Was he planning to *sleep* without telling her where they were going?

"Despite this trouble, you promise me Josiah is safe."

"He is. We're only minutes behind them, headed to the same destination."

The seconds ticked by, the *thump* of the carriage wheels striking the roadway the only intrusion. If Crispin wasn't going to explain, she'd hound him until he did. "I'm baffled if you'd like to enlighten me. Talk of rocks and burnt parlor floors. Disorder truly does follow this group of people you associate with, doesn't it?"

"Think hard, minx," he murmured, his gaze returning to the window. "It will come to you."

She frowned to hide her smile, straightening her spine as if she sat in her family's pew in Northumberland. He believed her intelligent enough to figure this out—and he was right. Crispin Sinclair and Jasper Noble were at their core the same man. Her childhood friend had never treated her with anything but respect, had never conversed with her in a contemptuous tone, choosing to speak only of issues he presumed a weak female mind could comprehend. They'd held long discussions about literature, art, *life*.

Conversations held before—and after—attraction had snatched them up in its teeth.

Raindrops began to strike the roof of the carriage and trail lightly down the windowpane as they bumped along. Cece recorded the play of light across Crispin's face, the hollows beneath his cheekbones, his full, pouting lips. The stubble he'd not had time to shave off his jaw darkening his skin to the point of piracy. As she stared, color rose on those high, hard cheekbones, his neck lengthening with his swallow.

Like it or not, he was beautiful.

Complicated. Intelligent. Courageous. So much so that England's government had trained him to work for them and likely paid him handsomely for the risk. Too, hidden deep, he was *kind*. She'd never forget the bruises his father had inflicted upon him and the tormented look in his eyes for days after. Circumstance had changed him... but nature was nature. As a boy, he'd rescued a stray dog and volunteered to rebuild the sagging church roof. He'd given donations in secret to a family in need when his father had refused to help. He'd been kind to her, a young woman society steered clear of. If he'd staged a diversion to end the country party, even engaged the dubious Leighton Cluster in his plot, she merely needed to determine *why*.

Cece smiled, glancing at her slippers to conceal it.

It was really quite simple.

He wanted her, though he wished he didn't. She felt sure he had no idea what to do about it.

Well, that made two of them.

"I'll give this charade a week. With suitable arrangements at your home, of course. I assume that's where we're headed."

Turning his head, his gaze slowly took her in. From the tips of the boots peeking from beneath her riding skirt, up her legs, her waist, her breasts, where he lingered, licking his lips. Her nipples pebbled in response, a sensation she worked vigorously to conceal. By the time he made it to her face, she was riveted, restraining herself from climbing in his lap. The pitch and sway of the carriage could shake them to glory, she well knew. The impulsive young woman would have done it, but that was no way to negotiate if she wanted more.

Because friends would be lovely—but ownership would be better.

As she'd let him own her. She wasn't asking for anything she wouldn't properly *give*.

After waiting an eternity for his reply—the man was certainly more patient than the boy—she extended her leg and nudged his calf with the toe of her boot. "Where?"

He tracked his gaze down her body this time, leaving a trail of heat behind. "Bloomsbury. You'll have a bedchamber in my townhome, Countess. Respectable, on the up and up. As good as any baron would provide. You, Mara, and Josiah, guests like any other. Nothing more to it."

She laughed, unable to hold it back. "You kidnapped me for nothing more than that?"

In a rare show of reticence, Crispin cracked his knuckles and knocked his boot to the floorboard. There was more he wasn't telling her. "Actually, there's a trivial dilemma, minx. A favor, of sorts, I wish to ask of you."

A favor he needed of *her*? What could he possibly—

"You hypocrite," she whispered, realizing the only thing he would need aside from her body—and he wouldn't ask for that in such a deferential tone. A kiss, he'd back her into the wall and *take*. Desire, why, he'd made her come while staring directly into her eyes, daring her to withhold her pleasure.

Forgery was all he would ask of her with reluctance.

Likely *all* he would ask, period. She'd suffered a moment's insanity imagining it was anything else. "No," she said, crossing her arms over her chest.

Scowling, Crispin rocked forward on the seat, his long legs invading her space and making her own tremble beneath her skirt. "It's for Xander Macauley. Or our business, I should say. Thanks to you, they know I'm someone aside from Jasper Noble, leaving *me* to prove *him* a trusted associate. We need a signed document from a distillery partner in Scotland, a minor issue with a revision we're making to the brewing process. We're getting the approval, full disclosure, but between the travel to Oban, the submission of the papers to the solicitor in both countries, the process will take weeks. And the administrators check past signatures on contracts as policy, so we need a proper match. If we can submit here to get the ball rolling, that would be extremely beneficial. It involves a part on the Islington still, a piece Tobias and Dash figured out—"

"Oh, for heaven's sake, I'll do it!" She threw up her hands in defeat, struggling with the brutal sting that this was the only reason he'd staged this senseless diversion. She couldn't very well forge a document at a house party, loupe in her pocket at all times or not. "Although, you devious blackguard, don't for one *second* think I'll forget how you urged me to leave this behind, only to have you come crawling to me when my skill suits your needs."

In a show of annoyance, he moved in, cupping her chin and forcing her gaze to his. "Forge every damned document in London if you like if I'm there to defend you. Let them try to get through me to get to *you*. That's the difference."

The smoke-tinged fragrance drifting from his skin and the way his fingertips gently caressed her cheek drained away reason in slow, aching measure. Attraction rippled through her, along with that wondrous feeling of security—when she'd had little afforded her in this lifetime. Her father and her husband hadn't cared enough to protect her when this man did.

Before she did anything she couldn't take back, she had to know. "Was this farce merely a ploy to satisfy a business need? Starting a fire and ending a party merely because you need a signature?"

Crispin hesitated as his gaze skated away. Sitting back, his tells dove into play. His fist knocking out a rhythm on his broad thigh, his toe tapping against the scarred floorboard. Her heart warmed to realize what a poor poker player he'd make, at least with her. As a boy, he'd been the same, unable to hide his emotions from her.

Finally, he murmured, "He's long gone, minx. Don't expect him to show up ever again. The hope will destroy you."

It wasn't an answer. And it felt like a lie.

The falsehood sat between them with the past throbbing like a wound.

If this was a dare, she wasn't in the mood to ignore it.

Chapter Eight

"She's too young. Too reckless. Too willful. Half the time, I don't even like her.

But I want to kiss her anyway."

-Angry whisper by a baron's son to his father's groom after a sound thrashing on the archery range, 1813

H e wasn't even sure he liked her.

Debating this judgment, Jasper lingered in the doorway of the cramped garret Cece had reconfigured as her office, a slender slice of sunlight from the high window choosing that second to pierce the pane and float across her like a vision.

As if she needed anything else to make him notice her—when he'd been doing nothing *but* notice for the two days she'd been in residence.

The bubbling brew she'd created in his belly this morn with nothing but a look brought the memories rushing back.

He recalled the first time he'd seen her with crystal clarity.

A remembrance which came to him in odd moments. He'd been rendered senseless more than once in his former profession, consciousness leaving him as that first picture of Cece floated through his mind. The gray tint of a stormy sky at her back; her glorious hair falling over her shoulders much as it was now; the crook of her lips, a worldly smile for such a young woman. His vision had sharpened, he recalled, for no more than five seconds, a sharp pinch of knowing. Clear sight through the fog.

He'd only been sure, bloody certain, there was nothing ordinary about Constance Willoughby. And that she was to be a thorn in his side.

The love of his life, a realization coming later.

He glanced at the invitations in his hand, delivered by Tobias Streeter's runner after breakfast. They'd arrived alongside a package of contracts for the new distillery Jasper was to sign and review. Due in part to Dash's blaze and the most titillating country party of the century, Lady Edgerly was the latest temptation. Interested admirers had flooded the Duchess Society's office with requests since it was rumored the countess had taken leave after the fright she'd suffered and was not currently staying at Edgerly House. Her whereabouts were a mystery, adding to the fascination.

At times like these, Jasper was thankful he no longer inhabited a rung on society's ladder, though this lack placed him out of reach of anyone climbing it. Like a widowed countess, for instance.

Sitting behind the escritoire Jasper's footman had moved into the room for her, quill caught between her teeth, Cece hadn't looked up once in the time he'd been lingering in the doorway. Her attention was utterly fixed on replicating the signature for Xander Macauley. She didn't feel his presence when he could damned feel *hers* at every moment. In fact, aside from her forgery assignment, she'd been a proper guest. Dining with him, discussing inane topics like the weather and plans for his home, trivial bits of nought. If he'd expected mention of orgasms and stables, their passionate past, her uncertain future, perhaps a late-night visit to his bedchamber, he'd been gravely disappointed.

She'd been everywhere around the place, actually, just not with him.

He'd caught sight of her from his bedchamber window, laughing with Josiah as they threw stones into the small fountain on his lawn. Strolled into the kitchen to find her happily hunched over the chopping block, taking tea with his motley staff, their smiles of delight sending a quiver of what felt like envy through him. She has an easy, boisterous nature, joy flowing like rainwater from her. People *liked* her. When he'd never been easy around anyone, never understood how to give of himself without pieces being ripped away. His father's brutal lessons had imparted more than he wished.

Hide your emotions, boy, and no one will know what makes you tick.

Or what could destroy you.

When he'd already been destroyed by this woman once.

Crushing her invitations in his fist, Jasper stepped into the room. Who cared if Cece had admirers? Or if she was well on her way to a second wedded union? Hildy Streeter was so furious, he'd been told by a sniggering Xander Macauley, that she'd made it her mission to find the best man in England for the countess, a man who wasn't *him*.

The Duchess Society tended to win the wars they waged, he well knew.

Which is what Jasper bloody wanted, wasn't it? To be free of this bothersome chit? For the past to stay just that—in the past. Let someone else worry about her. Worry about the boy. Worry about the bloody medieval roof in Northumberland which had always given her trouble. He'd bet she was *still* chasing that leak.

Jasper kicked aside a wadded ball of foolscap as he crossed to her, his irritation mounting. She'd chosen a gown the exact hue of the roses blooming in wild recklessness beneath his bedchamber window. A dusky, pale sort of rose. Regrettably, the shade brought out the auburn streaks in her hair, color intensified by her continual lack of a bonnet.

Cece had never liked hats. She hadn't seemed to care about the freckles that appeared every summer, ones now starting to dot her nose and checks. Hell, she'd worn trousers much of the time on the privacy of her estate. She'd never followed society's rules, only giving in once. When her father forced her to marry Edgerly or face ruining her sister's chances on the marriage mart. No matter Jasper's anguish at the time, forsaking what they'd had was a sign of strength, not weakness. He knew it was his fault they'd been caught in a compromising situation.

The man understood. The boy had not.

Still, the man couldn't quite get over it.

Gradually, Cece glanced up. Her blush was faint, her smile virtually nonexistent. *Christ*, to know what she was thinking. Or better yet, tup her right there on that desk. Legs parted to let him in, fingers clawing into his hair in fearless abandon, tender mews like she'd uttered during their impromptu rendezvous in the stable streaking the air.

Because she *was* fearless. He was the frightened one.

When her lips tilted, her eyes darkening to the glistening green of rain-dew leaves, he guessed she'd grasped his thoughts even if hers were still a mystery.

His foolishness did not improve his mood.

To remind her of the man she faced, Jasper slipped a bejeweled dagger from the sheath he had sewn into his coat and sliced open an envelope, nothing a baron would ever do. The top one was from the Marquess of Anglesey. The missive was swarming with fanciful language, an invitation to luncheon with his mother at his home in Regent Park. The sot. His bloody *mother*. With a growl, Jasper dropped it to the desk and ripped into the next, the shredded envelopes fluttering to the floor.

Cece grabbed the card and after reading it, braced her hand on her ledger, leaned in, and yanked her mail from his hand.

On impulse, he seized her wrist, and brought her in. Eye to eye, so close their noses nearly touched, her swift breath striking his cheek. She smelled of peppermint and blackcurrant, scents lingering from breakfast. Honeysuckle from the Marseille soap his company shipped from France, bars he brought home because his mother had loved the fragrance. Taking note of those freckles, ones he'd memorized long ago in the twilight glow after release, gave his belly a deadening twist. He kept himself from pressing a kiss to the tiny scar cutting through her eyebrow... but just barely.

The girl he'd loved was in there somewhere. He'd need to forget that.

"So, this is your mood this morn," she murmured and tapped Anglesey's invitation against his lapel. "My question is, will my punishment require a weapon?"

This said, her gaze fell to the knife he'd dropped when he reached for her.

Jasper's mind clouded, his cock hardening beneath his drawers. *The lock on this door works,* a voice whispered in the wicked depths of his mind. *The desk is of a height. It's been months, you mad cur, months!*

Take her.

Thank God Josiah chose that second to issue a happy shout from the lawn that fluttered past the open curtains. He and Mara were planting flowers Jasper had supplied along the graveled back footpath.

Cece uttered a very unladylike curse and shoved him away. Jasper was pleased to see she appeared as perplexed as he felt. It was then he realized no match was being played here. He wasn't being made a fool. Maybe she'd had a plan at the house party. Maybe she'd even had a plan when she returned to London. Now, with his respectful kidnapping and that impromptu bit of lovemaking in the stable, she was as off her game as he was.

Obviously, neither of them knew what the hell they were doing. Exactly like when they were young.

A bit calmed by the insight, Jasper retrieved his dagger and slipped it home. If his hand trembled, she'd never know. If his shaft could pound nails, his trouser close was appropriately covering for him. "How goes the forgery, Countess?" From a quick inspection, he'd seen she was close to giving Macauley what he needed. The chit was a keen study.

Her eyes strayed his way as she shuffled through her papers.

He stood up straight, thrust his shoulders back. He was the tallest man of any she'd associate with. Five inches over the Marquess of Anglesey, he'd guess, maybe six. He'd grown after he left Northumberland if she cared to notice.

"Quit preening." She grabbed her quill and scribbled five signatures across the page, then shoved the sheet across the desk for his review. "I see you."

"You must be mad," he said and slipped into the winged armchair across from her, looking about to keep his gaze somewhere else. If he blushed, that would be the absolute end.

Cece had reworked the space to her liking, dragging threadbare items from storage into the room. The desk, the armchair, the chaise he'd seen Josiah napping on yesterday, pieces he'd never laid eyes on. He'd purchased the residence lock and stock from a retiring barrister the year prior. Fully furnished but in need of care Jasper had yet to give. A wife would take the manse firmly in hand, Nelson often reminded him.

Or a visiting countess.

Slipping his spectacles from a coat pocket, he fit the arms around his ears and leaned in to study the signatures. Pulling a contract over, he compared them to the original. "I couldn't tell which is the real deal if you asked me. You are a talented criminal, minx."

"The 's' is off," Cece murmured, her gaze fixing on his face. Then, she was trying again. A line of elegant scratches down the page of her folio, one after another.

Jasper had patience for picking locks, reconnaissance taking hours if not days, and devising the least brutal way to get information he needed—but not this. This chit would recreate a trifling signature a thousand times before telling herself she had it right. He'd have gone mad first.

He settled back in the chair, stretching his legs out as far as he could without bumping her desk. "Breakfast was an abundant affair."

She didn't glance up, having pushed him to the back of her mind when he'd been on the verge of kissing her again. "Hmm... yes, it was."

He didn't know how to ask, so he simply asked. "I'm guessing you had a hand in the first full fast being laid on my table since I moved into the place?"

Her quill halted on the page. Her lips curved in a sly smile. "Perhaps."

The smell of hot cross buns had dragged him down the stairs minutes after dawn, followed by the teasing aroma of sausage and fried bread. He'd stumbled into the breakfast parlor to find the sideboard littered with a bounty of tempting sights. Rashers, potatoes, biscuits, beans, coffee, tea. A bowl of oranges—a delicacy he sourced from the

Duchess of Leighton, who was a shipping magnet aside from a wife—and even a somewhat dejected bouquet of wildflowers he suspected had come from his equally dejected garden. Everything situated on a set of Minton china plates he'd never seen before.

Cece had gone rummaging for more than furniture in his attic.

Jasper hooked his ankle on his knee and watched her work. He didn't want to be charmed. Or exasperated because his home felt more like a home than it had since he'd moved in because *she* was there, bringing the fragrance of food and female with her. Somehow, she'd whipped his ragged staff into modest shape in less than seventy-two hours. Added little touches of whimsy to a residence that had been staid last week. The sound of her footsteps in the corridor and a boy's joyful laughter were keeping him up at night, making him dream dreams he'd crushed long ago.

She tapped her quill to the desk, her amusement leaving her in a thoroughly irritating burst of laughter. "Stop pouting."

Jasper removed his spectacles and cleaned the lenses with the dangling tail of his cravat. "Who's pouting?"

She hummed, saying a lot without a single word being spoken. Then, minutes later: "Would you like to read my mail to me in the event I need to reply to something today? Since I'll return to Edgerly House on Monday."

"Monday," he murmured, seeking to ignore the leaden pang this comment sent through his gut.

She shrugged a slim shoulder beneath that tease of a gown. "According to our agreement, that's the date."

"Indeed." He nodded to the stack of invitations. "You're quite popular, it seems."

"I'm an amusement, nothing more. A ducal fire, a countess' disappearance, what fun! When I return to Northumberland, no one will give me another thought."

I will. A bit crossly, Jasper fit his spectacles in place, then dragged the letters across the desk. To think, he'd once been feared by every felonious fugitive and foreign agent in England. "I can imagine nothing better than acting as your social secretary." Using his finger this time as his blade was safely tucked away, he ripped into an envelope. "Lord

Ambrose. Tea on the 17th." He tossed the embossed card over his shoulder, out of sight. "He's known to lose significant sums at Dash's hellion, so that's a no." He destroyed the next envelope and offered another judgment. "Baron Talmon. Ride along Rotten Row on the 19th." This card fell to the carpet by his boot. "Penchant for light-skirts. By penchant, I mean obsession involving multiple parties and the occasional animal."

He swore he heard her snigger, but when he glanced up, her expression was completely void of emotion. "A baron might be too low-slung a designation for a countess to consider, don't you think, Mr. Noble?"

Jasper settled back, seeing there was a match being played after all.

His nerve endings sizzled, anticipation flowing through him like a chill. Aside from generic spying, he'd also been the keenest arbitrator in the Crown's service. Verbal battles were his *specialty*. "Undoubtedly," he returned, running his finger along an envelope's wax seal. "I'd not reach lower than a marquess if I were you. Not for the proper arrangements. Barons are known for being wretched gambles, as you know. They disappear, they disappoint."

She mirrored his nonchalant pose. A trick of negotiating he wondered where she'd had the wherewithal to pick up. She traced her quill down the page of her folio, seeming to reflect upon his advice, calm as the day was long. "What piece of the Duchess Society's search wouldn't be considered proper? Not that I am, in truth, searching. This is a ruse, as I've said from the beginning."

Gotcha, he thought, the flare of arousal raising the hairs on the back of his neck.

Yawning behind his hand, he rolled his shoulders, hooked one boot atop the other, and shifted his body forward until his feet grazed her desk. When her gaze followed his movement and a fetching hint of color flowed across her cheeks, he made his decision. Five days left in this abduction. She wanted him; he wanted her.

However, Cece's son and companion were in residence. A staff who'd taken a shine to the countess were gadding about, leaving them less than alone.

It was dicey. A challenge, assuredly, to keep an affair under wraps.

The bigger challenge? To let Cece leave without tucking his heart away in her grandmother's scuffed portmanteau. The past wasn't what Jasper *wanted*. Crispin Sinclair was lost to the world and good riddance. Despite his demise, Constance Willoughby still had her hooks in the man.

The trick was to become *unhooked*.

Five short or unbearably long days left. Why not have them fly by in a whirl of passion and desire, instead of unrequited longing?

Frankly, he was fucking sick of longing after this chit. It was time to *do*.

Determined, Jasper lifted the remaining envelope to his mouth and ripped into it with his teeth. "Proper is what happens in parlors," he said, letting the slip of paper tumble from his lips. If Cece leaned forward and glanced down, she'd see he was aroused. He couldn't hide the erection straining his trouser buttons, and finally, he didn't care to try. "In ballrooms. On those god-awful rides through Hyde Park. Walks along Bond Street, ice cream at Gunters, tea at Twinings. The other side of the coin is the *improper*." He wiggled the final invitation loose without looking to see who'd sent it. "You don't need a titled bloke for those. Considering the stories about higher rank equating to inferior sensual skill, I'd say it's a sound decision not to go in that direction. My advice? Go for a rogue this time."

Letting the card flutter to the floor, he fixed his gaze on hers. Her eyes darkened as he stared, going an alluring, bottomless green. This was the color he wanted to see as he thrust his cock inside her. "If a countess was contemplating the improper, that is."

She didn't do what he estimated nine out of ten women who'd been overtly propositioned would. She didn't fidget with her teacup; she didn't cast her gaze to her feet; she didn't argue, blush, fan her face, or say he had it all wrong while knowing he had it *right*. Instead, she glanced out the window to check that Josiah was still playing. Seeing he was, she rose and crossed to close the drape while his heart thudded out ten hard beats. He could only stare in mute exhilaration as he heard her move to the door, close it with a *click*, then engage the lock.

If this was an indecorous offer, he was prepared to accept.

But Cece didn't come to him.

After a lengthy, aching minute, he glanced over his shoulder to find her leaning against the door. A devious expression sat on her face. He had no other description for it. Worldly, knowing, wise. Without a breath, she began to raise her skirt in sluggish advances. Exposing delicately boned ankles, slim calves, slender, creamy thighs. She wasn't wearing stockings, he noted with no little hunger. A chemise and a thin petticoat suitable for home were it. His arousal, already justifiably intense, spiraled like opium through his body. He hadn't liked the senseless affect the drug had had on him in his youth, but this corruption, he desired with his very being.

Cece crooked her finger in a come-hither motion. "We have thirty minutes until luncheon. Mara is taking Josiah to the stable to feed the horses. He particularly liked the dappled gray mare, the gentle one."

"Zelda," Jasper whispered, his shaft throbbing in time to his heartbeat. If she didn't get to the matter at hand soon, he was going to spill in his trousers like a lad. "The oldest mount I own. She was being abused in the market by a fruit vendor, and I bought her on the spot. She's not much for riding aside from a lad, I'll grant you."

Cece froze, her fingers clenching around the rose silk twisted in her fists. Her lips lifted in what equated to a grimace. "I don't want to hear about Jasper Noble's thoughtfulness. I don't wish to yearn for an untouchable man. My beloved friend is gone. That's what you've been telling me over and over again until I can't hear anything else. This Noble fellow is all that's left. Fine, I'll take what he's offering. But you're asking me not to care about him, so keep his kindhearted deeds to yourself. Compassion isn't required for what we're discussing, or am I mistaken?"

Jasper held himself from pressing Cece against his oak door and tupping the breath from her. What she'd said meant something, and he couldn't ignore her candor if he tried. His curiosity, astoundingly, was greater than his hunger—because Constance Willoughby was the only person in his universe who'd ever really known him. "How am I unchanged?"

Silent, she continued raising her skirt until her quim and the wealth of ginger curls surrounding it were revealed to him. Her gaze never left his, daring him to look away, to *stay* away. She licked her lips, leaving them glistening—and he lost reason. His fingers clenched around the chair's arms as he started to rise. He'd been with many women, more than he'd wished to bed at the start of his London adventures. He'd gotten caught up in an identity that demanded a reprobate's reputation, and he'd been so successful that the affairs had begun to come to him.

For Crispin, the experiences had been an effort to repair a broken heart.

He knew without doubt as he hungrily observed her: he'd never witnessed a more sensual sight than Cece sprawled against a door, her half-naked body calling to him.

"How am I unchanged, Ce?" he rasped as he numbly levered to his feet. She needed to tell him before they were incapable of talking.

She tipped her head against the door and pegged him with a gaze as fiery as his. "If you hurt me, you'll hurt Crispin just as much. *That*, I can live with. Oddly, I trust you both."

She was right. A realization he hadn't faced in full. When it came down to the brass tacks of life, they were the same man. The knowledge snapped at him like a stray dog, teeth bared, ripping into his thirst.

"I confess to being a greedy woman. I want what you gave me in the stable," she whispered, her words a teasing echo in the sultry silence of the room. "This time with your fingers providing my pleasure. You know I liked that almost more than the other. It worked with the time we had, those stolen, risky moments in linen closets and dark corners. I didn't ask before. I didn't have the courage to tell you what I wanted, but now, I do."

The call of a bird through the open window sounded, and in the thankfully far distance, the happy shouts of a boy. The tick of a mantel clock reverberated through Jasper's skull, counting down his time with her. He gave the timepiece a rambling glance as he traversed the room, bent on destruction for them both. The young woman had loved when he'd fucked her with his fingers, a skill he'd, gratefully, been naturally gifted at.

A boon because he'd barely known what he was doing with the rest.

Jasper halted before Cece, air backing up in his lungs, hardly conscious of where to start when he wanted everything at once. His mind roared with need, his fingertips itched to touch. His cock pressed so painfully against his straining trouser buttons he feared them popping off. "I'm better now," he said, cradling her cheek and drawing her gaze to his. Murky, fathomless hunger spilled from her eyes. As he stepped in, hips brushing, heat from her core burned through the superfine of his trousers and drilled straight into his shaft, exactly where he needed it. "I have other ways to help you find pleasure, minx. Swift, explosive, *certain*."

The flash across her face was like lightning, gone before he could capture it. Jealousy, fury, and then shrewd, calculating desire. "I bet you're better now," she ground out before rising to her tiptoes and crushing her mouth to his.

Don't be angry, he thought as she drew his tongue into play. *You were the one I loved.*

The admission would only get him into trouble, possibly remove the orange blossom-scented bundle from his arms. *Shut it, Noble*, he told himself and yanked her skirt from her hand, wadding the silk in a tight ball at her hip and using it to anchor her body to the door. Standing would do nicely. Quite. He'd make her come so hard he'd wipe the anguish from her face and replace it with stupefaction. Orgasms generally left him unable to form anything resembling a rational argument for an hour at least.

Tilting her head up and out of the kiss, she murmured, "Before we go further, I have rules."

He trailed his hand down her body, halting to cup her breast, his thumb teasing the sharp point of her nipple beneath layers he wished he had time to remove. With her ragged gasp ringing in his ears, he nibbled her cheek, her jaw, the tender spot beneath her ear. "Of course," he whispered against her dewy skin, having lost the gist of the conversation ages ago.

Her plump breast fit his palm like her body had been crafted for him. He imagined he could feel her quim enveloping his shaft, the moist folds marking his pant leg. Desire was fogging the lenses of his spectacles, for God's sake.

Who the fuck cared about rules?

She bit his neck to get his attention. "The first being, I want control."

Cece knew all about Jasper Noble.

Supposed spy, astute capitalist, rookery thug. The hat box under her bed was bursting with articles ripped from gossip rags, mentions of him increasing in number after he joined the Leighton Cluster. Unsuitable women, reckless behavior, and mounting wealth making his power in a town built on titles and elite birthrights a shaky but ensuing premise. The mystery surrounding his ancestry only heightened the enticement.

Women loved him; men feared him. And the rest wondered just who the hell he was.

As her words registered, his face blanked, and his cheeks sharpened with color. "Control."

Cece was pleased to shock him. To shake him up. Although, the only sign of it was his fingers clenching around the gown he'd gathered at her waist.

He hadn't made it a question but rather a statement.

His head was downcast, his eyes drowsy with desire. Being this close, she noted things she'd forgotten. Behind the shimmering lenses of his spectacles, his irises revealed a hint of auburn stippled throughout the fierce blue, giving them a depth and beauty unlike any she'd ever seen. She traced her finger down the scar trailing into his collar, painfully aware of his shaft pressed hard and ready against her hip. "Since we're not looking for more, let's make it a game, this affair. Five days of enjoyment without examination. The past finished, the future out of reach. Pleasure and pleasure only, no regret involved. As you've asked, we'll let our memories go."

His lids lifted. Emotions flew across his face like pages flipped in a book. She grasped only one: *need.* "You have my undivided attention, minx."

She pulled her bottom lip between her teeth, knees shaking. He'd said he was better now—but she'd found him wonderful *then*. Their summer of love had been magical. Intimate. Remarkable.

"The way you're looking at me is burning me up, Ce," he whispered as his hand tilted her hip higher, shifting his cock tightly between her aching folds.

She'd never propositioned anyone. Her seduction of the young man from Northumberland had been love and desire mixed with graceless experimentation.

This was different.

She knew herself—and Crispin had admitted, damn him—he knew *women*. Tucking back her fear, she trailed her finger down his cheek and over his jaw. "I'll find you when I want you. When I can get away, when we'll have the promise of privacy. I dictate our interludes. Anywhere I say, any *way* I say. I'm not asking for the baron, by the way. I desire the ruffian. Why not use his boundless experience for a good purpose? *My* purpose."

Exhaling, Crispin braced his hand on the door, fingers spread for purchase. When he pleasured her, if he pleasured her, she suspected this would be the only thing to keep them standing. "Dangling fantasies before ruffians is a dangerous ploy, minx."

When he made a move to take off his spectacles, she shook her head. "Leave them."

The muscles in his jaw tensed as a small sigh left his lips. "Done."

Cece studied him in those brief moments before they lost control. Towering over her, lean muscle and hard-bitten intent, the scent of leather and sweat from his morning ride tinting the air and threatening to devour her, he was mouthwatering, a vision *beyond* her dreams. "Is that an agreeable option, Noble?"

He glanced to the window, his broad shoulders rising and falling. "We begin now?"

With a hum, she drew lazy circles around the buttons of his waist-coat, over his lean tummy, before maneuvering her hand between their bodies, and continuing the caresses along the length of his rigid shaft. "What better time is there to start?"

His head fell back, his eyes sliding closed. "Take control, Countess, and I shall endeavor to allow it."

Cece smiled as her body ignited. To hell with his forgotten title and to hell with hers. The Countess of Edgerly could go to the devil for all she cared. Jasper Noble—brute, scoundrel, seducer—would suffice. Perhaps he was the sincerer man of the two.

Did it matter that he'd forgotten the girl?

Truthfully, the woman didn't need him to remember.

Tunneling her fingers through his hair, Cece yanked his head down and seized his lips in a kiss intended to dominate. In seconds, intention spiraled away from her, leaving only awareness of their brief time and urgent need.

Cece's fingers danced over his trouser buttons, awkward but effective in opening his close. The slit in his drawers was wide, his shaft popping free without inordinate effort. *Oh*, to be a man with such casual liberties. Her lips left his to edge along his jaw, biting and sucking.

He growled in response and crowded her into the door. "Fast. Quiet."

She pressed her lips to the flushed skin at his open collar, wrapped her hand around his cock, and stroked. She hadn't done this with anyone but him, her husband never caring to allow her free range to touch him. She and Crispin had made love three times... but had played for months before going that far. Stolen moments exactly like these in linen closets and locked parlors, explorations into body and, for her, soul. She didn't mind stepping in where they'd left off.

She drew her thumb over the plump crown of his shaft, wetness dewing her skin.

"Again," he whispered, undone. So she did.

Gasping, his fingers trailed between her thighs, searching through her damp curls as her skirt tumbled over his arm. He shifted to bring her closer, his arm curling around her shoulders to cushion his hold. He retook her lips as he slid his finger inside her, his thumb pressing over the nub of her sex. He wasn't taking the time to finesse her in any way, a path to swift pleasure his goal. He stroked in a measured pump, working his long finger inside her. "How's this? As wondrous as you remembered?"

She worked to match his rhythm, curling her fingers tightly about his cock. What she hadn't remembered was the weight of him in her hand, the length and breadth of his member. She'd had no experience, no understanding of size or shape, no way to know he was built like a god. Added to this wonder was the feel of his crown brushing her thigh, bare skin to bare skin.

They kissed in haste, hips bumping, driving each other into a frenzy. The air charged and layered with sounds of pleasure. The door shook on its hinges as he moved her against it, time and time again. He shifted, adding another finger to the project. "I could lift you up, wrap your legs around my waist, and have you, Ce. Fuck you blind right here. Next time, and there's going to be a next time. I won't be denied. I won't deny *you*."

Imagining it, her head fell back, her moan reverberating about the room.

"*Shh*, darling Ce," he instructed, his voice cracking.

Fast. Quiet.

Later, she would have trouble recalling what had occurred in precise detail—although she spent hours rebuilding the scene. His hot breath striking her neck, her lower lip caught between his teeth, his arm pumping, her hand fondling. Moist heat, rushed breaths, and fevered skin, half kisses and a grinding rhythm creating less-than-nimble caresses.

He trembled, the shudders rolling through her and starting her downfall. She murmured senseless bits of encouragement to get him to topple with her, rocking against his carved parlor door. Nearing her release, she cupped his bottom, the flex of muscle as he thrust into her hand ruining her. It brought to mind the image of his body atop hers, her thighs spread, his hips wedged neatly between them.

This mental picture, one stolen from her memory whether he liked it or not, was all it took.

Hooking her leg about his waist, she shivered as sensation rippled up her body and out her fingertips. The dots scattered across her vision were the color of shooting stars and campfires, the summer day blue of his eyes. Wishes and dreams and promises for which there were no words.

Recognizing she'd fallen off a cliff, Crispin kissed her to contain her cries, his tongue replicating the act she'd imagined. They were locked in pleasure, relentless, panting souls mislaid by passion.

"I can't hold off any longer. Your wet heat is killing me. I want to slide inside you so badly," he whispered in her ear just before his seed spilled over her fist in a series of hip-jerking bursts. His groans were muted, pressed into her cheek, her neck. Chest heaving, his hand skated from between her legs to grip her waist as his head dropped to her shoulder.

Pleasure was a welcome spiral, an astonishing moment of having left life behind.

And then she remembered it all. Desire was violent, muddled, and magical.

Seconds ticked by as they clung to each other before recollection of their circumstances took hold. Crispin kissed her temple and her cheek before releasing her. Cece swayed, and he caught her to hold her steady. Brazenly, she brushed her lips over his, drawing him in for one last, hot, lingering kiss.

They didn't speak during the repair of hair and clothing. Without comment, he cleaned her fingers with a handkerchief and returned it to his pocket as if wiping his spend from a woman's hand was a thing he did every day. *Perhaps it is*, she reckoned with a sting to her heart.

After escorting her to the desk, he returned to unlock the door, leaving it open a hairsbreadth in some ridiculous display of propriety. Charmed and depleted, Cece slumped into her chair as he righted his crooked spectacles and whispered to himself.

Laughing, she caught his attention. "Your, um..." Her cheeks fired, the feel of his shaft riding her palm a lingering whisper against her skin. "That is, you're not quite restored."

She wagged her fingers, indicating a spot below his waist.

The top of his trouser close was undone.

Glancing down, Crispin sighed. Pewter buttons glimmered in the lamplight as he fumbled to right the omission. Taking a hard breath, he anchored his shoulder against the doorjamb in long, lean perfection. He was a *vision*—a faultless masculine vision. She blew a stray lock of hair from her face. While she felt like a wilted flower ready to drop.

"Strange, isn't it, Ce? We're as harried as we were back in the day, finding any nook available. I haven't done anything of a sensual nature with this much clothing in place since, hell, since then. I'd not even consider it when it's actually quite marvelous. I don't wish to know how long it's been for you. I don't care to ever know, should you think to tell me." He frowned and dabbed at the sweat beading his brow. Pausing in a deliciously erotic move, he lifted his hand before his nose and drew the scent of her into his lungs. "Your quim smells like a slice of heaven, minx. Abiding by those rules of yours, I humbly request a taste. A writhing, tearing-sheets-off-the-bed taste."

Yearning in its rawest form flooded her as ribald images roamed her mind. Reacting, Cece fumbled with her quill, spilling ink across her folio. How could her actions possibly match her bold words about controlling this man? Her late husband hadn't known what he was doing in the bedchamber, and worse, he hadn't cared to learn. Teaching *her* had been an impossibility. The few times they'd muddled through the process had been humiliating and dreadful. Lonely, acute, and without relief.

Much to her envious dismay, she had no experience while Crispin had *leagues*.

His gaze met hers, his eyes having darkened to a fiery, hardened cobalt. A lock of ebony hair lay tumbled across his brow, those streaks of gray at his temple flashing in the muted light. His cheeks were flushed, his lips held in a hard line. The mulishness of his stance wasn't lost on her, nor was his blatant magnetism. Against her will, she was drawn to both. "Don't back down. Not when you have me resting neatly in the palm of your sweet little hand, ready to expire from lust."

She glanced to the window as Mara and Josiah's voices drifted through the open pane. Her thighs were damp, her nipples ached, her brain buzzed. The scoundrel across the room was clear about being unattainable, though he was willing to share a piece of himself—simply not the piece she'd expected to recover. To survive with her heart intact, she must cease thinking of him as that sweet young man.

Crispin Sinclair needed to be allowed the death Jasper Noble had begged for.

When she looked back, she found him putting himself into proper order, smoothing his hair and ironing his hand down his waistcoat.

Shifting from one polished boot to the other in some internal dance of agitation.

She smothered a giggle. He seemed jumpy and a shade irritated. What man was cross after being brought to hasty orgasm? Would it make her an evil woman to tease him, just a little?

Disinterestedly, Cece wiped at an ink stain on her hand. "We don't complement each other in any way but one."

He glanced up with a snort. "When two people are this explosive together, Countess, there doesn't have to *be* any other way. Would you prefer we take leisurely walks through my sadly neglected garden, spilling our secret hopes and wishes? Didn't the boy bore you with enough of that prattle in his youth?"

She'd loved those talks, a fact she wasn't about to tell this arrogant reprobate.

So, she tried another tack. "The gossip rags are full of your exploits. The women—" Slapping her quill to the desk, she held back from saying more. She was treading into territory a woman on a sensual hunt wouldn't.

This is about sexual congress and nothing but, Cece! Stay the course.

He crossed to her, braced his hands on the desk, and leaned in. Apparently, towering over her was his specialty. Next, he'd think to slip that fancy dagger from his pocket and shred her gown with it. The thought lit her *up*. "They don't mean anything. They never did. If this is a game you feel I'll win from the outset, you're wrong. You're winning already because you don't have to do anything to make me want you more than I have any woman in existence, Ce. It's simply *you*. Take your five days and use me. I'll teach you everything you want to know and more. Then leave me to punch holes in my walls while I imagine you utilizing your newfound knowledge on another man."

She settled back in her chair, stunned by his honesty. She took a breath to calm herself and instead took two steps back. His scent had shifted with their adventure. He now smelled of leather, man, and *her*. Arousal wasn't far away, not nearly far enough to protect her. Plotting, she drew a small circle on his knuckle with her quill, leaving black ink glistening on his skin. His hands tensed, but he didn't move. Not one inch. She gathered he wouldn't when presented with such a dare. "I'll find you after Josiah and Mara are asleep. Leave your door unlocked, Noble. We'll strive to make a writhing mess of your sheets."

He exhaled softly, his shadow falling across her as he rose to his full, glorious height. "Deal."

When he started to turn, she grasped his wrist, holding him in place. "I want my taste as well. Don't think I won't ask for it this time."

His pupils expanded, his chest lifting. "I'll count the seconds, Ce."

Then he left her. A woman caught between desire and foreboding.

Chapter Nine

He's your best agent. And, regrettably, your most reckless. His past has left him without care.

-Internal communication to Chief Intelligence Officer Browning

He was nervous. Pacing the room like an expectant father nervous.

"Buck up, mate," Jasper whispered and knocked aside the curtain, peering into the inky blackness without a true sense of what he was searching for in the night or the woman. With a curse, he stalked to his desk to check his timepiece. The best watch in England, his Bainbridge stated exactly ten minutes had passed since his last review. He'd finally removed it from his pocket after the silver case had grown warm from repeated handling.

Circling the room, he noted the changes to his bedchamber. Fresh flowers—violets, hyacinth, and a slightly wilted bunch he believed were carnations—adorned a once dusty vanity. The scent of linseed oil and lemon rode the air, very faint but *very* noticeable. An antiquity or two sat on shelves that had been vacant. One vase in particular he rather liked, although he'd no clue where it had come from. He imagined his mattress felt lighter and his sheets crisper, both redolent of a teasing scent as well.

For a retired operative, this was comfort in the extreme.

When he'd been able to bed down on jagged cobbles, a lumpy carriage seat, an uneven floor. An hour of slumber sufficient if that's what the assignment allowed. He'd waited in a grimy alley outside a public house for two days, maybe three, on the Dublin case without a lick of sleep. And gotten those papers without one drop of blood—many thanks, his own—being spilled.

Jasper sighed and gave his spectacles a nudge, his watch a look. Three minutes.

Striding across the room, he picked up the pretty vase and rolled it between his hands. Halting, he tipped it into the sconce's light. *Coalport* was stamped in black letters on the base. *Damn*, he thought, *those are rare pieces.* He and Xander Macauley had imported a set just last year and were actively seeking more. A marquess in Mayfair had a fine passion for them.

He'd clearly lost his touch if he didn't recognize he had a veritable treasure trove of valuables in his home. Spying wasn't far from thieving, now, was it? Also, he'd gotten soft if he couldn't wait more than a few hours for a tup. Wasn't the game of cat and mouse supposed to make the end result better? It always had before because that had been the entirety of it.

But with her, of course, the game wasn't the *game*.

Bloody hell, he wanted Cece *now*.

He didn't wish to wait. He didn't need diversions to improve the outcome. Heightened anticipation was inherent. With the others, he'd required a bit of added enticement, a nudge to push him over the cliff. With his youthful fascination, his first love, he'd not required a damned thing. The want for Constance Willoughby—mind, body, soul—was a pulse, a connection running through his veins. A part of him, a feeling *and* a life force.

Sex was an infinitesimal factor, actually. Not close to the whole bit. Which was the scariest statement a man could think.

Cross with himself, Jasper shoved the vase on the shelf. He'd sunk so low. He was no longer the kind of man the Crown would demand for challenging projects. They'd use him as a high-styled runner. Put him behind a desk. Confiscate his blade, his pistol, and shove a batch of correspondence in his hand. Like Allen, that waste of an agent who'd been assigned the missing feline cases.

Though he didn't need a blade or a pistol. There were a hundred ways you could render a person senseless with a cravat. A pair of stockings if nothing else was available. He laughed into his fist. Christ, with his years of training, he didn't need a *weapon*.

Frankly, there were many things a man could do with a cravat.

With a jolt of hunger, his gaze sliced to the door, left open a smidge to encourage visitors. Cece was late, possibly not coming. A sensible choice on her part. Completely understandable. Jasper needed to be objective about this mission, a skill never failing him before. He was no prize. Crispin Sinclair, maybe that bloke had a chance with a countess—but Jasper Noble was a wretched bet. He had a well-deserved reputation and had promised the lady nothing but a night or two of passion.

He would leave her without looking back—and she knew it.

Why would she say yes?

Additionally, troubling but true, he carried the desperate sort of manner that comes with a man who's done things. Vile, regrettable things. It was why he avoided mirrors and freakishly clean shop windows. Others might not know what they were seeing, but he did. When he left Northumberland, he said goodbye to everything, and now here he was, trying to reconnect an amputated limb to a quivering baron's body.

Which made significant questions zing through his mind.

If the surgery was successful, could he really let her go in five days? Was that rubbish truly his plan after all this? Yearn for the woman for nigh on twenty years only to let her go once he got her back?

Jasper forced his hand between his ribs to contain the tickle in his chest. He hadn't had a coughing attack necessitating medication in years, nor had he stumbled over his speech in any way that was noticeable, even with a blade pressed to his jugular.

Cece would not reduce him to a trembling boy, by God.

That's when he heard it. The gentle whisper of a footstep. The creak of aged planks running beneath the corridor's equally aged carpets. Jasper burst into motion, his boots striking the floor as he swung the door wide.

Only to find a boy of the trembling variety he wished to avoid standing on the threshold.

"Sir," Josiah whispered and gave his nose a good scrubbing with his fist.

Jasper took one look at the lad's beaten pose, his bare toes curling in on themselves—not to mention the sniffles arriving every other second—to understand this was a post-nightmare stopover.

It was not the visit he'd been hoping for.

Nonetheless, he wasn't about to send the lad away like his father had when he'd shown up at *his* door. Going to his knee so they were eye to eye, he tipped Josiah's chin until his watery brown gaze flowed into view. "Let me guess. You're looking for a bite to eat, and you can't remember the way to the kitchen."

Josiah paused mid sniffle, his lips parting, the nightmare temporarily forgotten. "A wee nibble might be nice."

"I think I can help." Jasper beckoned him into the chamber.

"But," Josiah said, glancing over his shoulder, "the kitchen is that way."

Jasper crossed to the sideboard and proceeded to fill a small plate with *wee nibbles* and a tumbler with a wee dram. "Indeed, it is, laddie, but I keep a modest supply of food here. Bread and cheese, some crackers. An apple or orange when I can get decent ones from the market or one of my shipping partners."

Josiah followed him to the sideboard and popped up on his toes, glancing with interest at the food being assembled on the plate. "Ain't you—" He halted as if he'd uttered a foul word. *"Aren't* you afraid of vermin getting at it?"

"You sprinkle a spot of vinegar around and no vermin."

Josiah's eyes widened. "Truly?"

"An old rookery trick. I swear it works. In the event you're ever concealing sweets in your bedchamber, which I am *not* saying you should."

Josiah sneaked a cracker off the plate and bit into it. "Larks."

Jasper collected information as rapidly as he would have as an emissary. The boy had been raised in a rough environment. His bearing spoke of self-protection, his accent of the stews. It was a wonder Cece had taken him in when he'd shown up on her doorstep. Society wasn't welcoming to the poor and vanquished—and countesses weren't known for being kind to bastard ragamuffins of their late husbands. Only *his* countess, it seemed.

Jasper wished this illuminating fact didn't make him fall a little in love with her.

He really did.

Starting to hand over the laden plate, he changed his mind after seeing how small the boy's hands were. He couldn't have been more than five or six at most. "Here, before the fire, Jos. You have your nibble, I'll have my drink, then we'll go to sleep with full bellies and serene minds. I say that's as good a plan as any."

They settled before the hearth, the dance of a blaze Jasper had made sure was built to last for hours sending amber light across them. Sadly, this wasn't the romantic setting he'd been hoping for. But it was calming, nonetheless.

Jasper leaned against a chaise, stretching his legs out before him. He hid a smile behind his glass when Josiah mirrored his pose, tucking his scrawny shoulder against him. Children scared him in an elemental way, being the brutally candid beings they were, but he respected them for it. "I keep food stuff in my bedchamber because I often have trouble sleeping and..."

Hearing the truth glide from his lips, Jasper frowned and tossed back a slug of remarkably excellent whisky. He should know because it was his. And Tobias Streeter's and Xander Macauley's. Stunned, he stared into the glass, wondering why he'd slipped into honest territory.

"Night terrors," Josiah whispered around the crackers he'd shoved in his mouth. "I get 'em, too."

"Night terrors," Jasper repeated, never having heard the expression.

One that was quite accurate for his state when he woke after dreams of the past.

"Me mum called 'em that." He pushed a piece of Cheshire cheese in his mouth and chewed as if it was his last morsel. "My first mum, that is. I'd wake with them something awful or so she told me. I don't much remember. About her or the visions."

"I had them when I was a boy, too. At least I think I did." In his childhood, he'd snapped out of sleep with his chest aching so badly he'd believed he wasn't going to take another breath. Asthma did that to a person, and if that wasn't terror, he didn't know what was. His father's advice had always been the same. *Go to sleep, Crispin. Be a man.* Unfortunately, his mother was long gone, and there was no one like Cece to step in to offer so much as a moment's comfort.

Josiah slowed enough to swallow, then took a fistful of bread, and devoured it. For a slip of a boy, his appetite was impressive. "Girls are fragile and monsters are strong, so I came to your door. Your frown would be terrifying enough to scare them away."

Jasper filched a cracker off the plate while there was something left. "Monsters?"

Josiah hummed around a sliver of cheese. "Like the wicked one under my bed."

"Ah," Jasper murmured, chewing, beginning to perceive the situation. "I see."

"It's real," Josiah said, a hint of defensiveness entering his voice. He straightened his slump against the chaise and thrust out his chest. "It is."

"I believe you, Jos." He rocked against Josiah, shoulder to shoulder, an age-old symbol of masculine bonding. "But I also think monsters are sometimes as lonely and scared as little boys. Maybe he wants to protect you. Because I've got no children of my own for him to protect, you see, he's just now showing up. We'll tell him how much you'd appreciate his guarding over you on the morrow. Maybe leave him a small peace offering, even."

Josiah pondered this counsel while consuming every scrap of food that remained. Then, he licked his thumb and dabbed up the crumbs.

"Mara says you're a cheat, and your word is like mist. Here one day, gone the next. A rotten berry in the batch."

Affronted and amused, Jasper sputtered, whisky catching him at the back of his throat. The coughing fit was short but dramatic enough to have Josiah taking immediate action and slapping him hard on the back.

"I'm fine," he said, waving the boy away, more breathless than he'd like.

Josiah harrumphed, a trick he'd probably gotten from his sour governess. "Sounds like you're set to heave up a lung."

Jasper waited until he knew neither a stutter nor a cough was forthcoming. "Touch of asthma that catches me off guard from time to time."

This spot of news stopped Josiah in his tracks. His lips parted in shock. "Honest?"

Giving himself a second to assess the situation, Jasper readjusted his spectacles, wondering what Josiah imagined him to be. Or worse, what he'd heard adults whispering about him. Children apparently heard things you didn't want them to. "I was quite a mess as a boy if you desire the truth of it. My mother also passed away when I was a lad, leaving me with a father who wasn't, how shall I say it, very sympathetic to a son who stuttered and had a passing relationship with a condition that left him gasping for air at odd moments."

Josiah patted Jasper's knee, his compassion everything Jasper hadn't received as a child. "My father was grand. He wouldn't have thought to treat me poorly over some silly lung rattle. My mums told me all sorts of wonderful bits about him."

Jasper glanced into his glass, then took a measured sip. This didn't match what he knew about the Earl of Edgerly. The man's rumored proclivities and unjust temper were the main reasons—aside from Jasper's ill-fated love for the earl's intended and her penchant for forgery—that he'd put up such a fight against the earl's marriage to Cece. His father had left him bruised and bloodied when he'd tried to intervene. While Cece's father, despite them being caught in a compromising situation Jasper had tried to repair with his own proposal, had simply had him removed from the estate by two strapping footmen. Chaps Jasper could have, after a year of training, over-powered without a thought.

"I'm sure he was the kindest of men," Jasper finally said, in lieu of speaking truthfully about a nob who'd married the woman he'd wanted to. His animosity had no place in the boy's heart.

Josiah traced a thread in the carpet, hummed a little ditty, and wagged his toes before getting to what was really on his mind. Leaning in, he whispered, "Mara says you were a spider or some such. Them types that hang out in alleys on dark nights getting information."

Jasper rested back with a sigh. *Spider*. A slang rookery term for a *spy*. Come to think of it, he had lingered in many a dark alley seeking information. Suddenly, he wanted to get this Mara into a quiet parlor and advise her to keep her opinions to herself. If the entire bloody town knew what he'd been, however, perhaps he hadn't been as compe-tent as he'd thought at maintaining his cover. "I had an occupation that I liked and was, for a time, good at. But it was risky and gave me many regrets and still does to this day. Hence, food in my bedchamber and night terrors."

Josiah yawned and shifted his slender body, propping his cheek on a pillow lying near Jasper's feet. "Why be sad when someone made you do them?"

Jasper dropped his head to his hand, feeling a tad drowsy himself. "What do you mean?"

Josiah scrubbed his fist across his nose, though his sniffles were long gone. "Like a mum or da, you had people telling you what to do, right?" He shrugged a slim shoulder and snuggled into the blanket Jasper had hoped to wrap Cece in after he divested her of her clothing. "Why feel bad about what you were made to do? I don't love taking baths, but I have to, so why bother too much about it?"

Jasper lifted his head, his chest expanding with a forgotten breath.

Out of the mouths of babes.

He had been doing his job, every blessed moment. He'd never shown up at anyone's door unless they asked for it. He'd never used undue force unless he'd had no choice. Moreover, he'd suffered right along with the criminals he'd tracked. A blade had been held to his neck on more than one stellar occasion. A bullet had been removed from his leg. His body was littered with scars showing how hard-working an agent he'd been.

He'd fought for every scrap of success and had nothing to apologize for or grieve over. He'd made a life when the one he'd been handed at birth had chafed. More than chafed, it had pummeled.

The verdict felt final and wondrous. And to think, the insight had come from a lad he'd known but for a week.

As Jasper watched Cece's darling son slide into slumber, he tried very hard to keep from falling in love once again.

Chapter Ten

The Earl of Edgerly is nearing his end, although he's chosen to stay in London with his female companion of many years. As expected, his countess remains in Northumberland.

—Private report to Agent Noble from an intelligence officer assigned to the central region

Cece was happy someone was having a delightful week.

With a thoroughly uncouth oath, she wiped her palms on her skirt, leaving streaks of soil from her foray into gardening. She didn't usually fiddle with foliage and such in Northumberland. Although she couldn't afford a gardener, her aging groom had a way with plants and was quite talented at maintenance—and he was getting too old to ride, so this left her with a reason to continue to pay him. (Though it left her without a groom, which was a problem.)

Nonetheless, the spot she was hiding in afforded her a wonderful view of Crispin's back lawn and the two figures crossing it. And the ruse of gardening a reason to be crouched in the dirt, spying.

When she wasn't the spy in this house.

Josiah and Jasper were laughing as they trudged across the overlong grass, hands gesturing wildly as they talked, crumpled lengths of sodden linen draped across their shoulders. Their shirts were damp, the thin cotton sticking to their skin. This presented more of a view than she'd thought wet material could of the man's physique. Cece held her breath and leaned in until a yew branch scraped her forehead.

Even with the sting, she didn't move... one... inch. Not with this gift given to her.

Crispin's body was a marvel.

Scars littered the parts she'd seen. His forearms, his hands, his neck. She'd taken peeks into his open collar, of course, and when the chance permitted, at every bit of him she could, even his utterly masculine feet. But this was a *generous* portrait, his shirt fully unbuttoned, exposing the trail of dark hair leading from his chest to his lean belly. The roll and sway of his hips as he strolled along. He had muscles, the genuine article, features usually attributed only to those who worked with their hands. Lowly men of trade, untouchables for a woman of her status.

Therefore, she'd never seen the like.

Even more intriguing, he had a menacing air about him, an aura that exuded danger. Mara had whispered things Cece believed to be mostly true. Her companion had been born in Shoreditch, where Jasper Noble was legendary. There was talk about him, Mara said. So much talk, so much mystery. Cece could see the reasoning behind his choosing to create his persona there. What better place for a baron's son to bury his background than a ratty little corner of London where barons never trod? Brilliantly and quite unplanned, she guessed, the mix of urbane and crude made him a man who couldn't be easily placed in a category.

Except to her because she'd known both sides of him.

Cece well understood being a person society and the public at large couldn't place.

Leaning down, Crispin grabbed a ball and tossed it across the yard for her son to retrieve, his brawny chest flexing. His trousers were riding low on his hips. *Very low.* As if he'd heard her whispered sigh, he hooked his thumb in his waistband and gave it a tug that then high-lighted other assets. He wasn't wearing drawers, and his shaft was a noticeable bulge settled to the left.

This was an intimate slice she'd not been allowed in her marriage. *Oh,* the wonder to be permitted to examine someone from head to toe and everything in between. Any time of the day—and as often as one wished. Before, she and Crispin had only had stolen moments, young adults exploring passion. Hurried encounters, similar to what they'd done in the stable and again in her study. Standing up both times.

They were grown now. She might not know his body well anymore —but she knew *hers.* She wanted his weight pressing hers into a soft mattress. She wanted to claw his back while he thrust inside her.

She wanted to hold his arms over his head and make him *beg.*

Cece brought her hands to her flaming cheeks and blew a breath through her teeth.

She needed to get Crispin into bed, and she needed this soon.

But he was balking. Since she'd found Josiah asleep in his bedchamber two nights ago, both of the boys adorably covered in cracker crumbs, her host had been avoiding her. Before she'd woken them from their resting place before the hearth, she'd taken a slow tour of the room and rediscovered, from the stacks of books cluttering every surface, that Jasper Noble was as much of a reader as Crispin Sinclair had been. She found he preferred earthy fragrances, and he kept a neat wardrobe but a messy bed she hadn't been able to take her eyes off of. He had a spare set of spectacles on his vanity, a sharp blade under his pillow, and a hair clip of hers she'd been missing for weeks on his bedside table.

A finding that sent a burst of longing straight through her. A feeling close to, but she hoped not exactly like, love.

It wasn't entirely a disaster as far as a kidnapping went that she'd hoped would lead to more.

They shared a table at breakfast and dinner, carrying on stilted conversations about the weather, London's political climate, and the intricacies of producing best-in-class whisky. He loved talking about whisky. Crispin helped her complete the forgery assignment for Xander Macauley and sent the package off under discreet cover, while promising it was the last illegal task he'd ask of her.

The promise came with the faint threat that it should be the last she'd ever do.

Last night, she'd beaten Crispin soundly at chess, then sat back while *he* gave Josiah an introductory lesson that led to his putting her son to bed and never returning to the parlor.

Clearly, he was wooing the boy, not the mother.

The truth of it was, he and Josiah were getting closer, a situation filling her with equal parts happiness and dread. She'd seen the way Crispin looked at him, and the way Josiah looked at Crispin.

Love when it first hit you was hard to conceal. She should know.

She assumed this was the reason Crispin was acting like a jittery colt around her and hadn't requested she return to his chamber. No quick orgasms in the various nooks in his home perfect for them. Not even so much as a passing kiss in a spare linen closet. Although she'd like the next experience to be one where they were lying down.

Their arrangement hadn't included attachment to a boy, and she could see the attachment was a conundrum for the man.

When she asked Josiah about Jasper, he'd told tales of spiders and coughing fits. Of protection instead of fear of monsters under one's bed. Adding that his new friend must be almost as good a man as his father. After all, Jasper had said so.

When the Earl of Edgerly had been a rotter.

Yet, boys deserved to think well of their papa—and she wouldn't tarnish this image. It wasn't such a difficult untruth in a world of them.

Hearing their footfalls crunching atop gravel, she shrank into the yew. She was sweaty from the heat, covered in bits of grass and dirt, generally unappealing. She was nothing but a Northumberland hoyden after all. Her mother's decree rang through her mind—*a lady doesn't present herself poorly and hope to attract a man.* With a fallen sigh, Cece dashed a lank of damp hair from her brow. Actresses and opera singers, the types Jasper Noble consorted with, never looked this bad. Ginger hair looked *horrid* with flushed cheeks, so she was often told. She must have been mad to think she could attract an infamous rogue for even a week.

The young man from her past simply hadn't known better. She'd been the first apple on his tree to pick. He'd no experience with which to judge. What was one silly chit when you could have one *hundred?*

The scent hit her first. The fragrance she'd dabbed on her wrists from the bottle on his vanity, a scent that curled her toes inside her muddy slippers.

Slowly, although she knew who she'd find, she glanced up into Crispin's sun-kissed face. He was so tall his head seemed to be in the clouds, that dusky hair streaked with gray a staggering vision next to the blue-white of the sky. Her gaze rose from his crumpled waistband up his long body. Droplets of water glistened in the hollow above his collarbone and dusted the dark hair scattered across his chest. A bead coasted down his cheek and over his lips, before rolling down his stubbled jaw. His eyes were wide, slightly startled, a sapphire glow pinning her in place. The beat of longing that vibrated through her would have taken her down had she been standing. As it was, she tunneled her fingers into the warm soil and held on for dear life.

In those seconds, the air pulsed like the blood beneath her skin. A measure she could hear in her ears and feel between her thighs. The memory of her cheek pressed into the sweet curve of his neck and her fingers stroking his hard cock as she came rolled over her like a wave. He swallowed hard, his only reply to her stare, and if she'd had more confidence, she would have said it was both of them caught up in the fury.

As it was, she was wholly unsure.

Moments later, Josiah stumbled into the shrub, sending leaves fluttering around her feet. "The pond is the best! It's muddy but deep enough to dive and was just brilliant fun! Mr. Jasper swims there most summer nights, he said. Can you imagine? In the dark? Ugh. What if a snake found you? Or a monster that likes water? Or a frog the size of a carriage?"

Realizing there was no hope for improvement, Cece rose while shaking out her skirt. Crispin observed with a hawkish gaze, his eyes a compelling shade similar to the depths of his blasted pond, a mix of guarded blue and black. At times like these, she could believe he'd once been a treacherous emissary.

What she couldn't believe is he wanted her enough to fight for her. He didn't trust what he felt like the innocent young man had. Her betrayal—if a marriage she'd been forced into could be deemed a betrayal—had scraped his memory clean. She guessed every emotion that hit his heart was dulled due to the injury.

"You have a spot of dirt..." Crispin flicked his hand in the air, leaving the rest of his consideration unspoken. He was forcing back a smile, damn him.

She scrubbed at her cheek and her chin, getting angrier as his grin broadened.

Josiah grimaced. "Oh, mum, you're making it worse. You need a bath something awful."

Crispin laughed, full out, though he tried to conceal it behind an elegant turn of his wrist. Her son's amusement wasn't far behind. The two of them would be considered a charmingly adorable duo if she wasn't the object of their ridicule.

Leaning over the hedge, she yanked the towel off Crispin's shoulder.

Which was a mistake. It brought him closer, only an inch or two, but enough to make a difference. His gaze locked on hers as his tongue came out to sweep his plump bottom lip. As they stared, a muscle fired off in his jaw, ticking madly. His teasing scent was embedded in the damp linen—and in her blood after she pressed her nose into it.

Glorious, the bouquet. In addition to the sight of him standing there, skin moist, his breath lifting his broad shoulders, his hands tensing into fists, a hearth fire of attraction.

She wanted to immerse herself in *this*. Forget about a lavender-scented bath in the tub upstairs. She wanted desire to cleanse her.

Crispin proved her jittery colt theory when he quickly stepped back. Too elegant a move to be called a stumble, but it was rushed. And defensive. "I'll deliver the boy to Mara," he said, having already turned and started down the gravel path leading to the manse's side entrance. "Come, Jos. Your mum is working."

Cece watched them go, her nerves rippling. She returned to gardening with fumbling inelegance and only half a mind on her task, restraining her inclination to run after the exquisite beast and make him admit, in a way only *she* would understand, that he wanted her. Being a mother didn't mean she couldn't be his lover. Couldn't he get on with this bloody affair?

Nevertheless, she wasn't going to push. Not yet.

Her amiable host swam every night, so she knew where to find him.

When he reached the pond, Jasper unknotted his cravat with fumbling fingers. The buttons of his waistcoat slipped from his grasp once or twice. With a furious exhalation, he wrestled with his boots and finally freed them. The wind ripped past, tossing his hair into his face. A storm was brewing around him *and* inside him. Cece's immovable green gaze striking him every other second during dinner had unsettled the hell out of him, though her demeanor had been nothing short of decorous.

She played the lady magnificently when she wished to. Better than he'd played the gentleman. Maybe even better than he'd played the thug.

He needed this swim. Needed the purity of closing his eyes and being enveloped. In his youth, it had been the same. His father's black moods had often driven him into the forests and fields bordering their estate. He'd worked his horse out well, night after night. It was simple maths. Physical activity fought back emotions one wished to hide. In this case, emotions one wished to *take*. Cece's need was vibrating off her and spinning through him, a battering ram of yearning. Did she think he'd missed that little trick of burying her nose in his towel and breathing him in? His pulse hadn't been steady since he'd stumbled upon her behind that unkempt hedge, looking like Flora, goddess of plants or sunlight or trees. He cursed and yanked the last button of his trousers free without care, noting the spot of mud the fastener tumbled into. He'd not paid attention in class, apparently, if he couldn't keep up with the gods.

What man yearned to tup a woman covered in dirt and straw? A chit with cheeks as rosy as the glorious hair atop her head? A countess who looked like a glowing country lass out for a summer frolic? A woman who, if she had more experience, would understand she could wrap a jaded former spy around her pinky, causing him to lose his senses, his heart, and his mind.

He bloody did, that's who.

He didn't know what he'd have done if her son hadn't been standing there, delighted from their afternoon adventure, the cutest child imaginable with his gap-toothed grin and radiant happiness. There was a little-used pantry off the kitchen that had a butcher block quite perfect, Jasper imagined, for what he'd been envisioning. His fingertips had tingled for an hour or more with ribald, truly filthy images charging through his brain. Until he'd gotten back to his bedchamber, taken his rigid shaft in hand, and cut his fever down a notch. Another standing with his back against the door, half-dressed pleasure session.

He was running out of time and Cece out of patience—and he couldn't blame her.

The sole rake left in the Leighton Cluster had promised a torrid affair and only given a fearful coward's folly. Because love had proven more dangerous than the spy game. He'd worked hard, for *years*, to forget the hollowness of leaving her. It was smart of him to question getting involved again, wasn't it? He respected the power of their connection; hell, he *feared* it. The reckless, lovesick baron's son was long gone. Heartbreak had stolen his innocence, then the realities revealed during his emissary career had slammed the lid on optimism, leaving a sorrowful ache in his belly that lingered as he walked London's cruel streets. The docks, the stews, those forbidding passages winding down to the Thames, felt like home because the faces he encountered there mirrored his bone-deep sorrow.

Still, his hunger for Cece was a fearsome presence, a primal, intoxicating bubble of breath in his lungs, a skipping pulse in his veins. Beautiful women had flitted in and out of his life with scant disturbance. He'd had a vase thrown at his head, and there'd been the minor fracas

with the MP's paramour, but otherwise, he was honest about his inten-
tions, a forthright if distant but skilled-enough-to-sway lover. Lust was
a straightforward emotion, uncomplicated if handled adroitly. Sterile,
short-term affairs were his specialty.

Chemistry, however, the tensing of a man's belly when he walked
into a parlor and *she* was there, the shot of joy that rocked you where
you stood when she smiled at you, *ah*, was the stuff grief was made of.
He'd been served that tasty dish for nigh on two years after Cece
married her earl. Strolling into a shop and seeing a chit who tilted their
head the way Cece did had crushed him. Her laugh ringing out as he
crossed a busy lane making him stumble, then head to the nearest
public house to drown his pain. There'd even been the opium adventure one summer, as desperate a plea as a man could make.

After a bit, the tremors of his heart had lessened to dull numbness.
Now, his body and his mind were coming alive after years of insensitiv-
ity. Somewhere along the way, since Cece had stumbled back into his
life, he'd gone from feeling modestly comfortable in his aloneness to
simply feeling *alone*.

Stepping from his trousers, Jasper tossed them on a stump,
deciding the matter right then and there. He was going to take this
swim, calm his fevered blood, and march to Cece's bedchamber after
the clock struck midnight and not one second beyond. He wasn't
above throwing her over his shoulder for the trip to his chamber like
some bedeviled caveman. He was going to live this dream, then he was
going to let her go with *both* of them accepting that their time had
passed. Cece needed to be someone's proper wife, Josiah, someone
proper's son. Jasper Noble wasn't up to either job.

They'd have until dawn to drive each other mad before the servants
and the child and the companion awoke. He planned to lose himself in
her. Taste her from head to toe and start all over again. Milk his cock
in her glorious body until he could not *think*. He coveted blessed
oblivion at her generous hands, lips, and teeth. She could bite him at
will this time.

His pulse scrambled when he heard the crack of a branch beneath a
light footfall.

Jasper didn't have to turn to know his minx had made it easy on him.

She wasn't a woman who waited for what she wanted, and he loved her for it. He couldn't admit it yet, but he knew he did. And he always had.

The sad part was he didn't have her courage.

She appeared through the mist like the goddess he'd envisioned, her flaming mass of hair trailing down her shoulders, the blunt ends dusting her breasts. A breeze blew over him and across her, a silent roar. In the distance, thunder sounded, a ripple beneath his feet. Her spencer glided down her body and fluttered away to reveal a simple dressing gown he was going to destroy in seconds. There was a visible moon this night, and she crossed to him through dense shadow and light.

As she closed in, he rubbed his aching chest. Rolled his shoulders. Prepared to talk. Stopped. Composed his pitch. His thumb tangled in the waistband of his drawers while he debated how to let her know she didn't have to seduce him.

He was *seduced*.

She didn't give him a chance to speak. Her touch was eager, her lids closing as she went to her toes to reach him, fingers curving over the nape of his neck, and pulling him in. He was almost thankful the emerald burn of her gaze had been extinguished. A growling wind circled them, the sensation of madness cascading in a passionate slide down his body. He wasn't going to stop her or stop himself. He wasn't going to apologize. Ask for her mercy, her compassion, her damned understanding for the choices he'd made.

And he wasn't going to make her explain hers.

He was merely going to take. And *give*.

Seizing her face in his hands, Jasper sank into the kiss, offering everything he had. His heartbeat became a pounding cadence in his ears, his fingertips, his belly. His shaft swelled against her hip, pleading for release. Hooking his arm around her waist, he lifted her from her feet and molded her body to his. Worlds merged as time slipped away. The past caught up with the present, firing his memory banks. "You're safe with me," he whispered against her lips, a sudden burst of rain-drops slicking their skin. "You always were."

Speechless, she pulled back enough for moonlight to swim across her face. Her eyes were teeming with helpless certainty—a potent mix he held no weapons to fight. A raindrop struck her temple and did a lazy roll down her cheek. He trapped it with his lips, drinking her in. She tasted better than his whisky, better than life. And he needed her. *Christ*, did he need her.

Thunder rumbled as the storm strengthened. Sweeping Cece into his arms, Jasper tucked her head into the nook of his shoulder and strode in a direction opposite the house. The cottage at the edge of his property was little used and roughly maintained. A lumpy bed, a sagging settee, and a scuffed desk fit for a man in hiding. He'd last had a guest there when Dash Campbell had a falling out with his wife that lasted exactly two nights before Theo came to retrieve her utterly apologetic husband.

Halting beneath the portico, Jasper shifted the luscious bundle in his arms and reached for the rusty key secreted atop the frame. Cece took the invitation and trailed her teeth up his neck, nibbling until his knees weakened. Groaning, he elbowed the door wide and released her to stand silhouetted in the doorway. Bracing his hand above her, he moved her against the doorjamb, and took the kiss to another level. Beyond persuasion, this soared to a request for admission. A plea to *join*. With a slanting lean to accommodate for their difference in height, he melded into her, her folds enveloping his cock with warmth and imagined moistness through two scant layers.

Breaking away, she ducked under his outstretched arm and raced, laughing, into the cottage, her hair trailing like amber mist behind her. He remembered this joy, an exuberance for life that he was in awe of. Kicking off her slippers, she gave him a saucy smile from the middle of the dark chamber and reached to grasp the hem of her dressing gown.

"*Cece*," he whispered when he realized what she was preparing to do.

Her gown was gone in seconds, damp cotton fluttering to the carpet at her feet. Heart dropping to his knees, he squinted, struggling to see her in the muted light. His damned spectacles were on his desk inside the house.

"Are you coming in, Jasper Noble?" she whispered from the darkness.

Rain began to ping the tin roof as he closed the door with a soft *click* and leaned against it. If she thought he was going to rush an event he'd waited years for, she was sadly mistaken. "Do you remember watching me?" He slowly lowered his drawers and wrapped his fingers around his shaft. "Before we found the courage to make love all those years ago?"

She hummed softly, her chest rising with a swift breath. "*Yes.*"

Keeping his gaze locked on her, he tugged his drawers off until he, too, stood unclothed before her. "Those stolen seconds stand as the most intimate of my life. I've never shared anything like it with anyone, giving myself like that. I never thought to—or tried—after you."

"The earl—"

Wrenching free of the door, he stopped her with a snarl and an outstretched arm. "Perhaps someday I can hear this, minx, but not now. Not yet." Circling her like a tiger, he went about the room lighting lamps until her body was revealed to him in its glory. *Damn*, he thought, nothing was faded about his memories. She was the most spectacular creature alive. "The picture of you has stayed right here bright as the sun"—he tapped his temple—"and will for eternity."

Cece didn't shy away when he halted before her. She let him have his moment, a lingering, teasing, tormenting review. She was slim of shoulder, plump and curvaceous of hip; her skin creamy against the lustrous amber locks fired by lamplight. Her nipple puckered when he grazed it with his knuckle, her ragged sigh tunneling through him like the finest brandy. It was the color of nutmeg, dark and peaked, begging for his attention. He couldn't contain the impulse as his lips closed the aroused nub, his cheeks hollowing with the effort.

Trembling, she touched him then, fingers curling around his waist in possession. The scent of orange blossoms drifting from her skin threatened to eat him alive. "No more talking," she murmured and

147

stepped back, guiding him toward the bed. "Because I fear you'll soon be trying to talk me out of this."

Laughing, he thought to caution her about the shoddy mattress, but his mouth was full of her. He'd moved to the other breast, recalling quite clearly that she loved having her nipples sucked and preferred it when they were sucked *hard*.

He realized when they tumbled to the bed and her legs shifted to allow him to settle effortlessly between them that this was trouble. So much trouble. His heart horribly involved when devotion simply didn't happen to him. He'd shut the door to many a bedchamber on his way out in absolute relief.

When this squalid cottage and the woman inside it felt like a *beginning*.

Bracing on his forearms to keep from crushing her, he cupped her cheek and brought her gaze to his. Her lids lifted, revealing eyes the color of burnt grass, full of dreams. A lock of hair trailed across her lips in invitation as his chest ached in longing and remembrance. The golden freckles dotting her cheeks were guideposts in the night. The scar splitting her eyebrow, another connection, binding them. As if he needed more. "I'm going to do wicked things to you until dawn, Constance Willoughby. Over and over again until we perfect the art. Fair warning. I'm going to talk, in lurid, exacting detail until you're begging for release. We'll take the time we never had before."

In response, she skimmed her hand down his back. Digging her fingertips into the tender skin at his flank, she released a hot breath against this cheek. "*This*," she whispered and raised her hips, rubbing her quim against the firm length of his cock, "is all you need to say."

The kiss erupted, igniting the air around them. She drove her fingers through his hair and met his tongue thrust for thrust. Bodies bumping, skin slick, breath charged. Caresses flowing into awareness, flowing into pleasure. The experience was unparalleled, a mix of old and new. He remembered the sound of her moans, but her whispered desires, as lurid as the ones he'd promised, were a revelation, her daring suggestions a blunt enticement to a man starved for her.

She directed and allowed him to direct. They touched, licked, sucked, giving playful encouragement and breathless counsel, making bets, and breaking them soon after. She only halted him when he started to slide down her body to taste her, his fingers dancing through the silken hair at her core in preparation for the assault.

The bed squeaked as she rose, her thumb digging into his shoulder to stop him. Though he didn't, not really, sliding his finger inside her moist channel and stroking as she watched, dazed. Her juices coated his skin, her scent his soul. She was ready, so ready. His neck was stinging from a bite she'd given him seconds before and sweat was beading on his brow. His arms were shaking, his knees weak.

He was losing his noted composure and couldn't have cared less.

Working her hand between their bodies, she grasped his shaft and lined it up perfectly against her slick folds, adding three enthusiastic base-to-tip caresses to ensure he didn't argue. He gasped, his brow dropping to her shoulder. *Hell's teeth*, her hands were clever, her body calling to him. And her smile? Wicked.

"You win. I'm begging," she gasped and sank to the bed. The move shifted her hips enough to send the head of his cock inside her. Merely a shade, barely a whisper. Not enough, not nearly enough. "Actually, I'm demanding it. The rest, we can... *oh*, later."

"Slow, love, slow," he urged on a gusty breath, wholly for her benefit. Settling his head between her legs and stroking his tongue across her sex would've guaranteed she came before he did. He'd admit it to no one but himself, but he often used oral service to keep a situation exactly where he wanted it. He gave pleasure and took only the small portion he needed for himself. There was never a need to give a woman *everything*. Instead, a steady pulse was dancing at the base of his spine, indicating an impending orgasm that threatened to be of the losing consciousness variety. He knew the type—or rather, remembered them with her.

Cece being Cece, she was having none of his standard sexual schemes. Grasping his buttock in her hand, she angled her knee alongside his hip and gave him no warning before she thrust him into her tight, silken channel, seating him deeply inside her. It was hasty, almost angry, and breathtaking. To be seized was a rare thing for a man. A rare thing for him, anyway, as he'd commanded every carriage he'd ever ridden in.

After this ploy, he was spellbound, spent. Meaning Cece got what she wanted.

Wrapping his arms around her, he let his weight fall and began to fuck her thoroughly and with little of his usual finesse. Later, he'd have trouble recalling exactly where he'd lost himself.

He only recognized the night was the most stirring of his life.

"Don't be vexed," she groaned against his neck, her body shivering beneath him, the tight muscles in her core squeezing him dry. Her teeth closed in on a tender spot beneath his ear as she rose to meet his thrust, another of her delicious nibbles, and his vision blurred. He gathered he *liked* being bitten. "We have time for the rest."

"Yes, yes, later," he thought he whispered. Or perhaps the words were buried, misplaced in the glowing sensation of being surrounded by her for the first time in forever.

Linking their fingers, he tugged her arm above her head and against the rickety headboard, stretching her body out beneath him, sinking until his pelvis knocked hers, and they were one form in pulsing motion. He couldn't fill his hands with her quickly enough. He ached for her essence. He was starved, dying of thirst, expiring from unexpended pleasure. And she seemed the same, meeting him measure for measure. They kissed, panted, growled. Tore at each other as if clothing remained when there was nothing but slick skin and desperation. The bed protested—he truly feared the act was going to kill it—rocking into the aged wall with loud thumps.

She arched her body with a feral moan and dug her nails into his hip, dragging him deeper, which he hadn't thought possible. Slowing, he glided his length inside her in prolonged, provocative strokes, closing his eyes to the possibilities, the bloody *wonder*. His hand tangled in her hair as he brought the glorious mass to his face and breathed her in. The scent of orange blossoms shot through him like a punch, bringing his release a step closer.

"Quit tormenting me," she huffed, her tight, clever body closing around him.

Curving his arm beneath her bottom, he shifted her, angling, searching for the ideal fit. One moment more... *there, oh, hell, there.* "I'm tormenting myself, minx."

She whimpered, her arm trembling where he trapped it against the headboard. Her hand at his hip guided his rhythm, demanding, until the only sounds filling the room were the recurrent slap of skin and consequent cries of ecstasy. Her thigh at his hip tensed, her body seizing. Releasing her arm, he caught her knee in his hand, and held her steady as he thrust—as he overwhelmed them both. There was no gentle way to bring them home. They were grinding each other into oblivion in his cottage's rickety bed, marking each other for doom.

Ruin was bliss.

Fevered, she took frantic hold of his shoulders and bowed into his thrusts. "Touch me," she whispered, her eyes emerald beacons lighting his path.

It was sound advice as he was close to the edge and wanted only to take her with him. Her sex was coated in her juices, the nub aroused, and jutting from her folds. He thumbed it, circling and pressing, the vision of licking her clean doing him in. When he whispered what he wanted in her ear, she groaned and shook beneath him.

Her convulsions around his shaft unleashed a blinding orgasm that set his heartbeat galloping free. The world around him faded to a single point: *her*. He held her close, wanting her, wanting this. Love and lust intertwined. They thrust and shivered, kissing and clawing, clinging, mislaid souls. Their scent permeated the space, sounds of pleasure rippling like waves across a shore.

Sliding free at the last, he spilled his seed on her thigh while shoving aside the pinch of anger he felt at withdrawing—when he hadn't wished to withdraw. Truthfully, he wished never to withdraw.

Cece knocked his hand away and collapsed to the bed, her release cycling out like wheels spinning madly on an overturned carriage. He watched bliss take her, then take her again. It lasted longer than his, a fact over which he was envious.

He hung his head low, his weight braced on his forearms. He wasn't sure he could feel his toes, now that he thought about it.

"Breathe," she murmured drowsily against his shoulder, "or you're going to faint."

His mind blanked, his lungs burning as he realized he hadn't taken in air in minutes. *Faint?* Actually, with the black swirls littering his vision, it seemed possible.

He pressed his brow gently to hers. "Give me a moment, Ce, then I'll move. I know I'm heavy, but I'm also a bit boneless."

She wiggled and sighed. "No, your weight... I love your weight atop me. I've longed for it."

This endearing sentiment was the last thing he recalled before sleep took him, fatigue overriding fear in realizing love had once again smacked him in the face.

Chapter Eleven

Are you ever coming back to Northumberland, Crispin Sinclair?
-Unsent letter hidden in a hat box under a countess' bed

fter the third intimate indulgence of the night, which ended with the shoddy bed collapsing beneath them, Cece let Crispin sleep. Currently, his long body was sliding off a settee unused to holding a man his size, the faint wheeze echoing through the small space tying her heart into a proper knot.

Whether the spy liked it or not, he had a touch of the baron's lung complaint.

Energized, her body positively *ablaze*, she'd tucked a small woolen blanket around him, ridiculous as it barely covered him, then went on a mission to retrieve their lost clothing. Her spencer was ruined but adequate enough to get her back to the house. His boots—Hoby, she'd guess—weren't in much better shape, the leather blackened from rain and muck. She hung the wet garments before the hearth but left his cravat in a wad by the door as it wasn't worth the effort. Nelson could try to clean it, perhaps.

Nelson, Cece thought and glanced back to the settee, love a steady *thump* gliding in between her rapid heartbeats. The young man had run from her but taken the cantankerous groom who'd been like a father to him.

This said something about Crispin not leaving *everything* behind.

Cece found a deck of cards left by a past inhabitant and shuffled while Crispin slumbered. She bit hungrily into an apple she'd located beneath a tree near the pond, one appetite appeased while others raged. If she'd had paper and pen, she would have practiced copying Jasper Noble's signature—which she hated to tell him wasn't far off from Crispin's. She laughed softly around a mouthful of fruit. He wouldn't be happy about this project.

But making a man entirely happy didn't seem the best course. She'd wanted Crispin to work for her, even if for only one night.

Propping her back against the wall, she finished the apple while letting her gaze caress every inch of him not concealed by that ratty blanket. The chamber smelled of dust, mildew, and spent passion, a scent she was largely unfamiliar with.

It was madness... but in this very moment, she wanted to look more than touch.

They'd been so crazed for each other, she honestly hadn't had the chance. She grinned, pleased, the ability to make him lose himself the bright spot of her *century*. His hand had trembled when he'd pressed his brow to hers and whispered he'd never forgotten her.

Never forgotten *this*.

He was lying on his stomach on the settee, his head adorably buried in the crease between his forearm and biceps, his hair a black-gray blotch against his sun-kissed skin. His shoulders were wide, his ribs compelling dints leading to a lean waist and slim hips. Unfortunately, his tight bottom—she could confirm it was tight because she'd held on to it at various points—was hidden by the coverlet. Tilting her head, she studied him, wondrously still aroused. He had the physique of a brawler when the young man had been gangly. Rippling muscle layered upon more muscle. He must box or participate in some sport to acquire such brawn. Cece searched around on the floor for a second apple and tore into it, wishing she could draw instead of forge. She'd fill pages with sketches of this stunning beast.

If only she could capture the vulnerability the man tried incredibly hard to hide.

He was difficult. Ill-tempered. Arrogant. He hated to lose when she *loved* to win. Yet, he treated Josiah with tremendous kindness. His staff adored him, and this she'd found to be a decisive assessment. While snooping in his desk, a flaw she hadn't been able to conquer her entire life, she'd uncovered documents about a project to remove boys from the workhouse and place them in apprenticeships on the Duchess of Leighton's ships, in his warehouse, and at the Streeter-Macauley distillery. Unlike most of society, he wasn't boasting about his philanthropic efforts. He was concealing them. Why did he want to conceal the good side of himself?

"I'll do better next time," he whispered drowsily from the curl of his arm. "Longer. Slower. More. A little surprised, you meeting me at the pond." He wagged his hand. "Off my game."

Cece choked on an apple sliver. What they'd shared could be better? Longer? Slower? *More?* However, the good news was there would be a next time. She also liked that he'd not been able to do his typical routine because she knew the bounder had one. She swallowed somewhat viciously. His *game.*

Flipping on his side to face her, Crispin stretched like a cat coming out of a vigorous nap, the absolute glory of him filling the space. The groan that whispered free of his throat was one of supreme satisfaction. He'd made a similar sound during the last round, from his position beneath her. Her legs straddling his hips, the speed and depth of their connection left to her, had proved to be a revelation. It was the control she'd asked for, given in full measure.

Images running wild, her throat went dry as the pulse between her legs began to thump. *Oh,* that provoking thump! It had gotten her into leagues of delicious trouble.

Holding out his arm, he wiggled his fingers. "Food, please."

Cece scrambled for the third apple. She'd saved the biggest and most beautiful one for him.

"I'm bloody starving," he rasped and tore into the fruit like it was a slice of roasted mutton. He'd yet to open his eyes, resting there like a sated tiger. She wondered how long he planned to lie there, the blanket having wiggled its way to his waist, baring much of him to her view. He was comfortable with nudity in a way she'd never been. Although he'd murmured his appreciation for her in between ribald descriptions of what he planned to do to her. Her gorgeous hair, her bountiful breasts, her pert nipples. He loved the color of her nipples. That admission just before he'd snaked them between his lips. She'd never imagined a man would value such a thing.

When he opened his eyes, she almost wished he hadn't. Wariness had returned, swimming amongst sea blue. He motioned to her with the apple, chewing slowly. Something about the scene had thrown him off. "You're wearing my shirt."

Breath stalling, she glanced down. The once crisp cotton covered her from neck to thigh. It had been an impulsive decision to slip it on, an intense need to keep him with her a moment longer. His spicy scent rose from the material every time she moved, catching her in its teeth. "I, um..." She shook her head, not sure what to say.

"Another image burned in my brain," he said and took a vicious nip of the fruit.

He'd lost every trace of Northumberland from his speech, his accent now caught between rookery docks and Mayfair parlors. At times, it seemed he didn't know who to be, thug or baron. "Are you angry with me?" She snorted against her wrist, truly amused. "After that," she added, gesturing to the wrecked chamber.

Dropping his head to his fist, he sighed into his fingers. "I'm vexed with myself. I was not as solicitous as I prefer to be. I got carried away, which isn't like me."

Cece circled through her memories of the night. Flashes of hunger, desire, *truth*. There'd been nothing charming or diplomatic about it, thank heaven. She wanted passion raw enough to break a bed. "You didn't corrupt me, Crispin. And you didn't when I was seventeen. I sought pleasure, the first time since then I've been able to. I *loved* it. Is this what you need to hear?"

"Crispin," he whispered, the name layered with anguish. "Can't you let him go?"

His torment unleashed a horrid yearning to uncover his secrets. To know the man as well as she'd known the boy. "What happened after you left me?"

With a sigh, he flopped to his back, tossing his arm over his eyes.

Placing the apple core on the floor, she shoved to a shaky stand. Her knees were as flimsy as wet straw from the glorious things they'd done in his ragged bed. Crispin tensed when he heard her approach, but he didn't try to run. Progress.

Lifting the blanket, Cece trailed her fingertip down the arch of his foot. He flexed his toes and gave an aggrieved growl that lit her up inside. Bracing his arms, he wrenched to a sit, giving her the opposite end of the settee. The blanket fluttered but landed quite magnificently across his waist. Once she was settled, his shirt covering her well enough but not fully, they stared, waging a silent war. No matter her intense love for him long ago, they hadn't gotten along every second. They'd bickered and battled, trying to best each other. She'd never felt better than when she'd beaten the baron's son at something. The brash, enchanting young man who'd stolen her heart.

Knowing there was no reason to delay, she dove into the deep end. "This person you've become, you love his life?"

He eased back, scrubbing his hand over his face. Stubble rode his jaw, dark as the night surrounding them. He looked exceedingly unreachable, but she wasn't easily dissuaded. Taking a final bite of his apple, he gave the core an expert toss that sent it sailing into the hearth. With an absurdly masculine smile, his gaze skimmed her bare legs, halted at her breasts, before meeting her eyes. His cock shifted beneath the tattered wool covering him, and he did nothing to hide it. "I have ideas for activities that don't involve talking."

She did the wrong thing. Laughed when it was clear he was exhausted and, if she wasn't mistaken, in a vulnerable state. The least vulnerable man in England. "But you so like talking during them."

He frowned while calculating his strategy. Massaged the finger he'd injured in some silly carriage mishap with Dash Campbell that Hildy had told her about, another Duchess Society warning against getting involved with a scoundrel.

Had he been this shrewd before? His tender nature must have hidden it.

Finally, he whispered, "What did you do after I left, minx?"

Oh, he wanted to put her on the defensive. Stretching her legs, she nudged his hand with her big toe. She liked rubs, and he'd been happy to accommodate.

He glanced at her foot like it was a smoldering lump of coal. He was too astute not to realize this was an intimate act. Simple... but intimate.

She had her own strategy, she'd love to tell him.

"After you left," she started before her courage fled, "after you left, I retreated to my bedchamber and refused to talk to anyone, including Edgerly, until the ceremony. I entered the chapel that morning—it rained horribly if you must know—determined to save my family's reputation and nothing more. My sister's chances depended upon my not making a hash of my life, which I supposed I'd done that summer with you. If you recall, we were found by a servant, possibly the worst of circumstances since news travels swiftly at the lower levels, a fact my father stressed to me. After bribing the staff and the marriage occurred, things settled down. Rose entered the marriage mart the next Season and found a wonderful man in a forest of vultures. Her husband is an American, not titled, of course, but wealthy enough to satisfy. Until their last breaths, my parents felt they'd done right by their daughters. They didn't care if I was dreadfully unhappy as long as society was appeased."

He frowned and rolled his shoulders. "The estate in Northumberland?"

"It isn't entailed, thankfully, so it came to me. The only challenge is, Edgerly wasn't clever at managing money. Neither, it turns out, was my father. Although, I have funds enough to survive if I'm careful from a small bequest from my grandmother."

Crispin glanced away during her speech as if he couldn't stand to gaze at her while hearing about her husband. But he'd taken her foot in hand, his thumb digging into her arch in a way that made her want to purr. "Some time, I'll ask more about your life with Edgerly, but for now, I don't think I can stand it."

She shrugged, a tad drowsy. His fingers were working magic. "There's not much to tell. He lived in London, and I lived in Northumberland. It turns out he didn't want an heir, if I'm allowed to be indelicate, as much as he wanted the concealment of a wife. His mistress of long standing was married, although her husband conveniently contracted cholera somewhere along the way. She was with Edgerly at the end, I believe. Was it wrong of me that I didn't care?"

Crispin blinked and touched the bridge of his nose. He was searching for his spectacles, an accessory which hid his eyes from view. The man was keen about self-protection. "I don't like to imagine him anywhere near you. I knew about his paramour and the other woman in Limehouse, the chit I'm guessing was Josiah's mother. All of London knew about them, including your father. I tried to talk to him. I offered to marry you the day we were found or any day he chose. A year later, if we needed to wait. That didn't end well, as you know. The conversation with my father went even worse."

Cece flinched, and Crispin's gaze raced to hers. She remembered the bruises on his face—the ones hidden beneath his clothing—something she didn't like to imagine. He'd often sported injuries from clashes with his father, abuse she presumed made it easier to leave Northumberland and never look back. "I know you tried to rectify the situation. I was never angry with you like you were with me. I was merely sad. A bone-deep, everlasting sadness."

He gave the heel of her foot an almost painful squeeze. "I was hurt. Tormented and misplaced, my own everlasting sadness spinning out in the hours. Although men show any slight with raised fists, don't they? Luckily, I found a profession that fit my mood flawlessly. One with a new identity and a solid smattering of violence wrapped into a tidy package. At first, I thrived on the danger, which made me an accomplished agent because fear is what ruins them. I would have run into a burning building back then and not looked back."

"You never wondered about me?"

Dropping her leg, he shoved to his feet and began to prowl the chamber. Unfortunately, he'd taken the tattered blanket with him and had it clenched at his hip. Cece rested back with a muted sigh, enjoying the sight of his muscles rippling as he strode about the chamber. Her fingertips tingled with the urge to touch. She had a long list of things she wanted to do to him. Do *with* him. It astounded her how much he'd changed—when how much she wanted him hadn't changed one bit.

She drew her bent legs to her chest and wrapped her arms around them to protect herself. "I wondered about you."

"I got reports," he returned almost immediately.

Cece's lips parted on a shocked breath. "Reports?"

He didn't stop pacing, merely sent a swift side-look her way. "I had contacts. I got reports."

She patted her chest, truly stunned. "About *me?*"

He gave the settee an angry nudge as he passed it. "About Northumberland. About my property and, yes, fine, about the property next door."

"About the *countess* next door, you mean."

He halted in the middle of the room and knotted his fingers around the blanket looped at his waist. A distant gaze, tight shoulders, fidgeting. A demeanor akin to Josiah's after he'd stolen a sweet from the pantry and hidden it beneath his mattress.

"I would have let you in had you showed up on my doorstep, Cris."

"And then what?" he snapped, fixing his attention on her. "It would have ended with us in bed, as mad for each other as we were tonight, wanting more, wanting everything because we were too bloody naive to realize happy endings don't exist. This isn't a fairy tale, Ce. What if I passed Edgerly on the street days after I left you, which I did once and barely kept from throttling him, only to think, is he going to Northumberland next week to see her? Touch her? Tup her? I simply couldn't do it. Insanity would have been *mine.*"

Cece rubbed her temple, where a headache was brewing. He'd kept tabs on her all this time. "Edgerly meant nothing to me, and you knew it," she whispered.

He shocked her by finding a teacup on a scuffed cupboard and hurling it against the wall. "Was that to be the madness we lived in?

Hidden mistresses and forbidden love? I wanted more for our memories."

Truthfully, she had as well.

The ferociousness surrounding him shouldn't have enthralled her, nevertheless, she was completely enthralled. More so when he sighed and dropped to his knees to pick up the broken shards. She could only hope the blanket slipped, giving her full view of his dazzling body. "I turned down the Order of St Michel three years ago. Top-secret, of course, to protect my involvement with the government. Xander Macauley would never speak to me again should he find out. The baron bit, which I admitted because you nearly forced me to, was enough of an impediment. They don't exactly want more titles in the Leighton Cluster. They have enough."

This said, he stared morosely at the shattered teacup cradled in his hand. Long seconds passed with only the sound of their breaths and the calm shift of the wind against the cracked windowpanes to bolster them. "I have no clue why I tell you things I've never told another person." His gaze struck her, his eyes the color of skies before a raging tempest. She guessed a storm was brewing in his soul. "*This* is why I stayed away, Ce, to protect us both. Our connection isn't typical. It never was. Better to be heartbroken, past not present. Scars of skin and heart eventually heal, even if they're unpleasant to gaze upon after."

"And now?" she asked past a parched throat. She was scared of his answer, fear twisting her stomach in a knot.

He dusted his fingertip along a jagged fragment of the teacup with the concentration of a surgeon. "You need a man with a sterling reputation, one who could be a father. I don't know anything about children. My mother died when I was a lad and my father, well, you know enough to know I learned nothing about love from him."

She wasn't going to argue a ridiculous point. Josiah was clearly as taken with Crispin as he was with Josiah. He could be a father. Saying she needed him for what they'd done tonight was also a waste of breath. Hadn't her hunger been clear for him to see? So, she would try this. "I might be willing to leave forgery behind if I had something else to occupy my time."

He placed the shards on a table at his side, braced his fist on his thigh, and stood. "Do tell."

Nervous, Cece smoothed her hand down his shirt, the bone buttons cool against her still fevered skin. A dangerous time for illicit love, dawn was peeking through a crack in the drapes and tossing slices of subdued light at their feet. This was one of *her* secrets. "I've been corresponding with a woman in London, someone involved in women's rights. She's particularly interested in topics involving child custody. She's working on approval of a legislative act for care of infants as voting isn't going to happen during our lifetimes. Caroline—"

"Norton," he finished for her.

Cece unfurled her legs and plopped her feet to the floor. "How do you know that?"

Crispin hung his head and laughed into his fist. "Damned if Dash Campbell doesn't have it right. We are drawn to the problematic chits. Have you told Hildy you're involved with Mrs. Norton?"

Cece gave a dismissive snort, feeling a bit like *she'd* hidden a sweet beneath the mattress. She was playing a role with the Duchess Society, much as he'd played with his government contacts. Who wanted to find a proper husband for an agitator? He was the only person she trusted enough to admit this to.

Muttering softly, Crispin scrubbed at the nape of his neck. "Maybe you should. Hildy meets with Mrs. Norton once a month, I believe. Tobias puts an extra footman at the entrance those days. Furious husbands are known to be vengeful from time to time. It doesn't surprise me you're thinking of getting involved with a matter possibly more dangerous than your charming hobby. What luck, that."

Cece smiled, his long-suffering tone warming her to her toes. *Hmm...* Hildegard Streeter was an agitator as well. This was valuable information.

They laughed at the absurdity of the situation, and he took a tentative step closer. "A dimple is denting your cheek, Countess, which means devilish things are circling that keen mind of yours. I wonder if I have enough time to make you forget your schemes and grand plans."

A high-pitched shout slid like a vapor beneath the door, interrupting them. The words were unintelligible, but the tone was flirtatious. And very, very feminine. Crispin halted and glanced over his shoulder, his oath bouncing about the shadowed space.

"Jasper Noble, are you set on taking a midnight swim?" Crispin's visitor asked from much too close to the cottage. "I'm happy to come along, though I found it quite cold last time."

"Behind me, minx," he instructed, pointing at a spot in the corner like she was a dog. "*Now.*"

As Cece saw it, she had two choices. She could continue letting men direct her life as her father and husband had done—or she could take the painful step of mucking it up herself, thereby choosing the life she wanted.

Even if she made a mistake, at least the mistake would be *hers*.

With a heroic inhalation, she crossed to the hearth, gathered up her muddy spencer, and hooked it over her shoulders. "Thank you, but I don't think I will."

Crispin palmed his chest with a pained expression. "Can you not do this? It's social self-destruction to walk out that door."

She fisted her spencer at her breastbone much like he had his blanket fisted at his hip. "You're right, it is."

The knock was light, three teasing taps. A kittenish laugh soon followed.

Crispin stalked to her, grasping her elbow, and giving her a gentle shake. "I never brought anyone here. Hell, I've never even stepped into the place before tonight. Nelson manages it."

"Yoo-hoo," came another call. The woman was determined. Cece would give her that.

A flush rolled across Crispin's cheeks. "It was only a bloody stupid swim."

Jealousy was a bubbling cauldron, the haze spilling across her vision painting the night. "Why bother with this old place"—she gestured to the charming cottage she'd dream about for the rest of her life—"when you have a perfectly adequate bedchamber across the lawn?"

His lids lowered as a muscle in his jaw began to flex. "I have a past, Ce."

"Trust me, I've been reading about it for years," she said, thinking furiously of the hat box beneath her bed.

"You have a past, too, don't forget. Damned if I don't try to."

She wiggled from his hold and straightened her spencer, preparing for battle. "Edgerly visited me five times during my wedded years. Five ham-fisted experiences, each worse than the last. Is that similar to your story?"

His eyes glowed a deep, dark blue as fury took him. "You have to accept me for who I am, or we have no chance. I don't wish to touch another woman. I *wouldn't*. You're all I want, all I've ever wanted. Everything else was my way to survive. I can't erase what I did to repair a broken heart, and I can't make things right by becoming Crispin Sinclair again."

"Do you love her?" Her fist clenched around the crumpled velvet until her knuckles whitened.

Crispin's lips parted, shock making him take a stumbling step back. "I've never loved anyone but you. This"—he flung his arm toward the door—"is a man being a man."

"You loved the girl, you mean, because she adored you. The woman?" She laughed softly. "You have no idea what to do about her."

Another knock sounded. "Jasper darling, I can hear you moving about in there."

"Bloody hell," Crispin whispered and closed his eyes as if he was in pain. "You've not got any of this right, Ce."

In that moment, Cece decided she was a country girl. An unsophisticated hoyden. A forger of exquisite talent but modest ambition. She wasn't educated in the ways of society, and she never would be. She wasn't fit to be the next in line for a man like Jasper Noble. He needed them rough-and-ready, women able to leave his bed and never think of him again.

Frankly, social self-destruction seemed better than hiding from view, like he'd done for the past twenty years.

Waltzing past him and out the door, Cece played the countess for the final time.

Chapter Twelve

I would consider an assignment in the northern district should one become available. Northumberland, for example.
-Missive to Chief Intelligence Officer Browning from Agent Noble

B y the time he escorted Lady Shandling-Miers home and returned to Bloomsbury, Cece was gone. Josiah and Mara with her. Nelson greeted him at the door with the sour mien of a disappointed father. No words were spoken, but the punch of censure struck deep. As did the overwhelming rush of emotion when he stepped into Cece's bedchamber and found nothing but her delicious scent and an emerald hair clip on the vanity matching the one sitting on his bedside table.

Another scar—this one to the heart.

She left the last damning message in her study. Her loupe, a piece he pocketed immediately and had warmed in his hand every second since. Along with a note that said: *I can create a past now, too. Thank you for showing me how.*

Jealousy was blinding and had him bracing his fist on the wall until it passed. He had shown her how. He was skilled, undoubtedly, but he wasn't the only man in England able to do the job. Also, he might be more trouble than he was worth.

A conclusion that left him hollow.

Accordingly, he did what heartsick men had for ages.

Drank a bottle of whisky, got tossed from White's—for the last time, management claimed—then nearly overturned his carriage on Bond. One of those ridiculous races he hadn't taken part in for years, and it said too much about his reputation that no one had been surprised to see him appear at the starting point. As the winning curricle passed him minutes later, he realized risky behavior didn't bring the exhilaration it once had. Exhausted baron-cum-hoodlums needn't apply.

What he'd experienced with Cece was the only excitement he needed, Jasper decided when he woke the following afternoon with a pounding headache and a fresh set of bruises on his shin from that damned race.

He'd never be well again unless he figured out a way to make her trust him. *Choose* him. Not Crispin Sinclair, she idolized that sorry chap, but Jasper Noble. The rascal who had former lovers showing up at all hours, begging for admittance.

The ghastly bet among bets of men.

Had he enjoyed this kind of attention, he wondered, as he counted the cracks in his bedchamber's ceiling? Sneaking in veranda doors left ajar and out servant's entrances with his clothing in disarray? Having vases thrown at him (once) and women vowing never to speak to him again (more than once).

As images of Cece wrapped around him, lying beneath him, gasping and clawing and panting, drenched him like bathwater, he couldn't honestly recall. It was as if the past had been wiped from his memory —except for his past with *her*. Despite a chit he'd taken on a swim months ago showing up to wreck everything, his night with Cece had been a dream. Passionate pleasure. Truth, laughter, and tenderness. While she'd slept, he'd counted her freckles just as he had in their youth. Serenity had never been this serene.

For the first time since his espionage days, he'd been where he belonged.

In the arms of the only woman he cared two shillings about. A countess who could be carrying his child because, one of the three times, he'd been careless. The thought of a brother or sister for Josiah shot a wave of warmth through him. If he didn't manage to muck this up, there might be a *family* waiting for him, the first he'd ever had.

With his head aching but his heart light, Jasper decided the best advice would come from men who'd been in similar dire circumstances. Later that afternoon, Xander Macauley answered his door, as he was wont to do, before Jasper could begin a second round of knocking. Rookery thugs didn't hold with employing majordomos. As Jasper crossed into the foyer of the terrace, the shouts of children and the yip of a dog from the floor above sailed past him.

The type of chaos Jasper wanted—he simply wasn't sure how to get it.

"I'm not here to discuss the apprenticeships," he stated before Xander could dive into business.

They were expanding a campaign Xander's wife, Pippa, had created to remove young men and women from city workhouses and place them in proper jobs in society households. The plan had run into opposition recently from several underworld criminals profiting on cheap labor, hence the men of the Leighton Cluster getting involved. Dangerous opposition they didn't want the Duchess Society ladies anywhere near.

Xander closed the door, his smile a shade past amused. "I've been expecting you all day, mate. Leave your umbrella in the corner, will you? Pippa gets cross about slick marble and busted arses."

Jasper halted and spun on his heel. With a groan, he gripped his temple at the fast movement. "How bad is it?"

Xander laughed and leaned against the door. "You haven't seen the *Gazette*, I take it?"

Jasper's gut shriveled. *Fuck.*

"Come," Xander said and strolled down the main corridor as if his friend's predicament brought a splash of sunlight on a rainy day. He was whistling, in fact. "They're waiting for you."

Jasper tossed his umbrella aside and followed with a creeping sense of dread. *Who* was waiting for him? He'd persuaded Lady Shandling-Miers to keep quiet with the rationale that exposing Cece meant she'd expose herself. The chit wasn't actually a bad sort, a spot of fun in the day, and she'd apologized for putting him in an unenviable position as well as coming to his home when she wasn't invited.

Even if he'd let her in before without an invitation.

Apparently, their swim had been memorable. At least for her.

When Jasper entered Xander's walnut-paneled study, he got his answer.

Several members of the Leighton Cluster were gathered there and appeared to have been for hours. Dash Campbell dealing cards behind a massive desk taking up much of the room. Tobias Streeter sprawled on the settee, a set of blueprints balanced on his lap. The Duke of Leighton kneeling before a crate filled with rocks, geology the love of his life outside his duchess. They glanced up when he edged into the room and gave him looks that ranged from entertained to irritated.

The incensed man started first. "I nearly burnt down my west parlor for your little romance, and this is where you end up taking it?" Leighton selected a stone Jasper believed was azurite from the pile, rotated it in his hand in review, then made a notation in the folio at his side.

"Nice hunk of azurite, Your Grace," Jasper said and received a look of amazement from a duke who didn't actually talk to him very often. Surprisingly, he'd scored high marks in geology, not that Leighton wanted to discuss this when he'd nearly lost a section of his home for no good reason—or so it appeared.

"I'd suggest my jeweler. Perhaps a tiara is in order." With a low hum, Tobias trailed his fingertip along a section of the blueprint. A self-made architect, he was building a set of row houses in Marylebone that were causing quite the stir. The toothpick jammed between his lips, a relic of his successful effort to quit smoking cheroots, bobbed as he talked. "Though I heard he retired some years ago. May have even passed on for all I know. He was quite aged when I patronized his shop."

"Stopped working, the poor sod, after your marriage put him out of business," Dash said with a crafty shuffle that had gotten him banned from every gaming hell in Town except his own.

"Couldn't be helped. Hildy isn't the jewelry type," Tobias returned without looking up.

Xander gave Jasper a shove that sent him stumbling into the room. "Enter the den of thieves, my fine chap."

Jasper glared over his shoulder. "What are you stealing?"

Xander's lips curved in a knowing smirk. "Why, hearts, of course. Except for you, it seems. A truth, innit, that certain blokes can't win at love?"

"I tried to stop it," Jasper said, making his way to the sideboard, figuring whatever drivel was in that gossip rag had told most of the story for him. "Stop *her*. Sometimes a train is racing down the tracks and tossing your body in front of it isn't enough."

Before he could pour a drink, Xander was at his side, filling a teacup and shoving it into his hands. "Trust me on this. You don't need more liquor. I can't see those gorgeous blues for the bloodshot. Not to mention a faint aroma of the foxed variety drifting from your skin."

Jasper angled his forefingers beneath his spectacles and rubbed his eyes. Was it his imagination or was it Cece's scent clinging to his skin? His heart dropped at the notion. *Blimey*, had he messed this up. "The lady who intruded promised to keep her mouth shut. She's actually a pleasant sort. I hope the column didn't name her."

"It didn't, though all of London recognizes the two in question. You and Shandling-Miers." Leighton tossed the azurite in the crate, stretched, then rocked back on his heels. "Servants talk, Noble. The information pipeline begins on the lower levels. Your staff must love your countess, however, because the column mentions nothing about her. It only details a midnight swim and a chit who'd come calling. The rest we pieced together, what with the fire you and Campbell set in my parlor and a missing former love. The usual."

"Lower levels? You bleeding nob." Xander snorted and took a sip from his tumbler. Apparently, the happily married men could have a drink.

"He's a duke," Dash said and flipped over a card that was, naturally, the ace of spades. "Prince of nobs next to, *lud*, an actual prince. Everyone is on a lower level."

"Don't think to run over there and propose if you haven't gotten around to it yet." Tobias frowned, unhappy with an element of his design. "Hildy was as heated as I've seen her since my own misdeeds before our marriage. Your charming escapade in the stable wasn't enough? According to her, you're prohibited from ever seeing her client again, no matter if you've been dallying with her since your youth. This decree is an exact statement, by the by. She knows exactly where the Countess of Edgerly has been staying this week."

Xander leaned his hip on the sideboard, a grin ripping across his face. "Stable? Hell if this day isn't getting better and better."

Miserably cradling his teacup, Jasper crossed the space to sink into an armchair one of Xander's children had drawn tiny faces on in black ink. "Would it be indiscreet to admit, among friends, that the countess has been the one dallying with *me* since the moment I laid eyes on her twenty years ago?"

This got the room's attention in the way a lecherous comment, however slight, will among men. Though the expression on Jasper's face was melancholy enough to quiet their mocking. More teasing would be akin to kicking a pup.

Jasper stared into the cup, counting the flecks of tea floating on the surface. There were exactly six. The number of times he'd made love to Cece in his life. Perhaps this coincidence meant something. "Am I too old to start over? She has a son, a wee lad. I worry I'm not up to the job. Either job."

The silence was deadly. Men rarely admitted to fear. Or love. This was *both* in three simple statements and one troubled question.

"I, um,"—Leighton cleared his throat, likely eons since he'd given advice of this nature—"made mistakes of monumental proportions with Helena. Mistakes I assumed took me out of the running. She isn't anyone's idea of a typical duchess, and I had to prove to her this didn't matter one whit. It still doesn't. I'm sorry I'm a duke, but there's no help for it. I'd have quit society long ago and run off with her if I could. As it is, I'm sane because of her. And happy."

"Well..." Xander swirled the whisky in his glass, debating what to say. Which Jasper could understand because he'd married Leighton's little sister, therefore delicacy was required. "My children love you if it's any comfort. Being a father is mainly being there every morning when they wake up, loving them with all your heart, then feeling terrified every second of the day until they go to bed. And doing it all over again. At least that's fathering for me. Is this a difference in station you're worried about? Pip and I were at odds about this from the beginning. And my being older."

"Meaning *too* old," Leighton said without looking up from his inspection of another rock, this one of indeterminate origin.

Xander saluted the duke with his tumbler. "His Grace-ness was anxious if I'm allowed to be frank. Can you see him picking me for his sister? If it is the class bit, go back to being the baron. He isn't recognizable enough for anyone to care, mate."

"I don't know him anymore. I couldn't pretend to *be* him if I tried." Jasper downed his tea and looked achingly toward the sideboard. "The problem is, he's the bloke she loves. Noble? Not so much."

"Love is a gamble, though, isn't it? Not like you're anticipating favorable odds." This from Dash as he shuffled before sliding a straight flush across the desk with a smile. He'd written a book on duplicitous behavior in games of chance that had made him an instant celebrity. When he was a low-born Scot, as base as Xander and Tobias combined. His success went to show how bloody ridiculous society was. "When you and I tossed that carriage on the way to get the wife, Noble, I'd have said it was unholy rotten luck for a Scottish lad. On the contrary, laddie. Theo took one glance at my bruised jaw and the wee scratch beneath my eye and love just slipped into place like me ring on her finger. We haven't been apart since."

"Your advice is to crash a carriage to get Lady Edgerly to trust me?"

Dash shrugged and flipped a card. "How about stealing another telescope? That stunt secured the Earl of Stanford the wife he wanted right quick."

"The stunt was Necessity's idea," Jasper murmured, his mood sinking. Dash was the handsomest man in England. Securing Theo, the wife *he* wanted, hadn't been a challenge with that face.

Anyway, when had they gotten the idea he was discussing marriage? He was merely trying to figure out a way to get Cece to talk to him. Marriage and futures and love could come later. Furthermore, he'd nipped the telescope because Xander's half brother, Ollie, the Earl of Stanford, loved star-gazing, and the woman who loved *him* figured it was the way to his heart. Jasper and Necessity were friends from his early rookery days, and he'd been happy to oblige, though he'd been unaware of the kerfuffle the theft was going to create. He'd contacted several key associates to find the damned thing, ignorant to the fact the telescope he'd chosen was among the rarest in the world. Actually, the museum was still looking for it. "You're in marriages of long standing. Settled and deliriously, sickeningly contented. How can you help me? I'm still assembling the chess pieces while you've already won the match."

Tobias sighed and glanced up from his blueprints. "None of us wanted to fall in love, Noble. I fought it like hell, as did every man in this room for their own reasons. The vulnerability you invite into your life when you tell a woman you love her and mean it is only vanquished by the enormity of emotion you'll feel for your children. To my mind, that's the piece you're missing. You're expecting to, as Dash so unexpectedly put it, know exactly what you're doing here, to have a solid bet placed before you roll the dice. Do you think this mindless foursome"—he gestured with his quill to the Scot, the duke, the ruffian, himself—"had it figured out? I didn't know if I was up to the task of being a husband and father, either. I believed, and still believe, Hildy is too good for me. My reputation was the foulest in England, yet in the end, I won the earl's daughter. How many part-Romani men do you know that have done such? Not with threats and intimidation, means I used to build my businesses, but by opening my *heart*."

The pinch in Jasper's chest was pure panic. These men were feared, yet they were besotted kittens behind closed doors. If the world only knew. Jasper coughed into his fist while he imagined the terror of opening his heart, *really* opening it—again—to Cece. His cough this time was ragged at the edges.

"You circled too fast to the literal heart of the matter, Streeter," Leighton murmured and pitched a gleaming silver stone into the crate. Stalking to the sideboard, he poured a whisky, crossed back, and shoved the tumbler into Jasper's hand. "Take this, man, before you hack up something essential." Snatching the teacup away, he scowled down at it.

"Lingering spot of asthma from childhood, Your Grace," Jasper whispered, the mist circling his vision drifting away as air streaked into his lungs.

With an unimpressed oath, Leighton popped the teacup on a table and went back to his rocks. He was a man of few words and cantankerous temperament.

Things his duchess loved about him.

"Thank the devil you're skilled with a blade," Dash said and dealt himself another winning hand. "Not too menacing if you had a spasm during one of your investigative missions. Me? I'd have gutted you where you stood."

Tobias rolled his blueprint into a tight scroll and tapped it on his thigh. "It was *her* we chose, Noble. Not a blindingly clear future laid out before us like some bricked path leading to a Mayfair manse. I design those for my clients, but I've never encountered perfection myself. The reprobate piece, we'd all achieved. To the letter. Which you've proven once again with this morning's edition of the *Gazette*. You do make it hard on yourself, friend."

Xander slipped a cheroot from his waistcoat pocket and gave it a sniff but didn't make a move to light it. His wife, Pippa, hated the things. "I suppose you need to ask yourself, do you want the countess or not? Pip stripped away my resistance one goading smile at a time until the man standing before her was a bloke I didn't recognize. A man who waltzed and laughed and loved without fear. Now, I know him quite well. I even, most days, *like* him."

Certainty stole Jasper's breath this time. Followed by a pulse of desire when he imagined Cece tangled in his sheets for the rest of eternity, memories to wash away the lonely ones. He could still smell her on his skin, he *could*. There wasn't really a way to move forward without her. Why *was* he making this so hard on himself? "I asked her to marry me when I was nineteen." At the hush in the study, he glanced into his glass, unable to survive if his cheeks caught even a hint of color while he gave this speech. "Truthfully, I asked her father, who thought a lowly heir to an insolvent barony too far beneath her. In addition to the asthma and a gangling height I hadn't quite grown into, I also had a trace of a stutter."

"Unbelievable," Xander said on a gasping laugh.

"My father was less supportive and judged it an ideal time to prove a lesson about adoration or the lack of it with his fists. I would have run away with her, but Cece"—he looked up with a pained smile —"Lady Edgerly, that is, refused because her sister was soon to enter the marriage mart. I'm sure the union would have been a disaster because we were young, too young, but I wanted it. I wanted *her*. Consequently, I left my heart in Northumberland, and the courage to grab it back hasn't been forthcoming. They taught me expertise with weapons in my profession, I'll grant, but nothing about this feeling business. The petrified nineteen-year-old boy remains inside me, I'm afraid. Terrified and gulping for air."

With a look of longing at his cheroot, Xander slipped it in his pocket. "You had your future stolen from you, mate. By God, fight to get it back. If I can convince His Grace the Grump over there I'd make a faultless husband for his darling sister, you can win this campaign. If the countess is vexed about an eager-to-play chit showing up on your doorstep, you're halfway there. If she wasn't cross as hell, then you'd have a problem."

For some reason, in this sad state, Xander Macauley's advice made perfect sense. Cece loved him, even if the words hadn't been spoken between them in years. Last night, she might have whispered *I love you* in his ear. He seemed to recall this in the midst of the madness.

She was the courageous one, after all.

Now, it was his turn to fight.

"Figure out what she desires besides you. The independent ones always crave something. Usually dodgy, including some element you won't appreciate." Tobias pointed the rolled blueprint in his direction. "Then offer it to her. That's what we did. But make it pretty, will you? Those abundant gestures women are so fond of."

"Give her a choice," Dash offered with another of his world-class shuffles, "but not really. Underhanded, maybe, but who cares if you get the girl."

Exactly, Jasper decided, and with his friends' help, began to plan.

Chapter Thirteen

"I'm going to marry the baron's son one day."

   -Whispered promise from a viscount's eldest daughter to her sister,
1814

"That scoundrel," Cece said and tore the sheet of paper into pieces. She tossed the slivers in the air and watched them flutter like snowflakes to the faded Axminster lining Edgerly's back parlor. She'd nearly perfected Jasper Noble's signature, a bold scrawl designed to evade, like the man. An effort to pass the time in an agonizing day and a troublesome project without her loupe.

What had she been thinking, leaving it there for him to find? As if he cared.

"Arrogant, adorable *rat*." Tapping her quill to the desk, she glanced at the mantel clock. Two days had slipped by without an apology, and this fact had begun to prick like a splinter wedged beneath her skin.

The time without him had given her the opportunity to run through every moment they'd spent destroying his wobbly bed.

Every magnificent, vexing moment.

He'd cradled her face and stared into her eyes as they sought their release, something the young man hadn't. Magnificent wasn't really the proper word for the experience.

Then, he'd averted his gaze as soon as the discussion turned to the future—this wholly unlike the baron's son. He'd known exactly what he wanted even if he didn't end up getting it.

Vexing, the entire situation. She was wrapped in memories of him whispering *minx* in her ear as he shivered and shook. *Oh, so* glorious. But after, while he held her in his arms, he'd claimed the times they'd made love in Northumberland were his first three sins—and that he'd added three more in his vacant little cottage.

Very vexing when she wondered if he was counting and had determined six sins was his limit.

The nerve, Cece seethed and ripped another sheet to shreds. *Sins.*

Although he'd said it with a smile, a tender tilt of lips she'd bruised with her own. Then, they'd gotten caught in another round of passion when she climbed atop him, the breaking-the-bed session. Heavens, they'd been wild.

With more time than she'd like for reflection because there was no man on bended knee apologizing to her, Cece was stunned to realize she not only liked the person Crispin had become, but she also loved him. The hint of vulnerability surrounding such a formidable man attracted her in ways the boy hadn't. He was ruthless, yet kind, determined, yet caring, his complexities bundled up in a captivating package. Truthfully, Jasper Noble's storied past would have been more than young Cece could handle. His scars and his cynicism, not to mention the fight she'd had to wage to bring him around, demanded a woman's will, not a girl's.

She'd presumed she was doing the right thing by refusing to hide in the cottage and let another scandal get the better of him—and her. Her reputation was finished in any case. What did a former lover of *her* lover truly matter if Cece owned his heart? She either married a rookery reprobate or retreated to Northumberland with her son and played a widowed countess never to be heard from again.

Both were, as Crispin had warned, social annihilation.

Nonetheless, she was finished living someone else's version of her life.

She sighed and glanced at the scorched copy of the *Gazette* smoldering in the hearth. Whoever had ratted had left her out of the story entirely. They'd fingered his former paramour... while leaving her untouched. She wouldn't put it past Nelson to send a note to a journalist, she really wouldn't. He'd begged her to stay after the debacle and put the "laddie," as he'd called Crispin for ages, out of his lovesick misery and in a proper place.

Cece hummed and rolled the quill across her lips. Was he lovesick? Crispin hadn't been honest about his feelings because he was now a crook, but she hadn't been honest, either.

She hadn't come to London to get to know him again.

She'd come to *get* him. Period. A sacrifice of pride she was willing to allow because she was the one who'd rejected him. Fair was fair.

Cece tossed another hostile glance at the clock. Enough was enough with this withholding business. They'd concealed emotions and lied about intent. Flirted, teased, and argued, like always. With their bodies still pulsing from lovemaking, he'd held her as if she mattered, as if *they* mattered. A glorious night spent in a ramshackle dwelling that looked near to tumbling down upon them. A shack she'd move into tomorrow if he'd promise to build another bedchamber for Josiah. She'd only need to transport her horse from Northumberland and find a way to return home every now and again. Her needs, aside from Crispin and Josiah, were little.

She chewed on her thumbnail and paced to the bookcase and back. *Where was he?*

The heavy footfall in the corridor had Cece swinging toward the door. Her heartbeat rang in her ears as emotion flooded her body. How was it possible to miss someone this much? On the other hand, she couldn't be too agreeable since the rat had made her wait two days— but extreme spite wasn't required. Cece wasn't the shrew type.

Love negotiations required a delicate balance.

She understood Crispin's world had collided with hers when a scoundrel who wasn't the scoundrel she'd been expecting stepped into the parlor. As Cece's heart raced, he leaned to angle his immense frame through the doorway, his smirk too satisfied for her to be anything *but* the person he'd been looking for.

"I've come to talk, that's it," he said and smoothed his hand down his chest. Lamplight struck the bands of gold on his fingers and the bejeweled buttons on his waistcoat. The air of menace surrounding him said more than words about what he'd do to a person if he wasn't happy.

He'd fit right in with Leighton Cluster should they be seeking a new associate.

Before she could think to run, to shout, to move, the knave shook his head and settled into an armchair with a lazy sprawl, practically the only piece in her home capable of holding him. She swallowed and took a step back, her gaze fixed on his hands. Signet rings, he was wearing signet rings. Grinning, he flexed to show them off. She imagined him ripping them from someone's fingers and then breaking bones.

"Sit. Please," he murmured in a voice recounting a life spent in the underworld, nothing half regal, half ragged like Crispin's about it. He motioned to her escritoire, his request a clear command. "We have business dealings, little miss. A shade early for brokering as I'm a man of the evening, but a guv must work with what he's given, I always say. You need better latches on your doors if I'm able to give a slice of advice. Once they start to rust and stick, they're fit for the rubbish bin."

Giving her time to obey, he straightened a cravat a duke's valet couldn't have done a finer job fashioning and kicked his polished boots atop a table that rocked wildly with the motion. "I didn't want to chance coming upon your boy and his keeper. They left not an hour ago by way of the park, so we have time. Children shouldn't be part of professional dealings unless there's a reason."

Well, Cece reasoned, her stomach clenching, *that settled that.*

Channeling Jasper Noble's enviable composure, Cece slid into the chair behind her desk. She pressed her palms atop her folio to control the tremors. Thankfully, they were slight even as her pulse thumped. "What 'professional dealings' could you possibly have with a reclusive widow with a dubious reputation? I'm a nobody, a country mouse."

Her unwelcome visitor flashed a smile of genuine amusement. "Country mouse," he repeated with a gusty laugh. "I can see why Noble fancies you. I'd never have guessed that filcher would get caught in some chit's noose. Refined matrons usually look like a piece of fruit left too long in the sun, but you, nary a wilt about you." He tilted his head, eyes the tawny color of one of the stones in his rings gleaming in the sconce's glow. "I reckon Noble's confusion is understandable as his customary taste runs to doxies, like the *lady* who came for a swim the other night. Society don't alter them much from the ones taking blunt for their services, only the posh attire and the polished speech acting as camouflage. Many a light-skirt's got a bigger heart. Anyhow, it's unfortunate your man can't keep his snug transactions out of the rags, that's the truth of it." He knocked his bootheel to the table. "Because it led me right to you."

"Has Noble done something which requires repayment?" She leaned in until the desk's scrolled edge cut into her ribs. "Is that what this is about?" Cece would be incensed if so, however, she had to admit she'd agreed to dance with the devil—and everyone knew where dancing with a devil got a girl.

Her captor gave a muscle-popping stretch and reached into the inner pocket of his superfine coat. Pulling a folded sheet loose, he rose and placed it before her. His broad shadow crossed over her, cutting out light and freedom. She was ensnared, his threats about everyone she loved seizing her as surely as shackles. He was handsome, she had to admit. A face that would fit nicely on a sculpture in the British Museum. "Actually, little miss, it's you I'm after. Noble's done many things commanding repayment, or so I've heard, but he doesn't step into my territory, and I don't step into his. We crossed swords only the one time over a shipping concern I wasn't willing to give up. We parted with a few bruises, a typical day on the docks. He knows better than to try to best a Spitalfields lad, and I don't usually go Shoreditch way, though I'd have no trouble slicing his throat should he become a prob-lem. That you're his woman complicates the matter, but I'm given little choice. Since he joined the duke's club, nobs aplenty, he's close to running a proper enterprise. *Legitimate* even." He muttered the last with pure venom.

Cece ironed the sheet flat, her breath catching. *Oh.* Glancing up, she tried to keep fury from her voice. Who was she to be cross about her own misdeeds?

"I can see you want to call me all sorts of ghastly names, so I'll give you mine. Dorsey. Famous in the stews, unknown by the swells, chum to the footpads who patrol our streets and the representatives who fashion themselves the men of betterment for this fine city because I pay them for their friendship." He bowed, a rather crooked attempt, then placed himself back in her groaning armchair. "I'm also known for fair dealings *if*..."

He left the conclusion of this meeting hanging on the word.

"Where did you get this?" The contract he had in his possession was one of the marital agreements she'd forged in Northumberland last year. A particularly difficult signature she'd worked on for days.

Dorsey smoothed his palm over his dazzling waistcoat, the plaid material and the gaudy buttons a strangely striking mix. "A cousin of a sister of a friend of a chap I use as an informant here and again. You're notorious for being the swiftest countess forger in England. Northumberland Gold, they call you. Bet that name's a surprise, little miss." Sighing sympathetically, he gave one of his rings a twist. "Figures Noble would find you first. He's got sound wits about him, he does. Mayhap I should have tried harder to forge a partnership back in the day. I'm beginning to respect the man."

Cece slumped back, as astounded as she'd been in her life. Crispin was right. Her hobby was dangerous. People talked, no group more than domestics where gossip traveled from household to household like a fever. However, in a hidden corner she'd never admit existed, she was thrilled to have a scandalous nickname. *Northumberland Gold.*

A woman holding such an unsavory honor was suited to a former spy, wasn't she?

"Don't look so pleased. I'd tan your hide if it were mine to worry over. Noble has quite a fight on his hands." He jacked his thumb over his shoulder. "Surprised he lets you reside here with those bum locks. Sad case for a bloke rumored to once hold a securities position."

Cece glanced at the clock once more, judging she had less than an hour before Josiah and Mara returned, meaning she had to solve this unexpected problem now. "I'm not his concern, Mr. Dorsey. He doesn't *let* me do anything."

Dorsey snorted, grazing his knuckles beneath his chin. "Right-o, little miss, you go on telling yourself that."

"I'm retired." She dusted her shaking hands together. "My last forgery, done and gone."

Dorsey held up a sliver of paper, one of the sheets she'd ripped to bits. Half a signature was clearly visible. Tucking the scrap in his fob pocket, he rolled his shoulders, his impatience finally showing. "Listen, Countess, I mean you no harm unless you find you can't oblige my proposal. Then harm is on the table, I'm afraid, for you and yours. I'm a thief and you're a forger, collaborators natural as can be. Think of it that way. Retire, if you genuinely mean to, in style. You come to Spital-fields, reproduce two signatures for me, only two, then I deposit you back from whence you came. Fit and fiddle, as they say. I'll pay you a handsome sum and promise to never bring you into my dealings again. And I'll knock anyone senseless who thinks to ask a favor of you, forever after. Northumberland Gold, no more. My protection, honest to the heavens, means more than Noble's after he went and got involved with that lovesick bunch in Mayfair. Kittens, the lot of them. A cluster of *fools,* by my judgment."

Cece pressed her hand to her belly to calm the nerves making it jump, no method of escape coming to her. "I don't need your money."

He shook his head dejectedly. "Try again. I had my investigator look into your financials."

"He's going to find me. Then, he'll find *you*," Cece whispered with more certainty than she felt.

Dorsey linked his fingers and stretched again, cracking his knuck-les. "I have no doubt. I'd overturn every cobble to find you were you my affair. By the time Noble shows, I'll have those names on paper. When he and I have a chance to talk, once he understands you're iden-tifiable in the criminal arena, he'll rethink his strategy. He'll know I can help you retire yourself—but good. Point of fact, his arrival as your savior will keep me from having to escort you home." He glanced around her parlor with a shudder. "Fuck's sake, I hate Mayfair."

"I don't have my loupe," Cece said, her final attempt at a stay of execution. She sighed at his blank expression. "It's a magnification device I can't work without. Not well, at any rate. What you have in your pocket are frustrated scribblings done without proper equipment."

Dorsey's grin was cunning as he got to his feet, his stance as smugly confident as Crispin's. "I can get you any tool of the trade you require, little miss. Don't imagine I can't. Not as hard as finding a fancy telescope, I'll tell you that. The museum is still looking for the bloody thing."

Cece sighed. Did everyone in London know everyone else's business?

Dorsey crooked his finger. "My carriage is parked in the mews. We'll discuss the particulars of our deal along the way. You'll find Spitalfields a welcoming place if you're with me. I'm king in those parts."

Cece scrubbed her palms on her thighs, beneath the table where he couldn't see. "If I refuse?"

Dorsey removed his watch from a fob pocket and gave it a chilling glance. "When is your boy due home?"

Cece took a fast breath, shoving aside fear. "Mara will be frantic when she returns to find me gone."

Dorsey pocketed his timepiece. "Leave a note. Nothing alarming, just the facts as you feel you can share them."

"*To anyone reading this missive, I've been kidnapped.* Is that what you'd like me to write, Mr. Dorsey?"

He strolled to her desk and bracing his hands atop the ledgers, leaned over her, tossing his immense shadow into her space once again. "Tell them what you will. Does she know about your hobby? Make it enough to keep Noble out of my way with time for you to sign two documents of extreme importance to the residents of Spitalfields. In return, I'll pay you a proper fee, protect you during your travels, and take my thrashing from your man if it comes to that. He should have known better than to let a jewel of such talent lie out and about for anyone to pilfer."

Slightly flattered when she shouldn't be, Cece shook out her skirts and rose with the dignity of the countess she wished to leave behind.

"There you go, that's the daring girl," Dorsey murmured and had the gall to tweak her nose as if she was his little sister. "Look on the happy side, as my ma always cautioned I do. Maybe this scare will right Noble's ship. You've never seen a man move faster than when he's lost the most important article in his world."

Chapter Fourteen

I'd like to make inquiries about a missing Northumberland baron.
-Recent communication from Jasper Noble to his solicitor

"These streets are even fouler than the ones in Limehouse." Jasper grimaced and yanked the carriage's curtain into place, obscuring the piteous view of poverty and grime that signaled their entry into the stews. His heartbeat had been galloping in his chest since he received the frantic note from Mara.

A day after Cece disappeared from Edgerly's terrace. A bloody, fucking *day*.

Tobias offered a dented silver flask Jasper was too tense to refuse. "Don't be speaking ill of my beloved borough, Noble. I suppose you feel Shoreditch is the gem of the East End."

The scent of stewed oysters and coal smoke was nearly choking him, his breath coming hard despite his effort to calm it. Not the best situation for a recovering asthmatic. Restless, he patted his chest, his hip, his boot. Pistol, blade, blade.

All was well, except for a missing countess.

Xander paused in the cleaning of his own weapon, a walnut cane with a blunt-edged metal tip you could render a man senseless with in one swing. "Down, boy. Dorsey isn't known for violence against women. He's done much for this community, as we have for ours. I've teamed up with him a time or two over the years. Thieves aren't always the villain in the novel. According to my darling Pippa, they're there to add the flavor."

"It's rumored he has a gaggle of sisters he's accountable for," Tobias said and took a pull on the flask before dropping it to the seat. "Chits who've managed to stay out of trouble, mostly, which is saying something in this district."

Jasper nudged the curtain aside. Checked his pistol and repocketed it. Tapped his boot against the floorboard. Reached to adjust spectacles he'd left behind. It never paid to get glass in one's eyes during a brawl. He'd learned that lesson the hard way.

"Sisters," Xander whispered with an edge of dread in his voice.

Jasper snorted. He didn't give two knocks who Dorsey was accountable for.

The bounder had dared take what was *his*.

Jasper pushed a smile through his anguish. Cece would be mad as hell to hear him call her that. She didn't want to be owned, which was too bad because they owned each other. He'd someday find the nerve to tell her, someday soon. Maybe today. Or tonight as he slid inside her and the dewy glow he loved so much turned her eyes a dark, luscious green.

The men readied themselves as their carriage turned into the narrow alley behind a warehouse they'd been advised was the center of Jackson Dorsey's thriving enterprise. It had been years since he'd gone racing off like this, his pistol drawn. For reasons he couldn't quite place, Jasper had gone directly to the Duke of Leighton when he'd gotten the note—possibly because he was the most intimidating of the bunch. Two of the duke's footmen brought as backup, brutish comrades from his military days, were clinging to the tiger seat. Leighton was in a second carriage with Dash, the Earl of Stanford, and the Duke of Markham. Nobs who knew how to fight and weren't afraid to spill blood when the occasion called for it. Half of London's nobility had come when he said he needed help.

He'd never again take for granted the support of friends. Somehow, his life was becoming more complete with each passing day despite his endeavor to muck it up.

Except, they were husbands now. And fathers. The Leighton Cluster had families, obligations Jasper could only dream of. He couldn't live with himself if anyone was injured during this undertaking. His misplaced minx was completely on him unless the situation was a trickier one than he could manage.

"I'm going in alone," Jasper stated when the carriage braked hard, pitching them forward on the squabs.

Xander banged his cane to the floorboard. "Like hell, mate."

Tunneling his hand in his pocket, Jasper curled his fingers around Cece's loupe. "Give me five minutes. I'm prepared. When I say I was presented with dire circumstances throughout my prior vocation, I beg you to understand I meant dire. You're here because the woman I love is embroiled in misfortune of her own making, I suspect, but I did nothing to stop it. I could have safeguarded her better, made her see my side of things. You're here to protect her, not me."

"Once you admit to loving a woman, it can't be taken back. It's a cosmic rule or something." Xander nudged Tobias' boot with the tip of his cane. "You heard him on the other, Street? He thinks he can make her see *his* side of things. Ah, how the mighty fall."

Tobias batted the cane away with a scowl. "A man has to fight his own battles on the love front."

Love. Jasper rubbed his temple, the ache accompanying this recognition a resounding, near-blinding pulse. "She'll listen after this. I promise you. Your job is to get her out of here, no matter what condition I'm in. Do you understand? Emotion has never played a part before, and frankly, this change concerns the shite out of me. I worry love will throw off my normal, uh, instincts."

"Killer instincts," Tobias murmured as he thumped the carriage roof to alert the coachman.

"I'll wait seven minutes and not a second more. Spitalfields isn't the place for a toff who played at being a spy, even one with killer instincts." Xander settled back, though he brandished his cane like he intended to use it to bash in a nearby skull. He was the protective member of their group, Jasper was forced to gratefully admit. "Would have been nice to be informed about her forgery enterprise before now. A tad late, innit, as we sprint into battle? Though I'm appreciative of the skilled effort she put into my recent project. She's a talented criminal, your countess."

Jasper searched for a reply but the stutter resting on the tip of his tongue stopped him. Damn Cece and her predicaments. Waving his friends off, he alighted from the carriage to the grimy cobbles and a locale redolent of desperation and hopelessness. Shoreditch hadn't looked this dismal in years.

He hadn't the time to assess the state of affairs. The comings and goings of the inhabitants of the warehouse, the closest exits, any guards patrolling. He was going in blind, a dodgy move that had taken many an emissary down. He was usually logical about such things. Careful, deliberate.

Except where *she* was concerned.

Jasper realized two things when he reached the main door to find it unlocked and unguarded.

Dorsey was expecting him. He'd been invited. Thus, for the moment, Cece was safe.

Breath slowing, the ache in his chest lessening, Jasper stepped into the dim corridor. Sconces were affixed to the wall every five feet or so, their golden glow drifting across the scarred floorboards as he crossed in and out of shadow. The scent of tobacco and raw wood swirled like mist, a calming scent amidst the danger. Unbelievably, beneath the expected aromas was the faint tang of linseed oil. What notorious thief's compound smelled like a home?

Jasper halted in the entranceway of the soaring main room and slipped his blade from his boot. It wasn't Tobias Streeter's immaculate warehouse of exposed pipes painted a blazing crimson and aged wood reclaimed from other buildings—but it wasn't the office of a thug, either.

Cece huddled behind a crude desk made of shipping crates, bent over her work. She wasn't tied to the nearest steel girder. Her beautiful face was unmarked of injury from an assailant's fists. Her clothing was only in modest disarray, the pale peach gown one he'd never seen before. Her hair had come loose from its clips, the flaming strands trailing over her jaw and down her neck, pretty much the norm. Dorsey sat opposite her in a buttery yellow armchair befitting a king. Jasper squinted. The man was reading *Dickens*, the only hint of his lack of education the blunt fingertip he trailed across the page, a signet ring with a ruby as big as a goose egg glinting as he moved.

Jasper's heart kicked, his brain ticking off observations. The scene looked homey, inviting, *intimate*. None of Dorsey's men were about. It was just the two of them. There was a teapot on the sideboard mixed in among decanters and bottles, one Streeter and Macauley's whisky. His whisky now. The dark-green emblem on the label identified it even without the aid of his spectacles. A cup and saucer rested beside Cece's elbow. As was her habit, there were crumpled wads of paper lying about. Scones rested on a plate, and if he could trust his nose, they were lemon.

This looked more like a rendezvous than an abduction.

The detail that unleashed Jasper's rage was the loupe in her hand. The one in his pocket burned at the notion that another man had purchased anything for her. Suddenly, the stuttering, frightened boy he'd been was standing there with him, love and angst turning him to dust.

He hoped like hell Xander Macauley counted the seconds correctly on his Bainbridge timepiece because Jasper was going to kill Jackson Dorsey if his friends gave him long enough.

Jasper lifted the blackguard from the chair he'd been sprawled in by the neck and forced him into the first wall they met. Dorsey's smile was grand, a celebration, and clued Jasper into the fact that love had indeed done what he'd feared.

He'd been *had*.

Dorsey's pulse jumped beneath the thumb Jasper pressed against his jugular, but his eyes, a bubbling amber reminiscent of one of the Duke of Leighton's gemstones, glowed in delight. One was noticeably darker than the other, giving them a sinister shine. "About time," he whispered for just the two of them.

Jasper jammed his knife into the wall beside Dorsey's shoulder without letting his grip lessen about the cur's neck.

Cece gasped, and from the sound of things, upended a crate in her effort to get to them. A teacup shattered, the Dickens tome thudded to the floor. Her footfalls were a striking cadence in line with the wash of fury swirling in his ears.

"Let him go, Jasper!" she shouted, thankfully using the only name she could. "He's a client! We have a deal."

Jasper swore and tightened his hold. "*Deal?*"

"Jealousy becomes you, guv," Dorsey said in a rusty croak that meant his throat was going to ache for days. "This attachment is what you've asked for after getting involved with that... sentimental bunch, your duke's cluster."

Cece grasped his sleeve and tugged hard enough to bring him back a step. In resignation, not because she could keep him from turning this into a violent occasion if he made the split-second call. He'd paid for his crimes and then some. His brutality, learned or a part of him since birth, had him waking in fevered remembrance in the dead of night. The asset had made him an excellent emissary—yet it was a part of himself he wished *heartily* to leave behind.

Dorsey coughed and scrubbed his fist over the bulging cords in his neck. "Leave him, little miss." With a tight chuckle, he wrenched Jasper's knife from the wall and presented it to him like a gift. "A man in a rage has to unbridle his emotion somewhere. You're his possession, or so he thinks. We protect what's ours. We're simple creatures at heart if you don't already know it."

Jasper seized the blade and instead of pocketing it, tossed it from hand to hand. The metal glinted in the light, sending a shower of silver across the planked floor. In response, Dorsey's underlings, three hulking knaves who made Leighton's footmen look like starving lads, materialized from wherever they'd been ordered to remain during his arrival, further proof he was an expected guest.

Jasper pointed the blade at him. "I'm here, per the plan. What's it you want from me? Though I should drop you on the spot for the method. I don't accept enticements of this kind anymore."

Stepping between them, Cece thrust herself into the conversation. The lust, the *possession*, exactly as Dorsey had stated, struck him like a stone. Her hair was a feral amber mass flowing over her shoulders, devastation Jasper longed to plunge his hands into and sink so deeply, he'd never come *out*.

Cece laid a hand on each man's chest and gave another of her trifling shoves.

Jasper gently knocked her hand away. "*Christ*, Ce, you trust this ruffian. Is that it?"

"I'm replicating two signatures of great importance and—"

"He wants me, Countess."

Cece turned on him, her eyes as green as a lost sea. "You're mistaken. About many things."

Jasper slid his knife in his trouser pocket next to Cece's loupe. "Tell her, Dorsey."

Dorsey strolled to the middle of the cavernous space, and with a flick of his hand, those damned rings flashing, his men retreated to their hovels. "You know how to ruin a rescue, guv, I'll give you that much. Unintentionally, as I'm no romantic, I'd set you up for a royal gesture of the kind chits love." He perched his bum on a crate and stretched with a ragged hum. "Blimey, you're not learning much from that love-starved group you've befriended. Macauley made signs for his wife when he was chasing her, did you know? Bought her a bloody *business*, then gave her the choice of a last name. Shrewdest proposal I've ever heard of."

Cece curled her fingers into a fist and thumped Jasper's chest, harder than the shove. "This ridiculous abduction was a ploy?"

Jasper stalled, resisting the urge to stutter, which he wasn't going to bloody well do in front of a man who could, possibly, be his enemy.

Turning on her heel, Cece crossed to Dorsey. Her gown—now that Jasper got a solid look at it—was divine. Frilly but understated, her style, the peach silk flowing down her supple figure like a dream. He didn't want to *want* her in that moment, but his body responded just the same.

"You arranged this charade to get Jasper Noble here?" She tapped her slippered toe on the planks and propped her insubstantial fists on her hips. "I want the truth Mr. Dorsey, and I want it *now*."

Dorsey glanced over her shoulder with a wicked smile. "*Ah*, guv, she's a champion in any race. You've chosen well."

"Blasted cur," Cece said and made her way to the crates serving as a desk, but not before one of Dorsey's henchmen got there to block her way. "Both of you, cheats and scoundrels."

Jasper was across the room in a flash, muscling his way in front of her.

"Little miss, I need those fine signatures, I do. Don't make my man break your man's arm for no good reason. You've done me a favor I won't soon forget. Jackson Dorsey makes good on any debt owed him. Ask anyone. The papers you signed are for the good of this community. We have workhouses overflowing with illness, the basest medical care in the city given to the people in this borough. Women are dying during childbirth, and the babes who survive enter an even riskier world. I have plans, but plans require dirty dealing every now and again. It's a despairing situation I've tried, without luck, to get Mr. Noble to support. Hence this, *ah*"—he gave his neck another brutal scrub—"what did you call it? This charade."

"Let him have them, minx," Jasper said in a voice that brooked no argument. "Then, we leave in peace."

Dorsey bowed his head regally. "Wise man."

Jasper could feel her vibrating at his side, her fury more than palpable. Cupping her elbow, he turned her to face him. Her cheeks were flushed, her lips trembling. He longed to hold her, kiss her, *save* her, but she appeared as untouchable as shards of glass. And some injuries a person had to feel the sting of. "Jackson Dorsey isn't an associate of mine, Ce. I received a frantic note from Mara, then was left to figure out where you were. I have no part in this, so don't make me pay for his crime. I was going to come to you on the morrow, I swear."

"Most of his crew are waiting in the lane." Dorsey shifted, and the crates gave a weak groan. "He's well represented. My majordomo of sorts is right now haggling with a duke about where to park his upmarket equipage. I never thought that'd be a statement coming out of me mouth."

"How many dukes are outside?" Cece directed her question to Dorsey. Jasper was apparently getting the silent treatment.

Dorsey grinned and rocked forward, almost off the crate. "Two, which is two too many."

With a huff, she elbowed the brute standing guard before the desk. "I'd like my loupe, if you please."

Dorsey gave his man a nod, and the unmovable force stepped aside to allow her to take it. "Your payment is in the envelope on the desk, little miss. And the favor I mentioned is yours should you ever need it. You know where to find me."

"Donate my fee to your philanthropic endeavors," Cece said and marched toward the door without looking back. "I'm asking a duke, *any* duke, for an escort home."

Dorsey snapped his fingers, and his sentry stepped into Jasper's path when he tried to follow.

"I haven't forgotten my training," Jasper snarled, the first time in his life he'd admitted to being anything other than an enterprising scoundrel from Shoreditch.

"Leave her, Noble. My gut is faithful about such things. I have four sisters, and I sense when they're hot to the touch. You don't want to get charred any more than you already have. I'd give this kettle a spot of time to breathe."

Jasper paused and yanked his hand through his hair. Why did everything he tried to do for Cece end up being doomed? Maybe *they* were doomed.

"Just so you know, harming your wee countess was never the plan," Dorsey drawled as he came to stand beside him. "I have a sister with hair that color. The oldest, Henrietta, the sprite who keeps me up fretting over her."

Jasper glanced at a man whose reputation was almost as forbidding as his, the last bloke in England you'd expect to find "fretting" in the dead of the night over his sister. "I figured, when I stumbled in to find you two looking so cozy."

Dorsey laughed but tried gallantly to conceal it behind his wrist. "She agreed to this farce to protect the boy. But I also mentioned you to secure the deal. Your name on my lips turned her skin the color of cream, guv. Quite fetching, I must admit."

"Solid play," Jasper whispered, unsure if he should start a fight he might not be able to win. He was exhausted. He was old. He wanted *peace*.

He wanted Cece.

"I wouldn't have harmed her... but the next bloke might. The infuriating women are the ones you have to watch closely, trust me on this. For my sanity, my wife will be beautiful but dull, count on it. As for you, your little miss is known in certain circles for having a valuable talent as she's made no effort to conceal it. I realize you're not sitting this low anymore, prowling the stews, to be aware. She even has a name, Northumberland Gold."

Jasper rubbed his eyes, a headache pinging through his skull. *Fucking brilliant.*

Dorsey slipped a key from his pocket and smoothed it between his bejeweled fingers. The metal was dull from handling, the move so mechanical Jasper wondered if he even realized it. "I'd be willing to partner with you to pension her. Let anyone and everyone know the countess is off-limits, her business closed for good. Under my protection as well as yours. Mine being the more daunting threat because I'm still in the game. When you now chum about with dukes and such. Nothing intimidating about a pack of toffs, am I right?"

Jasper grunted, impressed despite himself by Dorsey's crude savvy. "In return?"

"In return, you obtain a bit of information about a certain gent who stepped where he shouldn't. He's high in the instep if you get my meaning. Friends in lofty places, not someone I have regular access to on the east end, hence my coming to the man with the most connections in the bleeding country." Dorsey gave the key a kiss, aware of exactly what he was doing, and sneaked it back into his pocket. "I'm supposing you have ways to get me what I need, what with your former training."

"Who?" Jasper asked, his gut telling him the name wasn't one he wanted to hear.

"Devonshire."

Jasper turned to Dorsey, wishing he had a drink. The Duke of Devonshire was known for ruthless activities that would ruin a man if brought to light. It was a marvel he hadn't been killed for them by now. "You're making a powerful enemy if you target that bastard."

Dorsey shrugged, vengeance glowing in his eyes. The differing shades of amber in each, slight but noticeable, gave him a feral air. "I protect what's mine as well as you, guv. Right is right. You'd be helping me help a vile man go down."

"She's retired if I bring you this information?"

"My vow, guv. Although"—Dorsey began to crack his knuckles, one ringing pop at a time—"I have a workhouse undertaking similar to yours. I'm not above accepting help with it. Cruel times, if you get me. I have my own crew, like your cluster, but my lads are gutter-bloods through and through. A rough lot I'm working to better. A titled nob or two might be who I need to recruit, now that I consider it. Add a shine. Blokes who donate money and make change in the Houses like shine."

"The Rookery Rebels. I've heard of them. Every lowlife in London has heard of them. Fears them, per your plan."

Dorsey gave one of his gaudy rings a twist, his smirk two ticks past sinister. "Then you know what an able partner I'll be to you in this time of need. The Rebels, as we've been named, are a loyal bunch. You won't regret going into dealings with us. I've got your back, you *and* your cluster, when you need me."

"Send me the details," Jasper murmured and made his way down the shadowy corridor. This wasn't an alliance he'd anticipated forming, but one he could, conceivably, use in the future. Xander Macauley would be pleased, Tobias Streeter wary, the Duke of Leighton disgusted.

There were no guards manning the warehouse door, same as when he'd arrived. Curling his fingers around Cece's loupe, Jasper wondered which duke had offered to take her home. Markham, he hoped, because he'd speak better of him. Leighton would fill her ears with rubbish—all of it true.

"Good luck with your romancing," Dorsey called, the last thing Jasper heard as he strode into the mist-laden dusk.

Chapter Fifteen

She has such a mind of her own. I wish I knew how to change it.
-Crispin Sinclair's journal entry, 1814

W hen he arrived, Cece was sitting on a stone bench by the servant's entrance he'd broken into a few short weeks ago. She'd been waiting her entire life for Crispin Sinclair. When it was Jasper Noble who showed up.

He halted when he spotted her, his lips parting in surprise. Moonlight adored him, cutting shadowed hollows beneath his sculpted cheeks and casting a golden shimmer down his long body. He was dressed for a caper in head to toe black, the lock pick in his hand there one second and gone the next. Her man of mystery.

"I don't want to talk," Cece said because she didn't. They weren't going to agree. Either she gave in or he did. She accepted the man he'd become, and he accepted the woman she'd remain.

Only, she wasn't sure they could do that.

Her heart ached at the notion—but desire was stronger than heartache.

Cece didn't lead him to her bedchamber. Instead, she tugged him through the kitchen and into a scullery smelling of nutmeg and flour. The cookies she and Josiah had made earlier were on a tray in the parlor.

When the scarred pine door closed behind them, she pushed him against it and pressed her lips to his, offering herself. She recorded the mad flurry of sensation while urging Crispin to offer himself. It was only fair. Sliding his hands beneath her bottom, he lifted her high, giving her no choice but to loop her legs around his waist, her arms around his neck. Connected, *finally*, the lock pick tumbled to the floor, and he kicked it away with a ragged groan.

Thankfully, the kiss wiped her mind clean.

His ragged breath hit her cheek, his fingers curling around her thigh as he fit her body to his. His shaft was hard, and she was power-less to contain her cry when he ground himself against her core. His hoarse whisper floated free—*God, yes*—his need trailing like a hot ember down her spine.

In desperation, they toyed with each other.

Fingers tangled in sweat-dampened strands, in silk and pressed cotton, clips and buttons striking the planked floor. His murmured devotions tickled her ear as his teeth sank into the tender skin at her nape. The scent of spice and leather drifted into her throat when she pressed her lips to his jaw in reply. He cradled her face to hold her still and ravaged her mouth, his tongue circling hers until she couldn't have stood had he placed her feet on the floor. A ripple of wind drifted in the window and across her in a coy caress.

Pulling out of the kiss, he guided her gaze to his. His eyes were hooded, lost to desire, burning a bright, brilliant blue. She knew the same ferocity was mirrored in hers. His heart thumped, matching the furious rhythm of her own. She braced her fist on the doorjamb and shifted her hips, grinding against his cock, no words needed. His lids fluttered, his head falling back. It was the most sensual second of her life, watching him crumble.

"Upstairs," he whispered, the command streaking into the night.

"*Here*," she returned.

Then, she added seven simple words.

"*I want you to fuck me here*".

The world blurred as his control snapped. Arms tensing around her, his mouth captured hers as he carried her across the room. She twisted her fingers over his coat lapels, and when he placed her on the butcher's block, shoved the garment from his body and to the floor. They didn't disrobe any more than was necessary. His shirttail yanked from his trousers, the buttons opened by two sets of trembling fingers. Her skirt lifted and bunched around her waist. She'd worn nothing beneath her gown, her plan to have him the only plan she knew would succeed.

When he realized this fact, he went wild.

He teased her nipples through layers, thumbing the throbbing peaks as their kiss spun into eternity. His fingers danced through the damp hair at her core, lingering to slick her folds with her own nectar. "You're so wet, minx," he murmured, every delicious, dirty thing coming out of his mouth making her arousal soar. How he recognized her lewd side so clearly, how he *knew* she desired this, she couldn't say.

She dropped her brow to his shoulder as he worked a finger inside her. Then two. Slowly, too slowly, like he was storing the shape and feel of her to memory.

"Harder," she whispered and through the open neck of his shirt nipped his skin. "Faster."

Surrendering in his own way, Crispin wrapped his arm around her waist and dragged her bottom forward on the block. She didn't think to stop him when he dropped to his knees and shoved her thighs wide with his shoulders. The rush of pleasure when he sucked the nub topping her sex between his teeth was more than she could comprehend. Blinding, breathtaking *bliss*.

He understood how to destroy her. To turn any argument she might make to dust.

Tangling her hands in his hair, Cece urged him on, lifting her hips and helping him find a perfect fit. She'd never looped her legs over a man's shoulders... but the fit was perfect. Unbelievably, he allowed her to control the pace as she closed in on her release. It was similar to riding astride him in some debauched, utterly delectable sense. Except this was his tongue and fingers, not his cock. The image of his head nestled between her thighs, the indigo gaze he turned to her dazed with longing, sent her over the edge.

She used him as she found what the world was missing, and he gladly let her. The orgasm was endless, cycle upon cycle of sensation. He stepped up and in before the ripples of pleasure had left her. Before her vision had cleared or her breath returned. Before she could speak or make a move to continue their interlude.

"I can't wait, minx," he whispered and positioned the engorged crown of his shaft between her tender folds. There was no reason to wait—she was ready, and he was breathless. Before he slid inside her, she touched him, her fingers curling around his smooth length. The sight of him so rigid amidst a thatch of dark brown hair left her thunderstruck. He let her stroke him, once, twice, three times, before ripping her hand away and taking control. In seconds, they were joined hip to hip, her leg hooked around his waist and pulling him in deeper. They rocked and grinded without thrusting, a novel experience. A merging without aggression. With tendrils of delight still coursing through her, this gentle abrasion stunned in its magnificence. She'd never imagined such a feeling from so simple an act—during what was not a simple act at all.

He exhaled sharply as he grasped her knee and locked it against his lean hip. "I'm going to come soon if we don't slow down." His voice was tattered, his plea desperate.

She held her body still until he opened his eyes, blinking as she came into view. His hair was an inky tumble about his face, his skin dewy, his cheeks flushed. His pupils were huge, black forcing out blue. He looked close to losing his mind, his senses. He was nearing his limit —because of *her*.

"I want to watch you, Cris," she said and trailed her knuckle down the scar on his neck. She shifted her hips and squeezed her muscles around his shaft. He groaned, his throat pulling in a long swallow. The hand holding her knee tensed, his fingertips digging into her skin. "I want you to break apart before me. I want to be your fantasy."

His chest hitched, and he shouldered away a bead of sweat trailing down his jaw. Dazed, he echoed her words like a child, "You want me to break apart. You want to be my fantasy."

Statements with an edge of desperation attached to them.

She licked her lips in challenge, inviting danger, inviting *him*.

He pressed his brow to hers, his terse exhalation striking her lips. His gaze roved her face, calculating, deciding. "*Fantasy*," he repeated. Seizing her mouth, he dove into a feral, almost angry kiss. Then without comment or warning, he lifted her from the block, disengaged from her body, and placed her feet on the floor. She grasped him to keep from pooling into a sated puddle at his feet.

"Remember later you asked for this," he whispered as he turned her, bracing her hands on the block. "Hold on, Countess, because I'm going to prove you have always been my fantasy. My *only* fantasy."

Then he growled and took hold of her hips, positioning her. His arm came around her, his hand sliding north to find her breast, his thumb her nipple as he thrust inside her. He curved his body over hers and, knocking her hair aside, kissed the nape of her neck as he pumped. His skin was moist, his body hot, his possession complete.

She moaned and arched, sending him deep, while discovering how exquisite lovemaking in this position could be. How spots, before untouched, came *alive*. In response to her enthusiasm, his hand covered hers on the block, their fingers linking.

After this, it was a race forged on passion and need. Their moans and the slap of skin echoing about the space, creating a brutal union, raw and unrestrained. She couldn't imagine sharing this with another living soul. It was too intimate, too real. It was a part of her only Crispin could see.

The shimmer began as a heavy feeling between her thighs, a thickening of the blood in her veins. A raging heartbeat she couldn't control. Her body quivered like a bow, vibrating into his. He groaned as his arm tensed about her, drawing her bottom into his pelvis with a hard thrust.

"I'm not leaving you," he whispered urgently, his rhythm increasing. "Not ever again."

Yes, she thought, but the sound arriving from her lips was garbled. Pleasure had her in its teeth, and there was no escaping the fury.

Knowing exactly what to do to make her come before he did, his talented fingers found the aroused nub of her sex and, within seconds, had her crying out, trembling against him. "Now," she gasped, wave after wave rolling over her. "*Now*."

"We are each other's fantasy, minx," he vowed, his lips at her ear. "I am yours, you are *mine*."

If nothing else, about this they agreed.

He clung to her as he found his release and swallowed hers whole, interlocked puzzle pieces bent on delight. In those moments, they were given a rare gift. One body, one mind, one purpose. Staggering and wondrous.

Cece didn't recall sliding to the floor, Crispin's arms wrapped protectively about her, where they huddled until their skin cooled and their breath slowed. Releasing a watery sigh as he tried unsuccessfully to rouse her, he bundled her up in his coat and carried her to her bedchamber. Cleaned her with a moist cloth while whispering endearments she couldn't fathom, then tucking her beneath her counterpane like a child.

He'd taken her to a realm she had yet to return from.

She was dead to the world before her head hit the feather pillow.

Jasper checked the scullery twice before relaxing in the knowledge they weren't going to get caught over a misplaced cravat or stray hairpin. Cece's loupe had tumbled from his pocket at some point and rolled beneath the butcher's block, a desperate search forcing him to crawl about on his hands and knees to locate it.

He was jittery, nerves thumping, a restless sort of energy that had him pacing the length of the parlor while Cece's staff of exactly two placed breakfast dishes on the sideboard. They gave him curious glances but otherwise, as domestics were trained to do, didn't speak a word. He wasn't lounging about in her bed where he wished to be, his clothing was right as rain, his hair was only vaguely disheveled. He had the look of a titled aristocrat down pat.

He didn't appear to be a man who'd tupped their employer until she was near expiration.

Hell, until *he'd* been near expiration.

The grin was uncontrollable, a wicked slant of his lips flashing in the cheval mirror he passed. The night had been a revelation, a confirmation, a bloody marvel. He'd never had sexual experiences like the ones he had with Cece. He'd never wanted to stretch out beside a woman and talk after he'd laid her across a butcher's block and... gone a little mad. He'd never been anxious over an encounter. He considered himself an unselfish lover, he made sure pleasure was given if at all possible, but he'd never worried about securing *love*.

"Love," he whispered and strode to the window as panicky as a groom on his wedding day. Which was what he was going to try to convince Cece they needed. A wedding.

He tapped the dirty pane and squinted into a brilliant burst of sunlight. Her lawn was overgrown, the hawthorns in a dismal state. He recalled the information received from his investigator about her meager finances, the trifling funds Edgerly had left her. Jasper had blunt enough for both of them for three lifetimes... but something told him Cece wouldn't be overly swayed by a discussion about money.

Stressing again, he crossed the room to pour tea, then placed the cup on the sideboard without taking a sip. There were things to occupy his time while he prowled the space. Figurines on a shelf, staid portraits of Edgerly's ancestors, a quite unattractive group, lining the walls. Plates and napkins on the table to straighten. He paused in the motion of polishing a spoon with his sleeve.

Cece would accept his proposal, wouldn't she?

He had a plan, after all. Perhaps not as grand as Xander Macauley's and the "making two signs for Pippa" business, but he had a very solid strategy. An offer. One he would never, *ever* make for another person. He glanced at the folio on the table, documents delivered this morning by an overly compensated emergency messenger.

He was offering to become that damned baron.

To step back into a persona he didn't want. He wanted Constance Willoughby—Crispin Sinclair could fucking walk a plank for all he cared—and Cece wanted Crispin.

Tapping the spoon on his thigh, Jasper sighed and sank into the nearest chair. So, step back he would.

If that's what it took to win her.

However, *first*, he planned to offer Jasper Noble on a silver platter along with a side business of sorts he thought would make her happy. If she wavered, he was prepared to toss the baron in to sweeten the deal.

After he talked to Josiah, that is. She didn't have a father or brother to give their blessing.

But she had a son.

Josiah materialized as if Jasper had summoned him, sprinting into the breakfast room with Mara hot on his heels. His hair was damp at the tips, his clothing rumpled but clean. It was madness keeping a young boy in check, he realized with a slight, *very* slight pang of fear.

Josiah gave him a two-second glance and marched to the sideboard. Jasper had been around enough for the boy to accept his presence without question. This thawed the icy dread in his heart enough for him to jump in.

Mara, conversely, eyed him like a dead mouse the cat had dragged in. She was keen, that one. She knew exactly what his attendance at this early hour meant.

Jasper stepped in beside the lad before his keeper made it over, taking a plate, and starting to dish out food. "Eggs? Sausage?"

"Everything but them stewed tomatoes," Josiah said and danced in place. "An extra slice of cheddar if you will." He lowered his voice, a whisper that was no whisper. "Miss Mara doesn't give me near enough cheese. Or biscuits, now that I think on it."

Jasper smiled, picturing watching this boy grow up. Helping him mature into the man Jasper hoped he'd be. His own father had done a horrid job, and he had the scars to prove it, inside and out. He was determined to change the Sinclair pattern of parenting by example, starting today.

Jasper settled Josiah at the table on the shadowy side of the parlor. Thankfully, Mara took a seat by the window, giving them enough distance for some semblance of privacy. He felt as cagey as he would if there *was* a father to discuss his plans for Cece.

While Josiah shoveled in food, Jasper edged into a serious discussion. He spun his teacup three times on the saucer, earning a suspect glare from Mara, before he started. "Your mother is still asleep?"

"Headache," Josiah mumbled around a bite of toast. "I jumped on her bed, woke her up, and she about tumbled to the floor. Her hair looks like a crazy animal got into it, a nest of squirrels or something. Her cheeks were really rosy, too. Like apples. She had the blankets all clutched up at her throat like it's winter. Must be freezing or something. She's always cold."

This comment elicited another vexed stare from Mara.

Jasper coughed faintly, muffling the urge to pat his chest. He wasn't having an asthmatic fit in front of some stoney-eyed governess, that was for damned sure. "You see, Jos, I have a question to ask you. A very important question."

Chewing furiously, Josiah dragged his toast through a dollop of blackberry jam. "I'm listenin', Mr. Noble."

Jasper tapped his finger on the saucer, Cece's loupe burning a hole in his trouser pocket. "You see, I'd like you to call me something else someday. I don't feel much like a mister, actually. Jasper might suit us better for now."

Josiah stilled, the gravity of the discussion finally dawning on him, in part at least. "Jasper," he said, rolling the name around his mouth like a sweet. "For now... and then later?"

The gravity hit Jasper as well. He was offering to be this child's father. Cece's husband. His family was within grasp. He only had to convince everyone he was worth the effort. And the trust. "I would like to marry your mother, Jos. And have her—and you, of course—live with me in London. Or, if your mother wishes, for me to live with you in Northumberland. We'd have two homes, you see, if this makes you happy. Her father is no longer with us, so I've come to the man of the family to ask permission."

The toast tumbled from Josiah's hand. "*Me?*" he croaked and streaked jam-stained fingers down the front of his shirt. "I'm the man of the family?"

Jasper bowed his head. "You are."

Josiah scooted back until his tiny bum hit the chair's spindles. He straightened his shoulders with a grin. He'd lost a front tooth in the past day. Jasper didn't want to miss the loss of the next one. "I suppose I am, girls being so weak and all." He tilted his head, his gaze narrowing. "You ain't asked her?"

Jasper laughed; he couldn't help it. His hand covered Josiah's sticky one where it rested on the table. "I haven't, I swear."

Josiah thought on this. "If she says yes, you'd be my da? And I might have a brother or sister someday? I'm hoping it'll be a brother... but I'd try to be decent even with a silly old girl."

He squeezed the boy's hand, the kick of pulse beneath his fingertips flowing through him like a warm tide. Jasper's eyes stung, and he swallowed past the emotion clogging his throat. Cece could be pregnant as he'd not taken the normal precautions. He promised never to take them again. "I'd like that. A big family sounds wonderful."

Josiah got directly to the heart of the matter. "Is she still mad at you?"

Jasper paused, his lips parted. Was she? He had to be honest—Cece's temper ran hot, probably not a surprising reality to her son. "Maybe."

Josiah slumped back with a groan. "Oh, blimey, then. You're doomed. My ma doesn't hold much for fools, which you are, according to Miss Mara."

Mara gasped from her spot in the sun, apparently not far enough away for true privacy.

Jasper propped his elbow on the table and turned to the lad, prepared to argue his case, when Cece marched into the parlor, her gorgeous ginger locks contained by a multitude of clips, her pale-yellow gown crumpled but mostly presentable.

However, her cheeks blazed with color no one in the room could miss.

Uh-oh, Jasper thought as Josiah murmured the same beneath his breath.

"I'd like a moment alone with our guest," Cece said in a dulcet tone Jasper wouldn't have bet two shillings was genuine.

Josiah grabbed a scone as he edged off his chair. His whispered "good luck" as he strolled past gave Jasper more courage than a thousand fatherly permissions would have. Even Mara, who obviously believed him to be one rung beneath a court jester, gave him an encouraging smile as she guided the boy from the room.

Cece stretched him on the proverbial rack as she crossed to the sideboard and poured tea. She added sugar and milk, then stirred with clicking motions of the spoon.

Jasper counted the taps, getting to twenty before his patience deserted him. "Am I in trouble here, Ce?"

She turned to lean against the sideboard. He hated that his body thrummed at her steady regard as surely as it had when she'd drawn her fingertip down his hip. A flitter of sunlight rippled over her, lighting up her dazzling ginger strands. He wanted to touch her, *kiss* her, but she seemed unapproachable. "I don't know. Are you?"

Jasper exhaled and curled his fingers around her loop, an item she'd be vexed about him carrying around like a lovesick swan. He wished he had his spectacles on to provide a layer between him and her censure. Her gaze was brilliant this morn, an emerald slicing him to pieces.

To hell with it, Jasper decided and moved ahead with his plan.

Grabbing the folio, he rose and strolled to Cece, hemming her between his body and the sideboard. It was an approach meant to intimidate, a move a spy would make. It said a lot about her strength of character that she recorded it without a flicker of distress. She stood toe-to-toe with him, and bloody hell, he loved her for it.

He wasn't a tender man. Or, if he'd been at one time, tenderness had departed somewhere along the brutal path he'd taken. But he adored this woman with every fiber of his being—and she was right. In the depths of his soul, he *was* kind.

He just didn't want anyone but her to know it.

"You could do worse," he said, the most inelegant start to a proposal he'd ever heard.

Cece laughed behind the teacup she'd lifted to her lips. "I have done worse."

Not caring to discuss a topic set to anger them both, him particularly, he opened the folio and flipped through the pages before extracting a sheet. Turning to her, he offered the first part of his compromise. "Caroline Norton and Hildy Streeter wish to organize a women's rights group, and they'd like you to lead. No forging required, by the way. You may not enjoy being a countess, but in this case, the title can only help you. This project requires time, and a substantial bit of it, spent in London. I had nothing to do with this beyond telling Hildy you might be here more often. Consider me the messenger."

Cece licked her lips, sending a jolt to a part of his body he'd hoped was appeased for the moment after last night. The scent of her skin—teasing, delicate, sweet—drifted his way. If he tried, he could still taste her.

Taking the page, she scanned the message Hildy had sent him two days ago. "This terrace isn't mine for long, as I mentioned. Edgerly's cousin is moving in this winter. Therefore, I have no place to reside in Town."

Jasper took a subtle breath of courage. "I have a lovely residence in Bloomsbury in need of feminine consideration. I've been told my breakfasts could be greatly improved upon, according to Nelson, my wise beyond his venerable years valet. There's a back parlor that would make a suitable office if one were seeking such a space. It gets morning sunlight when London's weather is charitable. A better situation than the smaller space you inhabited last time. Roomy and it has shelves. And two windows instead of the one."

Cece pressed her lips together, hiding a soft smile.

She isn't angry, he thought, delighted and frightened to the depths of his soul. His life was shifting beneath his feet, his world's axis in a free spin.

She was going to say yes.

The air around him took note of the transformation and fairly crackled.

"I could find a tenancy, perhaps," she said and placed Hildy's offer atop his open folio. "Lady Thompkins-Reeve is retiring to the country and is leasing her home in Fitzrovia. Although I'm not sure I can afford it."

"No more sneaking around, minx," Jasper said, his patience leaking away on a fast exhale. "I'm not picking any more locks to get to you. I'm coming in the damned front door. You're *mine*. You know it, and I know it. I'm *yours*. There's never been a day since the first we met that this wasn't true, not for me."

Cece placed her teacup on the sideboard and smoothed her hand down her bodice. An image of her pert, pink nipple disappearing between his lips flashed through his mind. His body responded instantly, reducing his negotiating power instantly.

"You're missing a key element in this graceful argument of yours, Noble."

He frowned, wishing again for his spectacles. Amazingly, wishing she would call him Crispin in that husky voice of hers. "It isn't an argument, Countess," he murmured, "but more a proposal."

"Ah," she said and cleared her throat of laughter.

He didn't mind being laughed at. Not if she said yes. "Josiah gave his permission. I asked this morning. At least, I think he did. His mouth was so full of toast I can't be completely sure."

This statement shook her. *Finally.* "You asked Josiah about—" She stumbled, bouncing her hand between them like a ball.

Jasper paused, stunned, realizing he'd never asked her *the* question.

The legal document he lifted from the folio trembled in his hand. He presented it to her with his love, his future, his everything. "I want to marry you, Ce. My dream since I was nineteen years old, as you used to know. I told you often enough, asked you a thousand times as we walked the fields of Northumberland. I've changed in ways time decided for me, but in this, *nothing* has changed. My feelings for you remain. In fact, they're stronger than ever. I'm far from perfect. The truth is, I'm not good enough for you. Nevertheless, I want you with every beat of my heart. If one night passes without you, it's going to be one too many."

With fingers that also trembled, she took the paper, her cheeks blanching as she read it. Her gaze shot to his, her green eyes fever bright. "You would assume the title for me?"

"If that's what it takes. I don't need him, but I *need* you. I love you, Ce. I love Josiah. I want us to be a family." He scowled, a muscle in his jaw ticking. "Mara can come, too, I suppose, even though she despises me."

"She'll learn to love you. You have that effect on people." Cece dashed a tear from her eye. "We could be starting our family even now."

His vision blurred hearing these words outside the prayers circling his heart. "I want more children. I want it *all*. This news isn't going to scare me, minx, if that's what you're expecting."

Cece stepped into his arms when he opened them, crushing a baron's resurrection between them. "Crispin Sinclair can remain in the past. I don't need him anymore. I love the man in my arms with *my* entire being." She sank into him, seeking a deeper embrace. "Although I refuse to call you Jasper in private. That, I find I cannot do. And please, no more 'Countess' for me, not ever again."

Jasper caught her firmly against him. Cradling her jaw, he tilted her lips to his. The kiss was a tender invitation that spiraled into the promise of more. Her heartbeat tangled with his through layers he couldn't wait to strip from her beautiful body.

She sighed, sending the taste of ambrosia skimming down his throat.

Before they got carried away, he pressed his brow to hers. "My proposal arrives in three parts, darling Ce. You must let me finish."

She wiggled her hips against his embarrassingly rigid cock. "Is this part three?"

He trailed his lips down her cheek with a throaty whisper, "I'll make an addendum. Lovemaking is part four."

She stepped back, snagging his gaze. "What more could you give me, Crispin? If I have you and Josiah, I have everything I desire."

"If the baron's heir is unaccounted for, the title remains in abeyance. Happily, the vacant Sinclair estate is available for purchase through some legal wrangling, since it was an acquisition acquired through a wager. My solicitors dug this little nugget of a fact up after months of research. It would make quite the magnificent spread, two Northumberland estates joined into one. The baron's tenancies are rather profitable, actually, with enough blunt coming in every year to update your home and the attached outbuildings. Your stable was once in need of repair, as I recall. If a neighbor in the village happens to think I resemble the young man from long ago, I'll smile and accept the comment without reproach."

"The stable roof is near to caving in," she whispered. "The conservatory I've always wanted to restore could use some love. The dwelling with the arched windows and iron finials we, *oh*, we had our second kiss in. I'm afraid for Josiah to play in there, though he wants to, for fear of the place collapsing on him."

Jasper grinned, his heart swelling. "I remember that kiss. I remember them all. Your luck is holding because love is what I'm offering in any form you'll accept it. Nelson, I have to tell you, is very keen on moving north. He feels his health will improve greatly with cooler temperatures and less coal smoke, so I'm agreeable to accommodating him if you are."

Cece's gaze skated away as she began to chew on her bottom lip. "I'll have to sign over the Northumberland property when we marry?"

Ah, he thought, *so this is her concern.*

Cradling her cheeks in his hands, Jasper pressed a gentle kiss to her lips. Her skin was warm to the touch, warming him in return. Finally, he was coming home. "Ce, I'm flush. Not to be tastelessly frank, but I've no need for you to sign over your family home. In writing, upon our marriage, your estate stays with you. The spy game paid well as have my investments. Wonder of wonders, but I'm suited to trade, the least likely profession for a baron. I seem to have a mind for capitalizing on my monetary reserves, and my new friends have helped. The icing on the biscuit, my father would have loathed my association with the Leighton Cluster, even with a duke or two thrown in. Therefore, this piece brings me unparalleled joy."

"I'll be slogging about with the Leighton wives, then?" She frowned, realizing he'd had more to do with crafting her future path than he'd admitted. "You have it flawlessly planned, putting your former skills to fine use. I feel managed—and after I've spent the past month chasing you down."

Jasper laughed, his delight boundless. "Leighton wives? Hildy would be incredibly displeased with this nickname, and Pippa would sock you in the nose if you called her such. She's a force, that one, an ideal match for Xander Macauley." He trailed his hand down her body, over the teasing curve of her breast. "What about my effort to chase you, darling minx? I've never agonized over a woman this much in all my days, as you well know."

211

Cece's throaty exhalation whispered over his cheek. "Due to your extreme dedication to the project, I've decided to let you catch me."

"For how long?"

"Forever," she said and, curling her hand around the nape of his neck, drew him into the kiss of a lifetime. "Forever."

Epilogue

Another rogue has been officially inducted into the Leighton Cluster with the hasty marriage of Jasper Noble to the widowed Countess of Edgerly. These men are known for their passionate unions and their adherence to securing the most interesting partners.

-Newspaper clipping pressed between the pages of a scoundrel's wife's folio

Even after a year of marriage, Cece didn't understand everything about her husband.

Why he preferred his boots be placed by the front door rather than in his wardrobe, for instance. Why he chose coffee over tea most mornings. Why he felt he must ask her every five minutes how she was feeling, a common occurrence since she'd told him she was expecting a baby two months ago.

Their relationship was changing in the best of ways, and the mystery of it thrilled her most days. *Most.*

Crispin's past had come out in scattered fragments of conversation in the dead of night as they lay entangled in each other's arms. With every story he shared about his emissary work, his heroism diminished in the telling, she loved him more. The risks he'd taken for his country terrified her to contemplate. He was a complicated man. A generous, loving, exasperating husband and father.

Actually, she didn't wish to know everything about him. She hoped her search to understand such an enigmatic person would take her a lifetime.

Cece wrinkled her nose at the sound of a fist striking a jaw. The Leighton Cluster were gathered around a large bald circle on the Duke of Markham's lawn the men called the "testing grounds." The boxing sessions they held on the spot were brutal, but when there was a disagreement, this is where they resolved it. They were barbarians, to put it plainly. Why Crispin felt he and his friends must battle it out instead of discussing the issue like women did, she'd never understand. Another mystery.

However, she hadn't heard Crispin cough or seen him pat his chest in months.

Brawling was evidently an excellent cure for asthma.

As was an incredibly joyful marriage.

"Don't let their antics startle you," Pippa Macauley murmured from her sun-drenched spot on the duke's immense veranda. Lounging on a chaise and looking for all the world like a languid portrait meant for an art gallery, Pippa yawned lazily behind her hand. Her eyes closed, Cece hadn't even known she was awake. Who could sleep through the uproar of men tussling and ten children of various ages bellowing? The serene woman across from her, that's who. "They're fools, utter and complete, but boys must have an outlet for their energy, or they're miserable to deal with. Sometimes I think Xander is one of my brood, roughhousing and destroying furniture, coming home with torn clothing and bruised cheeks, then he kisses me, and I remember that's not the case."

In the event Cece didn't get her meaning, Pippa winked.

Cece sat back, her cheeks burning.

This was new as well.

Friends. A circle of incredible people closing ranks around her. Scandalous discussions and laughter. So. Much. Laughter. Cece hadn't realized how lonely she was until the Leighton Cluster entered her life. Her decision to come to London and fight for the man she loved had brought her more than she could have imagined. An additional joy was the upcoming visit from her sister, Rose, and her family. Her life was turning out to be wonderful.

Looking across the lawn, her heart skipped a full beat. Josiah was in the middle of a pack of children, dancing about in glee. He had a bow clutched in his fist, although he wasn't yet allowed to handle the arrows. She had done something right if her son was this happy.

They had a true *family*. The tears intruded, as they did all the time, and she fumbled in her skirt pocket for a handkerchief. It was right beneath the new loop she carried each and every day, one Crispin had given her on their wedding night. *To past and future love*, he'd had inscribed on the metal lip. He'd kept her old one, an item he claimed he couldn't give up.

"It's the babe," Hildy said from her place beside Cece, giving her a comforting pat on the arm. As the two who freckled horribly, they were sitting in the shade. "I cried, uncontrollably at times. Toby was frantic, though I tried to tell him it was normal to experience staggering bursts of emotion. We *are* carrying another human, after all. If only men had the chance to experience such a thing."

Pippa gave a graceless snort. "Oh, bother, as if! They'd not make it a day."

"They're simply not built for it, body or *mind*." The Duchess of Markham, called Georgie by everyone who loved her, tapped her temple with a smirk. "Can you imagine? Dex can't even find his left boot most days. If it isn't some fancy rock, he's hopeless."

Shooting Crispin a quick glance, Cece hastily dabbed her eyes. "Cris can't see me upset. He'll spirit me away to the nearest parlor. I've never taken so many naps in my life."

This said, she issued a huge yawn, causing everyone around her to smile.

No one batted an eyelash at her calling her husband by another name, something she did only among this small circle. In public, she called him darling or Noble, both to the grave displeasure of society. Their friends knew about his past, enough to quiet the questions, anyway. Besides, they had their own secrets; Jasper Noble's weren't the most scandalous. Every man standing on the faded circle on a duke's Mayfair lawn had a past they'd chosen to leave behind for a brighter future.

One filled with love, family, and friendship.

As if she'd whispered something in his ear, Crispin glanced over. Seeing the handkerchief in her hand, he frowned and gave his spectacles a nudge.

"Uh-oh," Hildy said, her voice threaded with amusement. "Here comes an anxious daddy."

"Another one falls," Pippa added with a drowsy sigh.

Cece watched Crispin give Josiah a nod, then set across the lawn with a long-legged stride that meant business. Watching him, her heart gave a tender leap. He was grace in motion, summer sunlight awash down his long, lean body. Amazingly, he'd gotten more attractive in the past months. His eyes were a clear, brilliant, blissful blue; his jaw stubbled as he preferred; his dark hair long enough to curl over the collar. He looked relaxed and content.

He looked *happy*. She'd fought for him and won peace for them both.

This realization gratified her to the ends of the earth and back.

"You're not going to argue, are you, minx?" he asked as he climbed the veranda stairs, coattails flapping. "You seem ready to wilt, and I can't have that."

"This promises to be a laborious five months," Pippa whispered, awake enough to share her opinion.

Hildy flapped her hand, shushing her. "Goodness, are you mad? Xander Macauley was the worst expectant papa I've ever seen."

"Jest all you wish, ladies, I won't be deterred," Crispin said with one of his charming smiles. They were meant to bend a person's will to his choosing and could be quite effective, Cece would admit.

Although these ladies had cut their teeth on charming smiles. They were a skeptical crew.

"I'm not going to argue," Cece murmured as he reached for her. She was, in fact, fatigued. She'd had no idea being pregnant took so much out of a person.

"Brilliant," he whispered for her only.

She hummed and stood, placing her hand on his chest. "Oh, *no*, not this time."

He only grinned and looped his arm around hers as he led her into the house. "I have no clue what you're referring to."

Last week, he'd rescued her in a similar fashion from a painstaking discussion about politics in Leighton's parlor. They'd ended up in the duke's linen closet, her back pressed against the door as they tupped like the world was ending.

Her prodigious hunger was another aspect of pregnancy she'd not expected.

When they entered the hallway, Crispin halted at the first door they encountered. "Care to show me your underthings, Mrs. Noble?"

She giggled, then covered her mouth in mortification. Women who organized rallies for legislative change and still dabbled in the occasional forgery did not giggle. "You are incorrigible, Mr. Noble."

He leaned to press a nibbling kiss beneath her ear, a spot meant to stoke a blaze in her as he well knew. "Is that a *no*?"

After checking to ensure the hallway was deserted, she pulled him into a kiss that finished with them breathless and clinging to each other. She wiggled her hips against his. "Is this a loop in your pocket, or are you thrilled to see me?"

He released a gusty laugh against her lips. "Both."

Reaching around him, she checked the knob, and found it unlocked. "It has to be fast. The children will be racing inside for luncheon soon."

He scrambled to shove her into a tight space that was, indeed, another linen closet. Strangely, the scent of linseed oil was becoming a mild aphrodisiac.

Locking the door, Crispin brought her in until they stood in a full-body press surrounded by starched linens and misty illumination streaming through the high, narrow window. Dust motes drifted around them like snow on a winter morn. The way he looked at her, dreamy and dazed, sent her spiraling. It was a blatant look of possession, of love.

She was dazzled, once again, by the splendor of him.

"What?" he whispered, his eyes glowing in the light.

"I just love you more than I can manage some days," she said and bowed into his chest. The tears stung her eyes, but she refused to let them fall.

His arms came around her. "Ah, minx, you're going to have me weeping along with you instead of taking you against this door. I'm no good at one while feeling the other."

"I disagree. You're good at both. So very, *very*"—she streaked her hand down his body, halting at his waist—"good at both."

Crispin caught her hand before she could touch him, his fingers linking with hers. "I love you and Josiah and our babe more than I can manage, too. I lie awake at night, watching you sleep, watching Josiah sleep, worry streaking about in the darkness. Yet, I'm finding love gives me strength rather than weakens me, as men expect it to do. Honestly, I feel stronger than I did with a knife pressed to someone's neck."

"Do tell," she said and laughed into his coat. The superfine wool was a gentle caress against her cheek, his breaths a calming echo in the small space. She broke his hold and touched him then, listening for the kick of his heartbeat beneath her ear. "I can be dangerous in my own right."

He groaned as she traced the outline of his shaft jutting against his trouser close. "Prove it."

Gazing at her husband, Cece smiled as his lids drifted low. From the time she was fifteen years old, she'd known. This man was her everything. "Don't worry. I will."

The End

Thank you for reading *Three Sins and a Scoundrel!*

This was the final book in the legendary *Duchess Society* series.

Have you read all books in the series, including the Christmas novellas *The Governess Gamble* and *The Daring Debutante*?

THE DUCHESS SOCIETY SERIES

Thank you!

Thanks for reading Jasper and Cece's second chance romp! I love this trope so much I have to keep myself from incorporating it into every book. As you know, this is the close of the Duchess Society series (for now). There are six novels and three novellas to keep you entertained for a while! This series has been really special to me and a JOY in every way. If you haven't read all the books, please do. Tobias Streeter (*The Brazen Bluestocking*) and Xander Macauley (*The Wicked Wallflower*) are reader favorites. Although, my fav couple may be Dash and Theo in *Two Scandals and a Scot*, which just got nominated for a MAGGIE, an Orange County Bookseller's Best, *and* a National Excellence in Romantic Fiction award! Dash has had a good year. Scottish men rule! And I recently released a next generation novel with *The Daring Debutante*, which follows Tobias Streeter's adopted son, Nigel, on his love story!

I will admit Jackson Dorsey, introduced here as Cece's benevolent captor, has sparked my interest. I wonder how he manages a rookery enterprise and four sisters? Hmm... perhaps there is more to come from him. The Regency Rebels, anyone?

You'll also note I once again had my hero, Jasper, wearing a Bainbridge timepiece, finest in England. Christian Bainbridge is a watchmaker I wrote about in the steamy, second chance, love-at-first-sight Regency novella, *Tempting the Scoundrel*. I based him on a real watch-maker of the period and all my heroes wear a Bainbridge!

I repeat this because it's so true: Stephen King said in *On Writing* that writers reuse themes. I adore crafting stories about brothers and male bonding. And, as you know, the Duchess Society is a series about the men in the Leighton Cluster. My series, *The Garrett Brothers*, is full of backslapping and brawling. And steam! In fact, if I think about it, the *League of Lords* follows this theme as well. All I can say is, sexy men and their complex relationships are my pleasure to write!

Visit www.tracy-sumner.com to sign up for my newsletter to receive the award-winning novella, *Chasing the Duke*, as my thank you. I know the number of books we publish in romance gets confusing. The **Books** page on my website lays it out nicely for readers.

Happy reading, as always! Historical romance is the best.
xoxo

THE DUCHESS SOCIETY
SERIES SUMMARY

THE MEN AND WOMEN OF THE LEIGHTON CLUSTER
(or as Dash calls them, The Leighton Lovesicks)
Much love to Mya Wall for her assistance!

THE ICE DUCHESS
Series Starter Novella
Dexter Reed Munro/Duke of Markham
Georgiana Whitcomb/The Ice Countess; co-owner of the Duchess
Society
Cat: Merlin
Tropes: Second chance, best friend's little sister, widow, first love

THE BRAZEN BLUESTOCKING
Tobias Fitzhugh Streeter/Rogue King of Limehouse Basin, by-blow of
Viscount Craven
Hildegard Templeton/Daughter, Earl of Cavendish; co-owner of the
Duchess Society
Cats: Nick Bottom, Buster (+ more to come in future books for this cat
rescuing hero)

Tropes: Forbidden romance, bluestocking, working heroine, match-maker, class difference

THE SCANDALOUS VIXEN
Roan Darlington/Duke of Leighton
Helena Astley/Self-Made Shipping Heiress, rookery girl
Cat: Rufus
Tropes: Class difference, enemies to lovers, fake courtship, working heroine, hero falls first

THE WICKED WALLFLOWER
Xander Macauley/Half brother of Oliver Aspinwall, Earl of Stanford
Philippa "Pippa" Darlington/Little sister to the Duke of Leighton
Cat: Rufus
Tropes: Class difference, age gap, friend's little sister, heroine nurses hero back to health, slow burn/pining
Orange County Bookbuyers' Contest Best Historical Winner
MAGGIE Finalist/Georgia Romance Writers
Carolyn Award Finalist
National Excellence in Romantic Fiction Finalist

THE GOVERNESS GAMBLE
Holiday Novella 2022
Chance Allerton/Viscount Remington
Francine Shaw/American heiress
Tropes: Class difference, curvy heroine, reformed rake, wallflower
New Jersey Golden Leaf Winner
New England Reader's Choice Finalist
National Excellent in Romantic Fiction Finalist

ONE WEDDING AND AN EARL
Oliver "Ollie" Aspinwall/Earl of Stanford, half brother of Xander Macauley
Necessity Byrne/Infamous landscape designer, rookery girl
Cat: Delilah

Tropes: Grump/sunshine, forced proximity, scarred hero, class difference, enemies to lovers
Hottest book in the series, according to readers!

TWO SCANDALS AND A SCOT
Dashiell Campbell/Author, cardsharp
Theodosia Astley/Sister to Pippa and the Duke of Leighton by
marriage
Cat: Mr. Darcy
Dog: Wordsworth
Tropes: Friends to lovers, marriage of convenience, bookish heroine,
reformed rake, class difference
National Excellent in Romantic Fiction Finalist
Maggie/Georgia Romance Writers Award Finalist
Orange County Romance Writers Bookbuyers' Best Finalist

THE DARING DEBUTANTE (NEXT GENERATION DUCHESS
SOCIETY!)
Nigel Streeter/Adopted son of Tobias Streeter
Arabella Macauley/Only daughter of Xander Macauley
Tropes: Grumpy/sunshine, friends to lovers, class difference, forbidden
love, friend's daughter

THREE SINS AND A SCOUNDREL
Jasper Noble/Rookery man with secrets
Constance Willoughby/Countess Edgerly
Tropes: Second chance/childhood friends, hidden past, reformed rake,
class difference in reverse (you have to read it to find out why!)

Also by Tracy Sumner

The Duchess Society Series

The Ice Duchess *(Prequel)*

The Brazen Bluestocking

The Scandalous Vixen

The Wicked Wallflower

One Wedding and an Earl

Two Scandals and a Scot

Three Sins and a Scoundrel

Christmas novellas: The Governess Gamble,

The Daring Debutante

League of Lords Series

The Lady is Trouble

The Rake is Taken

The Duke is Wicked

The Hellion is Tamed

Garrett Brothers Series

Tides of Love

Tides of Passion

Tides of Desire: A Christmas Romance

Southern Heat Series

To Seduce a Rogue

To Desire a Scoundrel: A Christmas Seduction

Standalone Regency romances

Tempting the Scoundrel

Chasing the Duke

About Tracy Sumner

USA TODAY bestselling and award-winning author Tracy Sumner's storytelling career began when she picked up a historical romance on a college beach trip, and she fondly blames LaVyrle Spencer for her obsession with the genre. She's a recipient of the National Reader's Choice, and her novels have been translated into Dutch, German, Portuguese and Spanish. She lived in New York, Paris and Taipei before finding her way back to the Lowcountry of South Carolina.

When not writing sizzling love stories about feisty heroines and their temperamental-but-entirely-lovable heroes, Tracy enjoys reading, snowboarding, college football (Go Tigers!), yoga, and travel. She loves to hear from romance readers!

Connect with Tracy: www.tracy-sumner.com

facebook.com/Tracysumnerauthor
x.com/sumnertrac
instagram.com/tracysumnerromance
bookbub.com/profile/tracy-sumner
amazon.com/Tracy-Sumner/e/B000APFV3G

Acknowledgments

Thanks to my book friends in the Sumner Inner Circle! You guys keep me sane and give me the push I need some days to keep writing! Kudos especially to Mya who suggested I have a companion of sorts for Jasper —Alfred Pennyworth to his Bruce Wayne. Intro the groom-turned-valet, Nelson.

Big shout-out here to Sebrena Bohnsack for the name Constance Willoughby for the heroine of this novel. Sebrena won a contest I participated in for a Colorado animal shelter, and we loved this name. It's from her two grandmothers! How charming is that? **Please** support your local shelter. Adopt, donate, foster. They need you!

Finally, thanks to the Wolf Publishing team for their patience and support with his book, and Estela for her kind assistance in managing the scattered pieces of a publishing business. Jasper is an enigmatic fellow and was a bit hard to get a story out of.

As always, happy reading!
xoxo

Made in the USA
Middletown, DE
15 September 2024

60993771R00146